Dear Mystery Reader

History plus mystery equals pure reading pleasure. As a result, the mystery genre is packed with historical series. But in this popular, crowded category, look no further than Elliott Roosevelt's Eleanor Roosevelt series for one of the most creative, accurate and entertaining around.

The concept is terrific. One of our nation's most beloved first ladies—Eleanor Roosevelt—becomes an endearing amateur sleuth in the hands of Elliott Roosevelt. MURDER AT MIDNIGHT is the latest installment in this successful, long-running series. When a prominent judge is found stabbed to death while spending the night at the Executive Mansion, Sarah Carter—a black White House maid—is arrested for the crime. Positive that the police have the wrong suspect, Eleanor is determined to find the real killer. While juggling all her White House duties, the First Lady of Mystery must somehow save Sarah from the electric chair and the city from a mad killer.

Murder in the White House is one "new deal" Ms. Roosevelt won't stand for in MURDER AT MIDNIGHT. I'm sure you'll be thoroughly entertained by this latest installment in the endearing Eleanor Roosevelt Mystery Series.

Yours in crime,

Joe Veltre

Joe Veltre
Assistant Editor
St. Martin's Press DEAD LETTER Paperback Mysteries

WORDS OF PRAISE FOR
ELLIOTT ROOSEVELT'S MYSTERIES

MURDER AT MIDNIGHT

"[Has] glimpses of world and national events and the ongoing business of the presidency, lending piquancy and historical interest to a well-honed plot. One of the best in the series."
—*Kirkus Reviews*

"Peopled with famous lights of 1933...Washington, D.C. is brought to life in the mirror of the White House. [This mystery] gathers to an Agatha Christie-like ending."
—*Publishers Weekly*

MURDER IN THE CHATEAU

"An entertaining historical mystery featuring a unique and incomparable heroine."

—*Booklist*

MURDER IN THE EXECUTIVE MANSION

"Memory Lane for some readers; an intimate history lesson for others."

—*Kirkus Reviews*

"Fans will relish this glimpse into White House life of the time and the parade of famous names."
—*Publishers Weekly*

MURDER IN THE EAST ROOM

"Page-turning...Roosevelt conveys a wonderfully intimate and authentic picture of the FDR White House and its inhabitants."
—*Baton Rouge Advocate*

THE PRESIDENT'S MAN

"Colorful characters and sinister double crosses enliven this lively yarn."

—*Los Angeles Times*

MURDER
AT MIDNIGHT

ELLIOTT
ROOSEVELT

St. Martin's Paperbacks

MURDER AT MIDNIGHT

Copyright © 1997 by Gretchen Roosevelt, Ford Roosevelt, and Jay Wahlin, as trustees under the trust instrument of the "26 Trust."

Library of Congress Catalog Card Number: 96-53530

ISBN: 0-312-96554-0

Printed in the United States of America

St. Martin's Press hardcover edition published May 1997
St. Martin's Paperbacks edition/April 1998

10 9 8 7 6 5 4 3 2 1

MURDER
AT MIDNIGHT

MAJOR DWIGHT D. EISENHOWER, carrying a worn briefcase, left the War Department a little after three. Just inside the door he stopped at a desk.

"Where to, Major?" asked an elderly man seated there.

"To Capitol Hill, Mr. Dooley," said the young major. He patted the briefcase. "Facts and figures for the Senate Armed Services Committee."

The old man nodded gravely, reached inside a drawer, and withdrew a small piece of paper. As Eisenhower pulled the paper nearer him and wrote on it, the old man shoved two nickels toward him. They were car fare: a nickel to take the major to the Capitol, a nickel to bring him back. Major Eisenhower wrote the amount—10¢—and the purpose of the cash withdrawal neatly on the little chit and handed it to Mr. Dooley.

"Give 'em hell, Major," said Dooley.

Eisenhower grinned broadly as he pocketed the two coins. "I'll do that, Mr. Dooley," he said.

The forty-three-year-old major hoped business on Capitol Hill would not keep him too late in the afternoon. He was an aide to the Chief of Staff, General Douglas MacArthur; the Chief of Staff had been invited to dinner at the White House

that evening, and the invitation included Major Eisenhower
and his wife. Mamie was looking forward to the evening, and
the major was anxious to get home, get changed, and not have
to rush.

Sara Carter looked at herself in the mirror. She was pleased
with what she saw. Her brown skin gleamed faintly in the late
afternoon sunlight from her bedroom window. She tipped her
head. She was just what they all said she was: one high-toned,
damned good-lookin' colored gal, with high cheekbones, perfect white teeth, proud eyes, an unblemished complexion . . .
What was more, she was proud dressed, in the uniform of a
White House maid. It was the best job anyone in her family
had ever had, and she'd had it two years. She felt good about
herself. And she had a secret or two, besides, that made her
feel even better.

"You dressin' t' go back t' the Whaat House?" her mother
asked.

"Workin' tonight," said Sara.

"How late?"

"Late. They havin' a state dinner tonight, an' I'm helpin'
clean up after. Also, whatever else they might want. Could be
three, four 'clock in the mornin' before it's all over."

"You stays late hours, that job. Seems to me you work
hard for what you gits."

Sara turned, lifting her chin high. "Workin' hard is how
I gits what I gits . . . an' I gits $12 a week, don't forget."

Her mother glanced around her daughter's room, at the
things $12 a week had purchased: mostly dresses, shoes, hats,
underwear—but also a six-tube Silvertone radio she had
bought from a pawn shop for $22.95, batteries and speaker
and everything, and the girl sometimes listened to places like
New York and Pittsburgh and Cincinnati; also a portable
phonograph that could play two records on one winding, with
two or three dozen records she bought for 20¢ apiece. Plus,

Sara handed over a $5 bill twice a month: room and board.

"Okay?" Sara pressed.

Her mother nodded. "Okay."

"Anyways," said Sara, "it's only just been two or three times I've stayed so late. And sometimes they hand me a little extra money for stayin' late."

A few minutes later Sara boarded a bus. She deposited her fare and walked to the rear, past a dozen vacant seats, to the part of the bus behind the rear door, where Negroes had to sit. She had to stand there, but it did not occur to her that she might walk forward and sit down in a white seat. On rare occasions when the thought did pass her mind, she knew it wouldn't be worth the trouble.

When the black Packard stopped in a no-parking zone in front of the Gayety Burlesque theater, the cop on the beat only nodded at the driver, smiled tolerantly, and looked the other way.

Ten minutes later a white-haired elderly man, erect and firm in his step, but holding a cane in a firm grip and pressing the pavement from time to time to assure balance, came out of the theater. People on the street recognized him—maybe by his great white mustache—and smiled, and two ventured a greeting. The old man returned their smiles and nodded. His driver helped him into the car.

"That worked out quite well," the elderly man said to his driver. "We have ten minutes to reach the White House. Quite sufficient. And I saw the whole show."

The driver handed him a small silver flask. The old man removed the cap and tipped the flask. With practiced dignity, he took a swallow of brandy.

"Better do it twice, Judge," said the driver. "You'll get nothing to drink at the White House."

"Hmm," said the white-haired man. He accepted the suggestion. "Yes. Conscientious woman, Mrs. Roosevelt. Serves sweet cider, I understand."

"So they say," the driver agreed.

"Well . . . It's an honor, anyway, I suppose."

The driver turned his full attention to the early evening traffic. He was driving Oliver Wendell Holmes, retired Justice of the Supreme Court, to dinner at the White House.

The limousine bringing General MacArthur to dinner stopped on H Street, and the general walked across Lafayette Park to the entrance to the White House. In May, the sun had not yet set at the dinner hour appointed by Mrs. Roosevelt, and the general did not want anyone to see just how he arrived.

The limousine was not in fact his. Well, in a sense it was his, and in a sense it wasn't. He paid for it, and for the chauffeur. But it was not his limousine, it was Isabel's; and, since he was going to dinner at the White House, she was going out nightclubbing. He had promised her he would leave the White House as early as he possibly could; still, he had to anticipate she would not be back in her suite at the Hotel Chastleton when he returned there. In fact, she might not return before he had to leave the suite and go to his quarters—and his mother—at Fort Myer.

Isabel . . . Isabel Rosario Cooper. He had brought her from Manila. She was exquisitely beautiful. She called him Daddy.

The general squared his shoulders as he walked up the drive from the gate to the North Portico. He wore black tie, not his uniform, and was conscious that even in mufti he was an impressive figure of a man.

In a guest room on the second floor of the White House, Judge Horace Blackwell struggled with his bow tie. His watch lay on the dresser, reminding him that he had but a few minutes to conquer this necktie and get downstairs. A half-full glass of rye sat beside his watch. He, too, was aware that Mrs. Roosevelt would serve nothing alcoholic in the White House so long as Prohibition remained the law of the land.

Before the necktie began to defy him, Judge Blackwell had been humming a little tune. All he had to regret in life, for the moment, was that his parents had not lived to see their son installed in a guest room in the White House. He had been living here for six weeks. In another two or three weeks his work for F.D.R. would be finished, and he would go back to New York. He could have another judgeship if he wanted it: a federal judgeship this time. But he had decided it was time to practice law for a while, to make some money. He had been in touch with a Manhattan firm that was very much interested in having Judge Horace Blackwell on its letterhead, and it was likely he would let them engrave it there.

He was forty-eight years old, a man distinguished at both ends of his face: by his thick, curly, iron-gray hair, and by his strong, square jaw. He wore round, gold-rimmed eyeglasses. He smoked cigars.

The necktie surrendered at last. He picked up the glass and slugged down the rest of the rye.

Who had they said was going to be at dinner? Justice Holmes. General MacArthur. William Faulkner. Senator Carter Glass. Jim Farley. Bill Tracy. And of course if Bill was going to be there, Blanche would be there. Judge Blackwell wondered if he could somehow arrange to be seated beside Blanche.

He stepped out of his room and turned to the stair hall. Just in time. As he hurried down the broad stairs, he heard the buzzer that meant the elevator was on its way down from the private quarters, bringing the President down to dinner.

Franklin D. Roosevelt, President of the United States since March 4, propelled his own wheelchair—a utilitarian thing of wood and steel he had learned to command—without the assistance of anyone. Sweeping out of the elevator lobby, he rolled into the great cross hall of the main ceremonial floor of the White House and turned sharply right toward the entrance to the State Dining Room.

The President, too—knowing that Prohibition would be honored in the dining room—had enjoyed his usual evening cocktails before coming down. Judge Blackwell wondered why he had not been invited to join F.D.R. at cocktails this evening; but he would not have wondered if he had known that tonight the President had sat during his ritual mixing and pouring with just two people, neither of whom would be at dinner—his political mentor, Louis Howe, and his longtime faithful secretary and companion, Missy LeHand.

Mrs. Roosevelt would have been welcome, of course. She always was. But she wouldn't come. She rarely did. Before-dinner drinks had been so long an element of her life that she conformed her life to the Prohibition laws about as much as did everyone else at her social and intellectual level; but she could be, and often was, impatient with the amount of time the cocktail ritual occupied. She did not emerge from her suite until the President was about to yell for her.

Louis and Missy, on the other hand, regarded what the President and Mrs. Roosevelt were about to do as something of a waste of time: to sit over dinner in the State Dining Room with oddly assorted guests, with widely varying interests, who were unlikely to be able to make any sort of memorable conversation.

It was Mrs. Roosevelt's idea to invite widely varying guests to occasional dinners, to let them bounce their ideas off one another. Tonight, though, she was not the author of the guest list. For tonight, the author was Jim Farley—professional pol, Postmaster General, and recognized chief of patronage. He had put the list together with an experienced eye, not this time for immediate profit, but for what the newspapers would say tomorrow morning.

Well . . . Not entirely for what the newspapers would say tomorrow morning. An important motive for Farley was to give Virginia Senator Carter Glass the opportunity to hobnob with some bigwigs—as big as Washington could offer this week. Justice Holmes. General MacArthur. William Faulkner. The President himself, for that matter. The senator was proving to be an effective supporter and advocate for the administration, but in Farley's judgment it could never hurt to reinforce.

Mrs. Roosevelt was not yet comfortable with her role as White House hostess.

Would she ever be?

An element of her insecurity was that she felt she was always under critical examination. Under, for example, the uncharitable eyes of her Roosevelt cousins of Oyster Bay, represented in the haughty and caustic Alice Roosevelt Longworth, daughter of T.R., who presided as patronizing *doyenne* of Washington society and never missed an opportunity to make a quotable joke at the expense of her gawky cousin, who had married what *her* branch of the family called "the feather duster"—meaning F.D.R. Under the eye of Sara, the mother-in-law, who felt she had *made* her son whatever he was. Under the eye of what Washington called the "cave dwellers": old society in a city where, if truth be told, there *was* no society—which fact had never discouraged those who pretended there was from being critical, as they had been critical of the wives of all the Presidents with few exceptions, from Abigail Adams to Lou Hoover.

Conscious that she lacked the style even of Grace Coolidge, with whom she was often compared, Mrs. Roosevelt saw no alternative but to create her own style; and she knew no way to do it but simply to be herself. And so, she *was* herself. And, in her most private moments, she said to herself, The devil take those who don't like it—something she would never let the world guess of her.

* * *

At the door to the State Dining Room, a young woman stood deferentially aside as the President passed by. He looked up and nodded at her as if he knew who she was, but she doubted very much he had the least notion. Even so, it was good of him to take notice of her and acknowledge her, and Barbara Higgins smiled warmly at him and resolved to remember the moment.

Maybe she was wrong in supposing the President had no idea who she was. The President did not overlook handsome young women, and Barbara Higgins was an exceptionally handsome young woman, with something partly bold and partly careless in her carriage and demeanor that was innocently voluptuous. She was not perhaps exceptionally beautiful but certainly attractive in a way that was singular to her. She had a full figure that showed through her modest dress. Her light brown hair hung to her shoulders—completely out of style. She was not readily overlooked, whether she meant to be noticed or not.

Though Mrs. Roosevelt was a gracious woman, kind to all the White House staff, she did not notice Barbara and followed the President into the room without a nod or a smile. Though the First Lady was a democratic woman—democratic with a small *d*—she was accustomed to being served; and, though she was thoughtful of people who worked for her, she did not find it invariably necessary to see them standing around. Or so Barbara judged.

Barbara glanced into the State Dining Room. A string quartet played, and the tables were set with white linen and glistening silver. She thought of herself as privileged to be this close to the State Dining Room in the White House, and the fact that she would never be invited to sit in that room herself did not generate the slightest resentment in her. In there was a world to which she aspired—who didn't?—but one she did not hate because it was closed to her. After all, class was class; and she was not of the class that got invited to dinner at the White House.

Rather, she stood outside the dining room door, waiting for her boss to pass by.

And here he came: Judge Blackwell, following not far behind the President, a little behind glorious old Justice Holmes, who escorted Secretary of Labor Frances Perkins on his arm. Judge Blackwell was without a lady. He walked alone.

"Sir," said Barbara. "The memoranda . . . You said to have them ready here."

Judge Blackwell stepped aside. People behind him went on into the dining room. He accepted two typewritten memoranda from Barbara Higgins, glanced at them momentarily, and accepted a pen from her hand and wrote his initials on each document.

"Thank you, Bobby," he said.

"Will there be anything else this evening, Judge?" she asked.

He smiled at her. "Uh . . . Get them delivered," he said. "Then . . . have a nice evening, Bobby."

She nodded. "I will."

Frances Perkins, Secretary of Labor, was pleased and also more than a little surprised that the ninety-two-year-old Justice Holmes had accepted the invitation to dinner. Since his retirement from the Court he had been something of a recluse, it was said—though it was known he took in the show at the Gayety every couple of weeks. She was apprehensive, too, about how he might react to being asked to take in to dinner a woman known in some circles as a "flaming liberal." Yet, as she might have expected, he was a courtly man; and she concluded he would have offered his arm and led Lucrezia Borgia in to dinner if the social situation called for it.

"Justice Holmes," she said to him as they walked to their

place in the dining room, "the President tells me that when he came to visit you shortly after his inaugural, he found you reading Plato in the original Greek. Surely that must be a difficult labor. Why do you do it, sir?"

The ramrod-erect elderly man looked down at her. "Why?" he asked in a tone that suggested the question was not well asked. "Well . . . To improve my mind, madam. To improve my mind."

William Tracy took his wife in to dinner. A short, yellow-haired, square-jawed man, he was another temporary laborer in the group the newspapers were calling the "brain trust." He was a professor of economics at Harvard. During the 1932 campaign, Governor Roosevelt had read his confidential analyses of the state of the nation's economy, on the cause of the Depression, on the means of digging out of the Depression—and Tracy had experienced the satisfaction of hearing his words echoed in the candidate's speeches. Now he had the pleasure of coming to Washington and having academic ideas—not usually welcome in Washington—heard and sometimes put into practice.

He and his wife did not live in the White House—very few of the braintrusters did. The Tracys lived in a boarding house on Eye Street, which was of course only temporary, and they expected to return to Cambridge before the Washington heat became unbearable.

So far as his wife was concerned, Blanche did not regard Bill's service in Washington as a worthwhile professional credential. She was a short, chubby, yet extraordinarily pretty young woman: twenty-five years old, with mocking gray eyes and lustrous blond hair. She was a Bostonian of ancient lineage, and she was accustomed to thinking of politics (and, to her, politics and government were the same thing) as low and sordid.

She could understand how a man like Franklin Roosevelt could become a politician. He felt his patrician status imposed a duty. And Mrs. Roosevelt had a duty to follow her husband's bent. But the rest of them . . . What motivated them?

Judge Blackwell's raised chin and provocative little grin caught her eye. There was a typical politician. A New Yorker. Something of a rogue. An air of fire and brimstone definitely hung about him. An Al Smith kind of New Yorker, with the effluvia of Hell swirling around him and mixing with cigar smoke and the smell of whiskey.

She smiled to herself. The judge was, of course, a libidinous rascal . . . and appealing enough to be dangerous. She lifted an eyebrow just enough to acknowledge his grin.

Mrs. Roosevelt glanced around the dining room. One guest had not yet arrived. It looked odd for a chair only three removed from her own at the head table to be unoccupied, and she hoped Mr. Faulkner would appear soon.

William Faulkner staggered out of a Washington speakeasy. He had been invited to the White House for dinner, had accepted the invitation, and had dressed in black tie. Having heard that Mrs. Roosevelt did not serve liquor at the White House, he had stepped into a recommended watering hole to fortify himself for the evening. Two hours later he stumbled onto the street and hailed the first cab he saw.

"Where to, buddy?" asked the officer as Faulkner climbed unsteadily into a Model-A Ford police car.

"The White House, driver," mumbled Faulkner.

" 'White House,' " the police officer repeated. "Yeah, sure. Need a ride, huh?"

Faulkner pinched a corner of his luxuriant mustache. "Indeed," he said loftily.

"Well, you just make yourself comfortable, buddy," said the policeman, "and I'll take you right where you need to go."

The officer had in mind the drunk tank at the D.C. jail; but when Faulkner was seated beside him in the Ford, he dug out of his jacket pocket his invitation to dinner at the White House. The police officer looked at that and turned right where he had meant to turn left. Ten minutes later he delivered William Faulkner at the door of the Mayflower Hotel, into the custody of a solicitous doorman who promised him that the White House was only five floors up. The policeman shrugged and pocketed the dollar Faulkner had given him—fare plus a tip.

"Utterly horrible," said Frances Perkins to Justice Holmes and the President. "The newsreels are in the theaters this week. You can see them capering around the fire, throwing books into the flames. If only they were all stark naked, the image of savagery would be complete."

She was talking about the infamous burning of books, which had taken place in Berlin the Saturday before. The German Minister of Propaganda, Dr. Paul Josef Goebbels, had staged a pagan ceremony at which young Nazis, mostly students, gleefully cast thousands of books into the flames of an immense bonfire. They burned the books of "degenerate" and "racially impure" authors such as Thomas Mann, Marcel Proust, H. G. Wells, Émile Zola, and Helen Keller.

"Inferior minds," said Justice Holmes, "are invariably the most intolerant. When they can't cope with ideas, they seek to suppress them. It has always been so. Kings, emperors, ideologues, religionists . . . What did the man say? I can't quote it exactly. 'The mind of an honest man is terrifying.' Something like that. Kings and dictators, priests and preachers—and some professors, for that matter—fear the mind of an honest man. So . . . they burn the books. But the mind of man will not be suppressed."

It was more answer than Miss Perkins had expected, or wanted, but she nodded and tried to commit to memory what Justice Holmes had said.

The President added something—"God save us from those who think God talks to them."

Justice Holmes nodded. "And God save us," he added, "from those who think they talk to God. In the friendly little chat between God and William McKinley, McKinley thought himself advised to go to war."

"Considering that McKinley's intelligence was roughly equivalent to Warren Harding's," said the President, "I am skeptical that he was capable of understanding or interpreting the word of God."

Sara Carter stood just outside the door, her lips slightly parted, staring at the assemblage in the State Dining Room.

"Move that, Sara. Don't just stand there and stare."

She glanced at Mr. Babbage, nodded, and pushed her cart of dishes toward the elevator to the ground level. She knew Mr. Babbage had let her stare as long as he thought he could, before someone took notice of her. She was grateful to him.

She had seen, not just the President and Mrs. Roosevelt, but also Justice Holmes and General MacArthur, and maybe later Mr. Babbage would tell her who some of the other people were.

As she trudged toward the elevator, she glanced back. It was a real privilege to work in the White House.

Barbara Higgins would not have agreed. Sitting at her secretary's desk in the Executive Wing, she stuffed the last of Judge Blackwell's memoranda in an interoffice mail envelope. She had telephoned for a messenger, but getting a messenger to deliver anything after five o'clock was all but impossible in Washington, and after seven entirely impossible. She had no choice but to deliver some of these envelopes herself—at least those that went to people the judge might see early in the morning.

Two envelopes went to the President himself. Barbara tried phoning Miss LeHand, his secretary, but was told by the switchboard that Miss LeHand had left the White House for several hours. All right. She could leave the envelopes at Miss LeHand's door, with a note that they were to be handed to the President first thing in the morning. That meant a walk back into the main house and up to the third floor.

Mr. Louis Howe . . . Well, he lived on the third floor, too. She could try his door.

Then—

Barbara was tired. She stretched her legs out in front of her; and, because she was alone, she pulled up her skirt and rubbed the skin of her legs above the tops of her stockings. She yawned. She could sleep right here, if there were a bed.

Major Eisenhower was amused by how much the President and Justice Holmes seemed to enjoy each other's conversation. Secretary Perkins spent most of her time leaning toward them, listening and laughing as the two men exchanged what had to be quips and maybe even jokes. This president was an ebullient man.

Mrs. Roosevelt, on the President's left, was compelled, apparently, to struggle to make conversation with General MacArthur. The place to the left of the general was vacant, putting the First Lady under an awkward obligation to talk almost exclusively with him.

The general was grave and dignified. He smiled, even occasionally laughed, but comradely good humor was not his forte. Between courses he lit cigarettes—one of the few men in Washington, besides the President himself, who would have smoked while talking to Mrs. Roosevelt.

The fact about General MacArthur, as Major Eisenhower saw it, was that he was imposing in uniform but rather ordinary-looking otherwise. With his cap settled on his head, covering his balding pate, with shoulders augmented by the pads sewed into his uniform jackets, with all his ribbons in place, his Sam Browne belt crossing his chest, his breeches tucked into varnished boots, the general was quite a man. In the shower room off the golf course, he shared the equality of nakedness.

For himself, Major Eisenhower understood full well that he was as impressive naked in the shower room as he was anywhere. If he was in any way impressive, it was from his midwestern modesty and sincerity. That was all he had, and he wondered how far it would carry him.

It had carried him this far. Mamie could write home, after tonight, that she had dined at the White House. That was a high and unanticipated privilege for a thirty-seven-year-old daughter of the Dowds of Iowa. It was a high and unanticipated privilege for a son of the Eisenhowers of Kansas. A man would have to be utterly insensitive to fail to be moved by his wife's quiet pride.

Judge Blackwell sat at the right of Mamie Eisenhower. He was a fascinating man, just the sort of man she had expected to find at a White House dinner: urbane, knowledgeable, articulate—a native of Manhattan and filled with all that special shrewdness that characterized the best of the native New Yorkers.

"A considerable achievement, I should think," he said, referring to her husband's position as assistant to the Chief of Staff. "Doesn't the typical major find himself in command of a desert post in Arizona?"

"Oh, Judge . . ."

"I am certain *you* have had much to do with his attaining this position. The army is not the least of institutions where a charming wife is an important asset to a man's career."

"Please . . . !"

"It is true. And I am perfectly certain it has been so. I am sorry we have not met before, Mrs. Eisenhower. Uh . . . Mamie. Do you mind? I won't be in Washington much longer, but I hope you and the major will be my guests for dinner one evening soon. Or, maybe, you and I can have lunch one day. I know we would enjoy that."

The First Lady had not yet learned to sleep comfortably in the White House. The rooms in the family quarters in the west end of the second floor were comfortable enough, though far from luxurious, but she had not yet subdued the sense that she was sleeping in temporary quarters, like a hotel room. She had a sense, too, that the White House was an institution, not a home, not even a hotel; and she was aware that the great house never really slept, that someone was prowling around all night: maids, stewards, Secret Service agents, policemen . . .

So it was that when a disturbance of some kind broke loose in the Center Hall, a few rooms from her bedroom, Mrs. Roosevelt was wakened, even alarmed. It was, after all, only a few weeks since Zangara had attempted to assassinate her husband in Miami. Zangara had been electrocuted for the murder of the Mayor of Chicago, who had been killed by the bullets intended for the President-elect; but the President and his family had to be alert to the fact that there were those who meant them harm.

She pulled a faded wool robe on over her nightgown and went out into the hall to see what was the matter.

She walked out of the West Sitting Hall, the living room of the family quarters, the place where the President held his evening cocktail ritual, and through the door into the Center Hall.

The door to the President's own bedroom suite was to her right. To her left was the second-floor elevator lobby and the elevator that carried the President down to the ground floor each morning, from where he was wheeled to the West Wing, the executive offices. To her right a little farther along was the door to the second-floor oval room the President had chosen for his study. Next on her left were the entrances to two guest suites—that is, bedrooms with baths—separated by a book storage closet.

WHITE HOUSE, CENTRAL PART OF SECOND FLOOR—1933

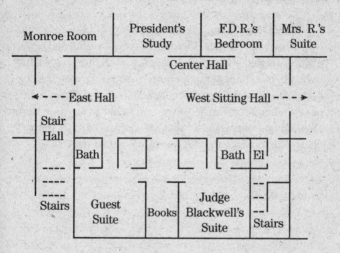

The disturbance centered on the door to the guest room occupied by Judge Horace Blackwell. A uniformed White House policeman stood at the door, as if he were guarding the room. Someone inside was crying.

When the First Lady reached the door, the policeman moved into the doorway and blocked it.

"Ma'am—"

"What's going on?" she asked, quickly irritated to be blocked from entering a room in the White House.

"There's been an accident, ma'am," said the policeman.

A shriek from the guest room dramatically contradicted the policeman.

"I had nothin' to do with it, I tell you! I swear! I just *found* him! An' I called for help, and you try to make it out that I killed him! I had nothin' to do with it!"

Mrs. Roosevelt glared at the policeman. "Stand aside, young man," she said firmly.

"Ma'am . . . You don't want to see—"

"Stand aside, young man!"

He did, reluctantly. She stepped through the doorway.

The body of Judge Horace Blackwell lay sprawled across a blood-soaked bed. A young Negro woman, her hands handcuffed behind her back, shook her head in anger and frustration. Tears glistened on her cheeks. Another uniformed officer stood alert beside her, as if to grab her if she tried to do anything violent. Another man, in civilian clothes, sat in a chair with a notepad on his knees, calmly writing.

II

"MADAM," SAID THE MAN with the notepad, "I should be most grateful to you if you would return to the private quarters. We have a murder to investigate here."

Mrs. Roosevelt stared skeptically at the man. "I have seen you in the White House," she said. "Just who are you? And what is your authority?"

The man rose from his chair. "My name is Pickering," he said with great dignity and precision in his voice. "Lawrence T.—for Thomas—Pickering. I am a senior agent of the Secret Service."

Pickering was a man of some sixty years, she guessed. He was slight: rail thin and of less than average height. His hair was light brown, as was his thin mustache, which was neatly, even severely, trimmed to leave a quarter of an inch between it and his thin, white lips. His nose and chin were sharp. He stood in a rigidly erect posture. Unlike most men, who were wearing double-breasted suits that year, he wore a narrow, single-breasted, light brown wool suit, with vest, white shirt, bow tie.

"I am pleased to meet you, Mr. Pickering," she said.

"Thank you. I know, of course, that you are Mrs. Roosevelt, and it is a pleasure to meet you; but in spite of that, I must ask you not to remain here. Investigation of a crime is a somewhat specialized endeavor, and intrusion upon a crime scene by anyone not essential to the investigation can do great harm. You might, for example, touch something and smudge a fingerprint."

She walked into the room and frowned over the body of Judge Blackwell. He was quite naked, and his body bore half a dozen stab wounds.

"Besides which," said Pickering, "this particular investigation is somewhat . . . indelicate. You really should not be staring, madam, at a naked man."

"*I didn't kill him!*" screamed the young Negro woman.

"So you have told us, repeatedly," said Pickering calmly and patronizingly. "But . . . madam— Please."

"Mr. Pickering," said the First Lady with equal calm. "You say you are a senior agent of the Secret Service. It is your function, is it not, to prevent harm coming to the President of the United States?"

"That is our major function," said Pickering. "We have certain other duties."

"None more important, I suppose," she said.

He nodded. "None more important."

"Yes . . ." said she. "And yet a murder has been committed barely ten yards from the door to the President's bedroom." She sat down in the second wing chair in the guest room. "I appears to me that you could use some help, Mr. Pickering. Indeed, you perhaps require . . . supervision."

"Would you care to have my resignation, madam?" he asked crisply.

"You can't resign to me, Mr. Pickering," she said with a little smile. "You must submit that to the Secretary of the Treasury. In any event, you seem to have made progress here. I see you've made an arrest."

She nodded toward the Negro girl, who twisted her

shoulders and tugged at the handcuffs that bound her hands behind her back. Pickering, too, nodded.

"*I didn't do it!*"

"Her name," said Pickering, raising his eyebrows and looking down on the girl, "is Sara Carter. She is a maid in the White House—as you can see from her uniform."

"And what makes you believe she killed Judge Blackwell?"

"She has no satisfactory explanation for being on the second floor at one A.M.," said Pickering.

Mrs. Roosevelt looked at the maid. "Why were you here, Sara?" she asked gently.

Sara Carter only shook her head and sobbed.

Lawrence Pickering sat down near Mrs. Roosevelt, in the chair where he had been sitting when the First Lady arrived. He picked up his little notebook.

"Officer Runkle was making his rounds," he said. "At . . . twelve minutes past one he observed Sara Carter in the Center Hall, just outside this room. He—"

"I run right to him and say, 'Judge Blackwell's dead! Judge Blackwell's been killed!' Why would I do that if I killed him? Why would I run to the first policeman I see and say, 'Man dead in there'? Why would I do that?"

"A reasonable question," said Mrs. Roosevelt. "Why would she, Mr. Pickering?"

"I do not know, madam," said Pickering with the tight-lipped precision she began to understand was a constant with him and not something dragged out for the moment to express annoyance and disapproval. "I can think of reasons. I would prefer to discuss them outside the presence of the suspect."

" 'Suspect . . . ' " muttered Sara Carter. "Is that all I am? Just *suspected?* If that's all, then why am I handcuff' like this? And I'm going to jail, ain't I? Why is that, if all I am is a suspect?"

"You are handcuffed the way you are because you got violent," said the uniformed officer. He turned to Mrs. Roosevelt. "Excuse me, ma'am. I'm Officer Runkle."

The First Lady smiled wanly at the officer and nodded. "I . . . am unfamiliar with procedures in Washington," she said. "You are taking her to jail? What jail?"

"The District jail," said Pickering. "We've telephoned for policewomen to come and pick her up."

Sara Carter turned toward Mrs. Roosevelt and faced her with defiance, yet with tears streaming down her cheeks. "To hang, is where they takin' me?" she said. "I got no chanct. They gonna—"

"We won't hang you," said Pickering. "You will be electrocuted. That is, you will if you are found guilty."

" 'Foun' guilty,' " Sara Carter repeated dully. "That'll be easy 'nough. She fixed her eyes on Mrs. Roosevelt. "I'm gonna be *lynched*, is what I'm gonna be. Like any other gal my color they decide they want to—"

The First Lady stood up abruptly. "No," she said forcefully. "No, Sara. You will not be lynched. You will have a fair trial. I promise you that. You know who I am. I am the President's wife, and you have my word that you will receive a fair trial."

After Sara Carter was led away, Mrs. Roosevelt sat for a long moment in silence, trying to stare as little as possible at the body of Judge Horace Blackwell: a ghastly sight but also, as Pickering had pointed out, a naked man. No one had moved him, or even covered him, since the arrival of a District police pathologist was expected any moment.

The body lay on its face mostly, though twisted sharply. Two of the wounds were on the back, and four were on the side, under the right arm.

"I would guess," said Mrs. Roosevelt, "that the first blow was struck while he was asleep, the second very quickly before he could wake fully, and after that he tried to roll away and the attacker kept stabbing him in the side."

Lawrence Pickering looked at her quizzically. He nodded. "I surmise the same," he said.

She rose and walked around the room. "Why do you suppose," she asked, "he was sleeping in the nude when a pair of pajamas lie here, folded, on his dresser?"

Pickering sighed. "My dear madam," he said. "May I once more urge you to leave this investigation to professionals? I am afraid you can only be . . . seriously embarrassed if you persist here."

She ignored the question. "He was drinking shortly before he went to sleep," she said, bending over to sniff at a glass. "The dregs of whiskey in this glass remain liquid. In a few hours the alcohol would have evaporated. A few hours? Perhaps sooner. He may have been too drunk to struggle. The autopsy will tell."

"What do you know of these things, Mrs. Roosevelt?"

She turned to face the Secret Service agent. "Only what a perceptive eye and an inquiring mind tell me, Mr. Pickering," she said. "Only what logic and common sense suggest. Are my surmises wrong, so far?"

He shook his head. "Not that I can tell. I surmise pretty much as you do."

"Then . . . the pajamas? Why—?"

Pickering sucked in his breath and drew his stiff body into an even more rigid, even more erect posture. "My dear lady," he said. "The answer lies before us. But I . . ." His lips whitened as he pinched them tight shut.

"You won't tell me," she said. "I must find out for myself."

Pickering closed his eyes and nodded curtly.

She glanced around. The judge's eyeglasses lay on the nightstand by the bed. In a large round ashtray lay the burned-short butt of a big cigar. And . . . And a . . . strange object.

Pickering stared at her apprehensively, watching her

stare at the object with the cigar butt in the ashtray.

"Oh!" she exclaimed, and her hand darted to her mouth.

"Do you know what it is?" he asked.

"I believe I do," she said. "Confirm it for me, please, Mr. Pickering. Tell me what it is."

Once more he lifted his chin high, and once more his lips stiffened. "It is, Mrs. Roosevelt, a condom," he said. "What is more, it is a *used* one. And I suspect it explains why Sara Carter was here."

"Let us not jump to that conclusion, Mr. Pickering."

Pickering rose from his chair. He walked into the bathroom and looked around, coming back into the bedroom after a moment. "You are interested to know why I ordered the arrest of the Negro girl," he said. "Why do I jump to the conclusion that she—"

"I did not mean to say you jumped to the conclusion that she is guilty."

He nodded. "Thank you. She was asked to work during the dinner, carrying trays of dishes to and from the pantry. After that she was asked to work downstairs, helping to wash dishes and pans. Her work was finished about twelve-thirty. She should have left the White House then."

"Twelve-thirty," Mrs. Roosevelt repeated. "Forty-two minutes before she was seen by Officer Runkle here on the second floor."

"The time from downstairs is an approximation," said Pickering. "As little as half an hour may have passed—enough time for her to have come here, engaged in illicit conduct with Judge Blackwell, killed him, and left the room."

"But that assumes a great deal, Mr. Pickering."

"Yes, except for one more thing. When she was asked by Officer Runkle what she was doing up here, she said she had come up from the kitchen to bring Judge Blackwell a bottle of seltzer water, which he had called for. That was a lie. In the first place, the ushers received no call from here asking for seltzer water. In the second place, there is no bottle of seltzer water in the room."

"I am afraid that *is* suggestive," Mrs. Roosevelt murmured thoughtfully.

"When Runkle told her she must return with him to the judge's room, while he confirmed the story, she tried to run from him. When he caught her, she struck at him. That is why she was handcuffed."

Mrs. Roosevelt looked around the room. "Where is the weapon?" she asked.

Pickering sighed. "At the moment, that's a weakness in the case. It could have been thrown from the window. We will search the grounds at daylight."

"It *is* a weakness if the knife is not found," said Mrs. Roosevelt. "Unless she threw it from the window, it must be in this room. Or in the bathroom."

"It could be under the body," said Pickering.

"The autopsy will show what size of knife it was," said Mrs. Roosevelt. "It may tell something more about it."

Pickering stared around the edges of the body as if he expected to spot the knife where he had not spotted it before. "Another suggestive point," he said, "is that Sara Carter is a Negro."

"And how is that suggestive, Mr. Pickering?"

"Well . . . It is well known that the knife is the Negro's weapon of choice. That and the razor."

"Mr. Pickering, *really!*"

"Don't be naive, my dear lady," he said.

"If that is an element of your proof, it is another weakness," she said. "And I find one more: one more glaring weakness."

"And what is that?" he asked, raising his chin and eyebrows and looking down his long thin nose.

"Motive, Mr. Pickering," she said. "What do you suggest was Sara Carter's motive for murdering Judge Blackwell?"

"The investigation will very likely produce one," he said.

"I should think it better, if that young woman is not to be rather quickly released."

Mrs. Roosevelt asked Lawrence Pickering to accompany her to her study while the body of Judge Blackwell was removed from the guest room. Two other, younger, Secret Service agents, who had arrived in response to Pickering's call, were given the task of searching every inch of the bedroom, closet, and bathroom, looking for the murder weapon or any other clue.

The night steward came up from the kitchen with a pot of coffee. Mrs. Roosevelt sat at her desk, still in her wool robe, nightgown, and slippers. Pickering gratefully accepted a cup of strong black coffee.

"I must, in all frankness, confess," said Pickering, "that investigation of murder is not my métier. My function in the White House is, as you suggested earlier, to protect the President. I am afraid, my dear lady, that you and I are amateurs at criminal investigation. I think we will have to call in professionals, probably from the F.B.I."

Mrs. Roosevelt sipped coffee. "The circumstances of Judge Blackwell's death suggest an embarrassing scandal," she said. "I think we should see if the matter cannot be handled within the White House, without summoning assistance from any outside agency—unless we absolutely have to do it. I will ask the President what he wants us to do. In the meanwhile, let us see what develops. After all, Mr. Pickering, if it proves true that Sara Carter killed Judge Blackwell, then the matter is closed. May I assume the District police will cooperate in keeping the matter confidential?"

"The District police," said Pickering, "will cooperate with the White House. Of that you may be certain."

"Well, then. Let us see what the autopsy determines. And you *will* continue to search for the knife?"

Pickering, as she had observed already and would continue to observe, did not like to be reminded of his duty. "Yes," he said loftily.

"Then, may we try to get some sleep?" she asked.

"Well . . . I should like to take a moment to review one matter, if you don't mind." said Pickering. "If Judge Blackwell was murdered by Sara Carter—or even, for that matter, if he wasn't—his life circumstances are of considerable interest. For example, the missing motive may be found in the man's character and background."

Mrs. Roosevelt nodded. "I understand. So . . . Let's see. Judge Blackwell is—*was*—a bit short of his fiftieth birthday, if I recall correctly. He was a native of New York City. His family were of modest circumstances, I believe. He secured a good education, nonetheless, and—if my recollection is accurate—received his degree in law and was admitted to the bar about 1912."

"His career was interrupted by the World War?" asked Pickering.

"Yes. He went to France, as I recall—as a lieutenant of infantry. I believe, actually, he was wounded there. Anyway, he became an assistant district attorney during the twenties. He gained a reputation as a crusading prosecutor. He brought some of Mayor Jimmy Walker's circle to justice and secured the convictions of a number of men who were cheating on municipal contracts."

"And was appointed a judge, as a reward," suggested Pickering.

She nodded. "I suppose you could say so. When my husband was Governor of New York, he appointed Mr. Blackwell to the bench. That was in the summer of 1931. When my husband was nominated for President, Judge Blackwell offered to resign from the court to devote himself to the campaign. Which he did. He has been serving here in Washington as a member of what some commentators call the President's brain trust. The President had asked him to make a close study of certain elements of the law, looking for effective ways of discouraging unethical stock manipulations. Mr. Blackwell had prosecuted some cases of the kind, and as a judge he had tried one or two. He believed federal law could be more effective than state law in preventing certain types of stock fraud."

Lawrence Pickering finished his coffee and put the cup aside, frowning. "Are you suggesting that 'malefactors of great wealth,' as your cousin Theodore Roosevelt used to put it, might have had sufficient motive to want Judge Blackwell dead?"

She shook her head. "I do not suggest that, Mr. Pickering. On the other hand, anything is possible, and while we lack a definitive answer to the question of who killed the judge, I suggest we list all possibilities as . . . well, as possibilities."

Pickering stepped to the tray and poured a second cup of coffee for himself. "We must then of course list the jealous wife as a possible suspect," he said.

Mrs. Roosevelt smiled weakly. "A jealous husband is not beyond the realm of possibility," she said. "A jealous wife . . . No. Judge Blackwell never married."

"A jealous husband . . . ?"

She shook her head. "The jealous spouse is the classic suspect. In the case of Horace Blackwell, there was no wife to be jealous. If the classic suspect is to be a factor in the case, it will have to be a jealous husband. But I have nothing specific in mind."

Pickering glanced at his watch. Mrs. Roosevelt glanced at the clock on her desk. The sun would rise in less than three hours.

"People he prosecuted . . ." said Pickering.

"People he sentenced," she added.

"But still," said Pickering with emphasis, "the murderer

has to be someone with access to the White House in the middle of the night."

"How very difficult is that, Mr. Pickering?"

Pickering's eyes dropped to stare into his coffee. "During the war," he said. "I mean, during the presidency of Woodrow Wilson, we made it rather difficult to enter the White House—that is, to get past the guards. We were afraid German spies might try to assassinate the President. Then, President Harding wanted to go back to the way things had been before, when a man or woman could walk into the White House anytime. That was part of what he called 'normalcy.' We never quite went back to that. But I would be less than candid if I told you that getting in and out is very difficult. It is if you don't know your way around. If you do—"

He shrugged, and she said, "If you do, you can wander in and out all night."

"Yes. Officers are on duty only at the gates and main entries."

"The murderer, then," said Mrs. Roosevelt, "is someone for whom the White House is no great mystery. That takes in a substantial part of the population of Washington, I imagine."

Pickering lifted his chin still again. "That is why," he said with his characteristic thin precision, "I do hope it turns out that Sara Carter murdered Judge Blackwell."

"And that," said Mrs. Roosevelt, "is exactly what is wrong. Wouldn't it be easy, wouldn't it be neat, to conclude that a young Negro woman stabbed Judge Blackwell to death, for reasons we cannot imagine but that were doubtlessly sufficient to her—?"

"Babs!" the President interrupted. "It is a matter for the Secret Service, for the police, maybe for the F.B.I. We—"

"EffDee," Missy LeHand interrupted. "EffDee" was what she called the President in private moments. "EffDee"—for

F.D.R. And private moments included moments when Mrs. Roosevelt was present.)

"Girl . . . ," said the President to Missy.

"Do you really want John Edgar Hoover prowling around in the White House?" asked Missy.

The President frowned, first at Missy, then at the First Lady. He was sitting up in bed, with his breakfast tray in his lap and half a dozen newspapers spread over the bed and floor. "I don't want Babs involved, even tangentially, in a scandal that could occupy entire front pages, from coast to coast," he said.

"I seem to have been somehow injected into the situation," said Mrs. Roosevelt.

"Well, inject yourself out," said the President.

"Really, Franklin, putting aside the unidiomatic—"

"Babs, you know what I mean."

"Think a minute, EffDee," said Missy. "Who could better protect your interests?"

"The F.B.I. . . . ," ventured the President.

"Would like nothing better than to enmesh you in a scandal," said Missy. "That's what Hoover lives on: scandals—except the one great scandal he represents. You can't trust that man. You know you can't."

"Babs . . . ," muttered the President. "Can I depend on you to remain on the outer edge of this matter: just looking after our interests and not sticking your nib into a criminal investigation?"

The First Lady had extraordinary energy. She did not quickly tire. But in the past few hours she had tossed in her bed, her mind troubled with the grisly sight of Judge Blackwell lying dead in a blood-soaked bed, coupled with the sight of a tearful young Negro woman being hustled off to jail—leaving behind the accusation that she was on her way to a lynching. Mrs. Roosevelt was tired.

"Franklin . . . ," she said wearily. "I know we can agree

on one thing. Sara Carter must have a full and fair trial. We cannot—even at the most remote distance—be parties to a lynching."

The President reached for the package of Camels that lay within easy reach beside his bed. He shook one out and inserted it in his holder. "Babs," he said as he lit his first cigarette of the day. "I deputize you in my name to see to it that no lynching occurs."

He sounded facetious, with the famous cigarette holder tipped at the angle that made him seem facetious; but the First Lady and Missy LeHand knew he meant what he said.

"No lynching, Babs. But no playing Sherlock Holmes. Just be sure the evidence against that young Negro woman is sufficient to justify the charges against her. And— Well, if the evidence is convincing, you must back away and let justice take its course. Only if it's not—"

Missy was grinning. Mrs. Roosevelt smiled.

"What kind of mandate am I giving?" The President chuckled. "I can only depend on your good judgment, Babs— of which I've had ample evidence over the years. Go to it, old girl!"

Mrs. Roosevelt was pleased to learn that Lawrence Pickering was in the White House and on duty by eight-thirty, though he had been as active through the night as she had—and maybe more. He still wore the suit he had worn last night, and she wondered if he had left the White House at all.

She herself looked fresh in a simple pink knit dress, with a strand of pearls around her neck. She wore also a small white flower on her shoulder. Tommy Thompson, her secretary, had appeared this morning wearing a flower and had brought one for Mrs. Roosevelt too.

"The grounds beneath the guest-room window have been closely searched," he said. "By five men. And they have not found the knife that killed Judge Blackwell."

"We might have wished they had," said Mrs. Roosevelt.

"Certainly," said Pickering, as if the idea that they might not want to find the knife had never occurred to him.

He suspected something. Mrs. Roosevelt was not ready to admit it, but she was forming within her the genesis of a hope that the Blackwell murder case might not be solved so easily as to convict Sara Carter. Apart from her native sympathy for the underdog—born in part from her childhood as the never-terribly-attractive orphan—she was troubled by the weaknesses in the case against Sara Carter.

Where was the weapon? How could Sara have disposed of it in a few minutes, so that a team of searching policemen could not find it? Besides, what was her motive? Why did Sara Carter want Judge Blackwell dead?

"The President authorizes us to pursue this case, Mr. Pickering," she said. "Without the assistance of the Federal Bureau of Investigation. I imagine my mandate, vague though it may be, is to see to it that justice is done . . . with as little embarrassment as possible to the new administration."

"My dear lady," said Lawrence Pickering. "Allow me to assure you that I am a great admirer of President Roosevelt and all he is doing. As a permanent staff member here, I am obliged to hold my political opinions *in pectore*, as they say. But— Well, I was a great admirer of President Hoover, as a man. I found him intelligent, honest . . . and— But, madam, President Roosevelt's boldness in addressing our nation's crisis has won from me an admiration I was prepared to withhold."

She heard this with some surprise. Pickering was reserved— No, not reserved. He was stuffy. "Very well then, Mr. Pickering. I believe we understand each other."

"Perhaps," he said.

"I mean, we understand what we are to do, how we are to handle this matter. Now, has any word come from the police pathologist?"

"Not as yet. He will send his report by messenger."

"And Sara Carter remains in jail?"

"In isolation," he said. "Where she cannot tell other pris-
oners that there was a murder in the White House last night."

Mrs. Roosevelt frowned. "Does Sara Carter have a family? Have they been informed why she has not come home?"

"They were visited by a D.C. officer this morning. He told
them she had been arrested and was being held on suspicion
of murder. He did not tell them where the murder occurred."

"She will tell them when they visit her at the jail."

"They won't be allowed to visit her. Not for a while, anyway. We can hold her forty-eight hours without letting her see
anyone."

"In forty-eight hours we may be able to release her," said
Mrs. Roosevelt. "I am still deeply troubled about the matter
of *motive.* I cannot think why that girl would have wanted to
kill Judge Blackwell."

"Two District detectives searched her room," said Pickering. "What they found may complicate the case. It may also
suggest a motive."

"What did they find?"

"Money," said Pickering. "They found $172 in cash. The
girl is paid $12 a week, so where did she get $172?"

"Savings?"

Pickering shook his head. "That is most doubtful," he
said. "They also found in her room a radio, a Victrola, and a
rather extensive wardrobe—more than $12 a week might be
expected to buy. She owns eight pairs of shoes, half a dozen
hats, dresses, coats, and a collection of . . . intimate wear, none
of it cheap."

"Does she have a . . . a boyfriend?"

"We haven't found out yet. They interrogated her for a
time last night, but she was defiant, and nothing much was
learned. The detectives intend to work on her some more this
morning."

"Telephone them, Mr. Pickering. Remind them that the case is a White House matter and that we will not tolerate oppressive methods of interrogation."

Pickering showed a pinched and uncertain little smile. "Very well, madam," he said.

"Tell them also that I will be coming by to question the girl myself."

"Is that wise? I mean, should you be seen at police headquarters? At the jail?"

"Tell the officers in charge that I count on them to arrange for me to visit Sara Carter confidentially."

III

"BEFORE THE WEEK IS ended," said the President, "the Congress will have the bill. Ordinarily, I like to avoid talking about bills we send up to the Congress before they get there, but in this case the cat seems to be out of the bag, so I guess I can talk."

A score of White House reporters were gathered around the President's desk in the Oval Office. Leaning back in his chair, cigarette holder atilt, Franklin Roosevelt was presiding over a press conference.

A few of the senior reporters sat. Most stood. All had notepads and pencils ready. They were sure the President would announce something significant. He never disappointed them.

What was different about a Roosevelt press conference—what none of the reporters have ever seen before—was that this President actually *enjoyed* hearing and answering their questions. Usually he opened with a statement: something he wanted to see on the front pages of their newspapers. Then he took questions. And the whole thing was a friendly exchange, often punctuated by little jokes and hearty laughter.

There were no microphones in the Oval Office during a

press conference. Like his predecessors, President Roosevelt
wanted his statements to be reported, not directly quoted. He
would speak on radio—and often. But he did not want the nation to hear the give-and-take between him and the reporters.
That was an inside thing. The people generally might not understand it.

"What's it going to be called, Mr. President?"

"The National Industrial Recovery Act," said the President. "That is . . . it will be an act when it's enacted. As of today,
it isn't even a bill, because it won't be introduced for a few
days yet."

"Let's see, Mr. President. That's N.I.R.A., isn't it? What
will the agency created to administer it be called?"

The President joined in the laughter in the room. "Another alphabet agency," he said. "National Recovery Administration. N.R.A. N . . . R . . . A."

"Mr. President, the Congress expects to adjourn in the
middle of June. Do you expect this legislation to be enacted
in the month that's left?"

The President laughed. "Well . . . I'm not going on vacation in June. Are you? The crisis our country faces is not going
on vacation. Men who are out of work aren't going to have jobs
suddenly, in June. I would imagine the Congress will look at
it that way. If they can't give this legislation full consideration
between now and the middle of June, maybe they'll elect to
remain in session a little longer."

"Mr. President, there is a story in the Chicago *Tribune*
this week to the effect that one of your sons will soon enroll
in a C.C.C. camp. Is there any truth to that?"

Once more the room all but glowed in the light of the famous F.D.R. grin. "Actually," he said, "I'm a lucky parent. None
of my chicks is unemployed. You've noticed, I don't even have
any living at home. There is no more truth in that story than
there is in anything published by Bertie McCormick."

Even the reporter employed by "Colonel" Robert Mc-
Cormick laughed.

Missy LeHand stood apprehensively in the doorway, listening for the question about the death of Judge Horace Blackwell. It was not asked. The story was not out yet.

While the President was holding his press conference, the
First Lady was meeting in the Blue Room with a delegation of
women, representing, as they said, women's clubs in eighteen
states. They had come, they said, to enlist Mrs. Roosevelt in
what they called a "crusade for decency."

Speaking for them was a formidable woman named Mrs.
Violet Barnes, from Cincinnati, who said she was a regent of
the D.A.R. She wore a cloche that covered almost every wisp
of her iron gray hair and her eyebrows besides. As many as
fifty buttons closed her maroon silk crepe dress from her
throat to her ankles.

"What a time it is," she said—obviously delivering a lec-
ture she had memorized—"to re-establish decency and morality in America! What a time!"

Mrs. Roosevelt sat with her head slightly tipped, a measured smile on her face, listening intently to the woman's fer-
vent speech. Her thoughts were on the murder of Judge Blackwell and on Sara Carter in the District jail. She had checked
to see if the judge's family had been notified of his death, and
learned that he had no family closer than an aged aunt and
uncle in Queens. They, it seemed, couldn't remember a
nephew named Horace. The judge's secretary, Barbara Higgins, had fainted when told the judge was dead.

"The repeal of Prohibition will mean the end of the
speakeasies. But it will mean the return of the saloons! What
a time! What an urgency to reassert Christian values!"

Tommy Thompson sat apart in a corner of the room
placidly taking notes on what the woman was saying—which

seemed to disconcert Mrs. Barnes, who apparently had never experienced anyone's writing down what she said.

"The dime novel! Indecent singing, called, I believe, 'crooning.' Utterly indecent dancing! Indecent magazines on every newsstand! Indecent cartoons in every newspaper! Indecent dress on half the women of America!"

The knife. They still had not found the knife. How could Sara Carter have disposed of the knife? If they did not find the knife, how could they convict the young Negro woman of the murder?

But would they try without it? And would Sara Carter be—as she vividly feared—the victim of a white prosecutor, a white judge, a white jury, who would send her to electrocution simply because she was a convenient suspect, simply because disposing of her would dispose of the case? A lynching . . .

Mrs. Roosevelt had promised her justice. But the matter would escape from her hands before long. If Sara Carter were indicted—

"And so, *we call on you!*"

Oh, dear . . . What were they calling on her *for?*

" 'A Century of Progress' they want to call it! The 1933 World's Fair, in Chicago! But on that midway they mean to exhibit indecency that would make even the Little Egypt of forty years ago blush! Are you aware, Mrs. Roosevelt, that they plan to allow that notorious trollop *Sally Rand* to take off her clothes and dance *naked?*"

"Umm . . . ?" was all the response the First Lady could generate for the moment. She had not heard that Sally Rand was to dance at the World's Fair. And nude? She hadn't heard that.

"Progress?" asked Mrs. Barnes shrilly. "Hardly! And that is one reason why we have come to you, Mrs. Roosevelt. We call on your to use your influence to prevent this outrage!"

The First Lady cast an appealing glance at Tommy, who only shrugged.

"Well, I . . . I'm afraid I have no influence on the selection of entertainment at the Chicago World's Fair." She smiled, in the vain hope she could lighten the moment. "They didn't consult me as to what they should—"

"But they will listen to you!"

"I'm not quite certain what I should say."

"We have prepared a letter for you," said Mrs. Barnes, jerking a sheet of paper from her handbag. "If you will but sign it—"

"I am afraid I *never* sign letters others have written for me," said Mrs. Roosevelt firmly. "I am asked to do so from time to time, and—"

"But *this* is a demand for morality!"

"Please leave it. I will consider it."

"There is no compromise with morality!" warned Mrs. Barnes.

"Oh, no. I am quite sure there is not. And I grateful to you ladies for coming here to give me the benefit of your views."

When she left the Blue Room, the First Lady was met in the hall by Lawrence Pickering. He stared inquisitively at the delegation of moral ladies who marched across the hall toward their exit onto the North Portico. Whatever else he was, Pickering was distinctly a judgmental man, and he was not subtle in his judgment of the club women. He pursed his thin lips and looked down his nose at them with scorn he made no effort to conceal.

"The autopsy report has arrived," he said to Mrs. Roosevelt.

"Does it contain anything interesting?" she asked. With a nod toward the door to the elevator hall, she indicated she wanted to go upstairs. "I mean, does it tell us anything we did not know?"

"I believe not," said Pickering. "However, you may wish to look at it."

When they sat down in her study and she scanned the

pages of the report, she saw why he would rather not summarize it.

Judge Horace Blackwell, it said, was a man with impaired heart function. His heart bore the scars of an old heart attack, suffered probably five years ago. He was overweight. His muscle tone was poor.

His death had been caused by six stab wounds, four of which had penetrated his lung, one his heart. Each wound was approximately five inches deep, approximately one inch wide. Judge Blackwell had, therefore, been stabbed with a hunting knife or something of that type.

The time of death was estimated as between 12:00 midnight and 1:00 A.M.

> The alcohol content of the subject's blood was 0.12%. With this quantify of alcohol in the blood, the subject was, at the time of death, intoxicated to the extent of severe impairment of function. It is possible that the subject was unable to resist effectively when attacked with a knife.
>
> The subject engaged in sexual intercourse and experienced orgasm within the last hour before death. Since the ability to perform the sex act is inconsistent with the subject's state of intoxication at the time of death, it may be inferred that the subject drank a considerable quantity of alcohol after sexual intercourse.
>
> A few loose pubic hairs, not the subject's own, were found entangled in the subject's pubic hair. These have been retained in an envelope marked "B."

Mrs. Roosevelt returned the report to Pickering. "So," she said. "It contains nothing inconsistent with our suppositions about the case."

"That is true," he said.

"When do we go to interview Sara Carter?"

"Whenever you wish," said Pickering. "I need only make a call before we leave."

"I want to speak with her alone for a few minutes, Mr. Pickering. She may be more forthcoming with me than she will be with you."

Half an hour later—having entered District police headquarters through a side door and walking through a maze of halls to avoid the public rooms and inquiring police reporters—the First Lady was admitted to what was called the women's isolation ward of the District jail.

The ward was a square brick room containing two small cells. Because Sara Carter was not to be allowed to talk to anyone, the second cell was not occupied. She was alone. The cell was furnished with a toilet, a basin, and a bunk suspended by chains. The heavy bars that confined her would have held a gorilla, or maybe even an elephant, Mrs. Roosevelt speculated, and Sara looked very small and weak behind them. She was wearing a loose and ragged knee-length cotton dress that had maybe once been white but was now a dingy gray. Her feet were bare.

She stood up when the First Lady came in. She looked warily at the matron and seemed relieved when that woman closed the door and left Mrs. Roosevelt alone with her.

"I told you they'd lynch me," she said to the First Lady in a thin, high voice.

"No one is going to lynch you, Sara."

"They told my mama I am charged with murder. They searched our house. Mama, she—" The girl paused and sighed. "She be frantic!"

"You could help yourself, Sara, if you would answer certain questions truthfully."

"Sure. Or maybe that would hang me," said Sara bitterly.

"Lying will hang you. You can refuse to answer questions, but you must not lie. It makes everything worse."

Sara gripped the bars that separated her from Mrs. Roosevelt. "This is as worse as it gits!"

Mrs. Roosevelt shook her head. "No, it can get worse."

" 'Certain questions . . .' Yeah. What was I doin' on the second floor at one in the morning? How come I had a little money in my room? If I answer those questions—"

"How can the answers hurt you?"

Sara nodded curtly. "They can hurt me," she said. "You're right. It can get worse."

"Would you consider trusting me? I mean, would you answer the questions in confidence?"

"What I'd tell you . . . you'd *tell.*"

Mrs. Roosevelt shook her head. "Maybe I could understand why you won't answer—"

"Like why I had some money—which they now took? Why should I have to explain why I had some money? You *know* why. 'Cause a colored gal isn't s'posed to have money. If I be white, would they want to know how come I had a hundred dollars or whatever it was? Would they?"

The First Lady sighed loudly. "I don't know, Sara. Or . . . Or maybe I do know. Maybe you're right: they wouldn't ask. And it's wrong. But you're hurting yourself by refusing to explain where you got the money. It's wrong and unjust, but you're hurting yourself."

Sara stiffened her back and lifted her head. "They can't prove I did it," she said, almost defiantly. "They ragged me an' ragged me about where's the knife. They ain' found the knife that killed Judge Blackwell. If I'd had it, they have found it, 'cause I was grabbed by the cop soon as I came out of the judge's room. They ain' no way I could have got rid of it. An' what's more, I can't tell 'em where it is, 'cause *I don't know!*"

"You weren't just on the second floor at one in the morning, Sara," said Mrs. Roosevelt gently. "You were in Judge Blackwell's room. Sometime you are going to have to explain why. You lied. You said you went there because he had called the pantry and asked for a bottle of seltzer water, and that isn't true. If you are to have any chance of getting out of here, you must tell us truthfully why you went to that room."

"Tellin' you that ain' gonna git me outta here," said Sara, shaking her head.

Mrs. Roosevelt paused for a moment, thinking about a question and bracing herself to ask it. "Sara . . ." she said reluctantly. "The autopsy done on Judge Blackwell's body shows that he'd . . . he'd performed the sex act shortly before he died. Was it with you?"

Sara shook her head vehemently. "No," she muttered. "It wasn't me. And when you find out who it was, then you'll find out who killed him."

Detective Sergeant Wilbur Rainey frowned over a white coffee mug and used a clean white handkerchief to wipe it all around, inside and out. Only when he was satisfied the mug was clean did he pour a mug of coffee for the First Lady.

"I'm sorry I can't offer you any cream," he said. "I do have sugar."

"That is quite all right, Sergeant Rainey. It is good as it is," she said as she took a sip of what had to be the worst coffee she had tasted in her whole life.

She was seated before the sergeant's olive-painted wooden desk, on a rickety wooden armchair. Agent Pickering sat on a folding chair.

Having poured coffee for her and for Pickering, Sergeant Rainey sat down and clasped his hands in front of him on a pile of papers. The office was a tiny room, not much bigger than Sara Carter's cell, and it was dim, cluttered, and shabby. The sergeant had crushed out a big cigar, in deference to Mrs. Roosevelt, but the room stank heavily of old cigar smoke and smelly butts.

Sergeant Rainey himself was a caricature, she thought:

the caricature of a big-city police detective—and perhaps consciously playing that broad role. He wore a checkered double-breasted suit with wide lapels, and the bulge of a revolver was conspicuous under his left arm. He wore also an ill-fitting yellowish wig, from under which his gray hair stuck out at the sides and behind. His face was pink, his eyes blue and watery.

"Nobody knows she's here excepting those that have to know she's here," said the sergeant, indicating by a jerk of his thumb in the general direction of the cells that he was talking about Sara Carter. "Nobody knows there was a murder at the White House last night—again, excepting those that have to know."

"We appreciate your cooperation," said Mrs. Roosevelt.

"She's sassy," he said, nodding in the same direction to which he had jerked his thumb. "We have your word not to sweat her too much. Without that word, I could get a confession in an hour."

"Whether she's guilty or not?" asked Mrs. Roosevelt.

Sergeant Rainey grinned. "Nothin' like that," he said. "Just apply what you might call psychological pressures. She's guilty all right. They all like lie that, the colored—anything to weasel out of trouble. Most of 'em scare easier, though."

"There's a weakness in the case, Sergeant," said Mrs. Roosevelt. "We don't have the murder weapon."

"Got somethin' just as good," said Rainey. "Fingerprints."

"I wasn't aware the room had been examined for fingerprints," said Mrs. Roosevelt.

"It was carefully examined," said Pickering. "Sergeant Rainey and his forensics crew arrived with the medical examiner."

"Her fingerprints were found— ?"

"On the lamp by the bed," said Rainey. "On the mirror over the dresser. And on a glass in the bathroom. She says all she did was stick her head in the door, saw the judge was dead, and backed away. But it isn't true. She was *in* the room—and in the bathroom."

"And that, I should think," said Pickering with studied serenity, "fairly well concludes the investigation."

"It might if we had the weapon," Mrs. Roosevelt contradicted him. "Tell me, Sergeant Rainey . . . did you find any other fingerprints—other than those of Judge Blackwell, of course."

"Yes, indeed," said Rainey. "As you know, fingerprints are taken of everyone who is employed in the White House, to be sure no one with a criminal record is hired. We found the fingerprints of two other White House maids—the women who clean the rooms—on the light switches, bathroom fixtures, and so on."

"Sara Carter," said Pickering, "was assigned to food service and did no room cleaning."

"We found two other sets," Rainey continued. "One belongs to Miss Barbara Higgins, Judge Blackwell's secretary. Her fingerprints were found on the same bathroom glass where Sara Carter's were found. Also on the surface of the nightstand by the bed. Also on the judge's hair brushes, both of them."

"Two other sets . . . Whose are the other set?"

"Ah, now that is a good question," said Rainey. "Whoever left those prints has never been fingerprinted—at least not so there is an F.B.I. record. The prints were on the windowsill and on the window glass."

"That person opened the window to throw out the knife!" said Mrs. Roosevelt excitedly.

"If so," said Pickering with exaggerated calm, "why wasn't the knife found below the window this morning?"

"Because whoever killed Judge Blackwell went out on the lawn and retrieved it," she said.

Pickering shook his head. "That window opens onto the

North Portico," he said. "The knife would have to have been thrown through the columns and then would have landed on the driveway. With a clatter that would very likely have alerted someone. I don't think so, madam. I really don't think the knife was thrown from the window."

Mrs. Roosevelt considered the objection for a moment. "Very well," she said. "I suppose you are right."

"We found the same print—a partial, I must admit—on one of the judge's cufflinks."

"What fingerprints were on the bottle of whiskey?" asked the First Lady.

"Good question," said Rainey. "None. It had been wiped clean. And there were none on the glass, either. I mean, there were none on the glass he'd been drinking from. Not even his own."

"Do you not find that an odd circumstance, Sergeant Rainey?" asked Mrs. Roosevelt. "If Sara Carter wiped off those fingerprints, why would she wipe them from a glass from which she had perhaps taken a drink of whiskey but not from the glass in the bathroom, from which she'd taken a drink of water?"

Rainey shrugged. "I've got no explanation for it, I'll say that."

"And there is no explanation as yet about the knife that killed Judge Blackwell. Where is it? How did Sara Carter dispose of it? Is there an air duct in that room? If so, let's open it and see if there is a knife in it."

"There is no duct," said Pickering.

"We found one more item of evidence," said Rainey. "I—"

"You intend to show *that* to Mrs. Roosevelt?" asked Pickering, coldly disapproving.

"I believe the lady is entitled to see what we have," said Rainey. He passed across the desk a manila envelope, fat for what it contained. "Found in his dresser drawer, among his own private things," said Rainey.

Apprehensive, Mrs. Roosevelt opened the envelope. She saw inside a bit of white fabric. She shook it out. The bit of fabric was a pair of women's panties: the new style, elastic and brief, with almost no legs at all.

"Don't s'pose *he* wore them," sneered Rainey.

"No, I don't suppose he did," she agreed.

"Sara Carter's, you imagine?" Rainey asked. "Sears and Roebuck? Montgomery Ward? Penney's?"

"As a matter of fact, no, Sergeant Rainey," said Mrs. Roosevelt. "This garment was *not* purchased at Sears, Roebuck or Montgomery Ward. This brand of ladies' underwear is quite expensive and is available only in some rather special shops. And I imagine that opens a new line of inquiry. Does it not?"

"Oh God!" moaned Pickering. "Still another line of inquiry!"

Mrs. Roosevelt shot him a malevolent glance. "It would be altogether too convenient, Mr. Pickering, Sergeant Rainey, to exclude all other lines of inquiry and use our investigation only to establish the truth of a preconceived idea of who killed Judge Blackwell. We understand quite well that persons other than Sara Carter may have had a motive to murder the judge—and indeed we have as yet failed to establish a motive for Sara. Let us not, then, close our minds."

"My mind is not closed," said Pickering stiffly.

"Would it be terribly difficult, Sergeant Rainey, to set in motion an inquiry as to whether or not this brand of ladies' undergarments can be purchased in Washington at all? We do understand, do we not, that the capital city is better known for a proliferation of dime stores than for shops that carry first-class lines of merchandise—as it is better known for speakeasies and cafeterias than for distinguished restaurants?"

Pickering laughed. For the first time, she heard him laugh unreservedly. "I shop in Alexandria!" he guffawed.

"I . . . uh. I, uh, guess we could call the manufacturer and, uh, ask—"

"Do so, Sergeant Rainey," said Mrs. Roosevelt. "Who knows what we may learn?"

"I still can't believe it," said Barbara Higgins. "I just can't believe he is dead. And I can't imagine why anyone would want . . ."

She paused to cover her eyes with a white handkerchief, and Mrs. Roosevelt poured ginger ale over ice and held it ready for the distressed young woman to take as soon as she saw it.

"Please understand," said Mrs. Roosevelt, "that we will find another job for you in the White House—or somewhere in the government. We understand that you came to Washington from New York to continue your service to Judge Blackwell, and we will not overlook that."

Barbara Higgins wiped her tears away. "I went to work for him when he left the court to devote himself to Mr. Roosevelt's campaign. And he asked me to come to Washington with him. I never dreamed I would work in the White House!"

Mrs. Roosevelt sighed. "You understand, dear, that we are doing all we can to discover who killed Judge Blackwell. I am sure you understand, too, that we hope to complete the investigation as confidentially as possible."

"Yes. I could— I could myself kill the man who—"

"It may have been a woman," interrupted Mrs. Roosevelt. "What do you know of the judge's relationship with women? He was not married, and—"

"He was a . . . a *man*," said Barbara Higgins. "He had friends. Women friends."

"Did you know any of them?"

Barbara shook her head.

"Barbara. We cannot overlook the fact that you are an

exceptionally attractive young woman. Did the judge——?"

To say this young woman was alluring would have been understatement. She was erotically beautiful. Partly it was intentional: she dressed and carried herself to be enticing. Partly it was innocent: she could not have been other than titillating if she had tried.

"Yes. He suggested a . . . relationship. When I said I would prefer not to, he was a gentleman about it. He asked once and never again."

"Then, did you know of others?"

The young woman shook her head. "Well . . . Only that there *were* others."

"How do you know that?"

"I saw his bills from florist shops. And other shops. He sent out gifts. The bills showed what he owed, not who he bought flowers and perfume for."

"Can you name the shops?"

She nodded. "Yes. Florist shops. I think one or two of his bills may be in my desk drawer yet."

"Lingerie shops, Miss Higgins?"

Barbara Higgins shook her head. "No. If he gave gifts of lingerie, I didn't know of it."

"To what extent, if any, Miss Higgins, did you see the judge drunk?"

"He drank. Like anyone. Like any American who is not a prohibitionist nut, he drank. I have never seen him under the influence. I have seen him under the"—she smiled faintly—"morning-after influence."

"His room," said Mrs. Roosevelt somberly, "was examined for fingerprints. Among those found were yours. Do you have any comment on that circumstance?"

Barbara Higgins stiffened, face and body. "You have to understand Judge Blackwell," she said. "He worked twenty-four hours a day. Or to say it more accurately, he was *engaged* in work twenty-four hours a day. If I had consented to live with him, in his apartment in New York, or here in the White House, he might have roused me at three A.M. to take a shorthand transcript of some thought that had come to him in the night. I intentionally put myself in a young women's residence hall, here in Washington, where telephone calls from men are not received after nine P.M., so the judge could not reach me."

"So your fingerprints . . . ?"

"In his room? Of course. I went there . . . Well, not every day, maybe, but very often. As long as I was where he could find me, he might call and say, 'Hey, Bobby'—that's what he called me: Bobby—'Hey, Bobby, come up and— Come up and do whatever. Take notes. Go over his marks on a draft. Pour him a drink. Help him get dressed. And, Mrs. Roosevelt, if I had agreed, it would have included . . . come into his bed for a few minutes."

"A few minutes?"

"A few minutes," Barbara Higgins repeated. Then she shrugged. "How do I know? I never did it. And that's why I didn't. I figured it would be *only* a few minutes. For a secretary, hmm? An hour for somebody else maybe. A few minutes for a secretary. Hmm? Okay? That's how it was."

"Well, then, Miss Higgins. Who do you suppose killed him? Do you have any idea?"

Barbara Higgins thrust her lips forward and rolled her eyes up as, for a long moment, she considered her answer. "I don't know, Mrs. Roosevelt," she said. "But . . . How is it the French are supposed to say? *Cherchez la femme?* Okay, do that. And, better yet, *cherchez* the jealous husband."

IV

"BABS," SAID THE PRESIDENT.

She had, as was not her usual habit, joined him and his closest friends for their early evening cocktail party in the West Sitting Hall. Tonight she took the time to do it. Missy was there. Louis Howe. Marvin McIntyre. The First Lady sipped a light Scotch, though it was still illegal and something she had promised she would not taste as long as Prohibition remained the law of the land. The President, who had never honored that law, had Beefeater gin for his martinis, plus J&B Scotch for those who wanted it, plus Cognac and champagne.

"Babs," he said. "Did you listen to Walter Winchell?"

She shook her head. "I never listen to Walter Winchell."

He laughed. "Well, all right. Nor do I. But he said something tonight." The President's voice turned to a bad imitation of the Winchell newscast: " *'Flash!* Washington! The *White House* is hiding something. Just where is Judge Horace Blackwell? Crusading New York prosecutor, later judge, lately braintruster . . . *missing*, not heard from since a White House dinner last night! Where—?' And so forth. Is the word out, Babs?"

While the President was saying this, Mrs. Roosevelt had picked up a copy of *Collier's* magazine, and now she read from an ad: " 'Luckies are kind to your throat . . . I know . . .

I've smoked them for eleven years.' So much for the integrity of Mr. Winchell." She tossed the magazine aside.

The President laughed, but he said, "Integrity is not the issue. Has the word leaked? Do we need to issue a press release?"

"We need to, Winchell or no," she said. "We must say, I am afraid, that Judge Blackwell was found dead last night, the apparent victim of foul play. Then we say the investigation into the cause of his death is being pursued intensively but that premature release of information would impede that investigation."

The President glanced around the circle. He trusted the judgment of each of these people. When no one objected, he said, "Okay. Get that out. And keep the lid on as long as you can."

The President would have his dinner from a tray, in bed. Missy would eat her dinner from another tray, sitting close by. They would talk, play records, and listen to the radio. Mrs. Roosevelt would dine in the private dining room with a few guests, who tonight were her friends Lorena Hickok and Elinor Morgenthau, plus her daughter Anna.

An usher came to Mrs. Roosevelt's side while she was with her friends. He bent over and whispered in her ear.

"A Mrs. Carter would like to see you," he said. "Martha Carter. She is the mother of Sara Carter. A distraught lady, I am afraid. Shall I—"

"Take her up to my study and serve her tea or coffee," said Mrs. Roosevelt. "Tell her I shall be up in a few minutes."

A little later the First Lady went up to her study to sit down with Sara's mother. The heavy Negro woman was sitting rigidly erect in a chair. The coffee and tea sat on a tray on a table beside her, untouched.

"Miz Roosevelt," she said immediately, even before the First Lady could greet her, "my girl din' kill nobody." Tears spilled from her eyes. "I *know* she din'. I *know!*"

Mrs. Roosevelt sat down in a chair facing her. "You may well be right, Mrs. Carter," she said. "Let's talk about it. But first— Please, let us have some coffee or tea. And some cake."

It was apparent to the First Lady that Mrs. Martha Carter had probably never before been invited by a white woman to share coffee and cake—much less, of course, by the wife of the President of the United States. It was a poignant moment, watching the anxious woman, who had apparently not understood the tray was for her, suddenly understand that she was not being condemned for coming here but was being offered dessert and coffee.

"Coffee or tea?" asked Mrs. Roosevelt gently.

"Uh . . . Uh, tea . . . please, ma'am."

"Milk? Sugar?"

"Yes, ma'am."

As Mrs. Roosevelt poured, she said, "I visited with Sara today. She is not comfortable, of course, and she is very worried; but she is all right. She is concerned that you will be worried."

"I *am* worried," said Mrs. Carter.

"So am I," said Mrs. Roosevelt. "She is not telling the truth, Mrs. Carter. That is the worst thing. She is not telling the truth."

"Sara do that sometime," said Mrs. Carter sadly.

"She seems to have had a great deal of money. She owns expensive things. And the police found $172 in cash in her room. She is paid $12 a week, Mrs. Carter. Where did she get that kind of money?"

"She work hard."

"Yes, and I understand the White House sometimes has paid her extra money for working late hours. But that does not explain all the things that cost money and the $172. She has only worked two years. How could she save that much?"

Mrs. Carter shook her head and turned down the corners

of her mouth. She took a tentative sip from her tea, handling the cup with care as if it were something of great delicacy. "I fear'd she fancy, ma'am," she said.

"I beg your pardon?"

"She's *fancy*," said Mrs. Carter indignantly. "I think . . . I mean she gits money from *men*."

"Ohh . . ."

"Mebbe I wrong. But where else it come from, that kind money?"

"Ohh . . ." A thousand thoughts raced through Mrs. Roosevelt's mind. "That could explain—"

"How many nights she work after midnight?" asked Mrs. Carter. "She say many. What boss say?"

"We can find out specifically," said Mrs. Roosevelt, "but I have to doubt she was required to remain in the White House after midnight more than once or twice since I have been here."

Mrs. Carter nodded. "I figger," she said.

"So you think she . . . This is most distressing, Mrs. Carter."

"Distressin' you? Distressin' *me*."

"Yes, of course."

"She nineteen years old," said Mrs. Carter. "I make her go school, get as much learn as a colored can git. She smart girl."

Mrs. Roosevelt nodded. "Eat your cake, Mrs. Carter. And tell me if Sara ever mentioned the name of Judge Horace Blackwell."

"He the one she s'posed to have kill?"

"We have not as yet released the information that Judge Blackwell is dead. I am going to ask you not to talk about the case to any newspaper reporters, or to anyone else for that matter. I have great doubt that Sara is guilty. I have promised her that she will have a fair trial. I will do everything I can to see to it that she does. But I must ask for your help and cooperation."

Mrs. Carter nibbled cautiously at her slice of cake. "They say you honest woman," she said.

The news release Mrs. Roosevelt had dictated had been typed by Tommy Thompson. After Mrs. Carter left, the First Lady read the terse words:

> The White House announced this evening that Judge Horace Blackwell, a Special Assistant to the President, was found dead in his White House quarters early this morning. A spokesman indicated that the judge was the victim of murder. A suspect is being held, but the spokesman emphasized that the investigation is continuing. The investigation is being conducted by agents of the Secret Service with the assistance of detectives of the District of Columbia police.
>
> Judge Blackwell, who was 48 years old, was formerly a district attorney in New York City and won acclaim for his successful crusade against corruption in municipal government . . .

Satisfied with the draft, she left it on Tommy's desk with a note telling her to hand deliver it to the White House press office early in the morning and to have a copy delivered by messenger to Detective Sergeant Wilbur Rainey at District police headquarters.

The release, which would reach the newspapers during the morning, would radically alter the character of the investigation.

Next, Mrs. Roosevelt carried out a little investigation of her own. She had asked Pickering to obtain for her a small quantity of rye whiskey. He had obtained a pint, which he said was the smallest quantity in which it could be had.

She lined up three glasses on her desk. Into the first she poured about a quarter of an inch of the amber fluid, into the second about half that much, and into the third only enough to wet the bottom of the glass. She noted the time.

For the next two hours she read correspondence and memoranda and signed letters Tommy Thompson had typed for her during the day—from time to time glancing at her three glasses of rye. By the time she was ready to go to bed, all the whiskey in the third glass had evaporated; the bottom was dry. In fact, it had been dry for well over an hour. Nearly all in the second glass had evaporated; though the bottom was still wet, a brown residue was forming, which would soon be dry. In the first glass, where she had poured a quarter inch of rye, liquid remained, though it was changing color as the alcohol evaporated and the remaining fluid thickened.

Remembering the condition of the rye whiskey she had seen in Judge Blackwell's glass—a tiny quantity but still liquid, still light in color—she concluded that he had probably taken his last swallow of rye, emptying the glass but leaving dregs, no more than half an hour before she examined the glass. Officer Runkle had said he saw Sara Carter just outside the judge's room at 1:12 A.M. Mrs. Roosevelt had been aroused by the disturbance in the hall and had arrived at the room no later than 1:20. If her whiskey experiment was accurate, that meant the judge died no earlier than 12:50.

She resolved to repeat the experiment tomorrow. She had plenty of rye whiskey left.

Mrs. Roosevelt's first morning activity was her visit to the President, who was sitting up in bed as usual, eating from his breakfast tray and looking hastily through the newspapers. Missy was already with him, reading the papers too, and occasionally folding a paper and marking a story with a red pen-

cil for his attention. Mrs. Roosevelt showed the President the
press release on the murder of Judge Blackwell and asked him
to instruct Steve Early to get it to the reporters as soon as possible.

"Goodbye the peace and quiet of a spring morning," said
the President, but he handed the release back to her without
further comment. "Let's see if we can keep it confidential that
you are looking into the case. If *that* gets out, Bertie Mc-
Cormick will editorialize that I should appoint you Director
of the F.B.I."

She met Lawrence Pickering in the hall outside her
study. He had come up in response to her request for an early
meeting, and he said he had talked with the captain of the
White House police about the specifics of how the house was
guarded during the night.

"There are three levels of security," he said. "The most
closely guarded areas are two: the Executive Wing and the
second floor. After that, the White House itself—the entire
building—is guarded, but not so tightly as those two areas. Finally, the grounds are patrolled, and there are officers on duty
at the gates, but there is no question that a knowledgeable person could enter and leave the grounds at night, almost at will."

"How?" she asked.

"Oh, various ways. A person *could* climb the fence; it is
not so formidable. There are several little gates locked with
old-fashioned padlocks. In fact, I have brought one such lock
for you to examine."

He produced from his small black leather briefcase an
antique brass padlock: big, heavy, and apparently strong.
The key alone probably weighed as much as some modern
locks.

"Put in service during the Civil War, I should judge," said
Pickering. "When the army decided to protect President Lin-
coln a little more carefully. There are a dozen or so of them
in storage, which is where I obtained this one. The same key

opens them all. What is more, I suspect it would take relatively little skill and time to pick this lock."

Mrs. Roosevelt turned the big old lock over and over in her hands. "Why are these locks not replaced, Mr. Pickering?" she asked.

"Why are a thousand things not done?" he asked. "It is a matter of appropriations. Congress will not appropriate funds to improve the protection of the President."

"Or to replace threadbare carpeting or disintegrating curtains," she said. "So—"

"White House police officers patrol the grounds all night," he continued. "Two of them. Carrying flashlights. A would-be intruder who has seen one walk by knows that another will not appear for half an hour at least—and then will be announced by the beam of his light."

"How very intelligent," she said scornfully.

"Tradition, madam," said Pickering. "A powerful force for small minds."

"Oh, this is an education for me, Mr. Pickering," said Mrs. Roosevelt. "So how are we protected inside the house?"

"Two officers patrol the ground floor and first floor, all night," said Pickering. "Two. We have suggested four. Or five. The available funds dictate that it shall be two."

"Two . . ."

"No matter how devoted a guard is, madam, he becomes wearisomely bored as the hours pass, night after night. How alert is he?"

"Not as alert," she said with sudden severity, "as anyone who wants to slip past him."

"I am afraid that is true, madam. I am only one of those who has pointed this out. President *Theodore* Roosevelt, in his ebullience, could not believe anyone could want to murder the President—in spite of the fact that he arrived here only as the result of the murder of President McKinley. President Wilson was realistic. Presidents Harding and Coolidge . . . Well— And

President Hoover was committed to reducing government spending."

"As is President Roosevelt, do not forget," said the First Lady. "I am sure you know, he has criticized President Hoover for excessive spending and has pledged himself to achieve more economy in government."

"Let economies be effected where they will, madam," said Pickering. "It remains possible for an intruder to penetrate the White House and—as you yourself so cogently pointed out—to commit murder only a few yards from the door to the President's bedroom."

"Yes." she said quietly. "Here on the second floor, one of the most tightly guarded areas."

"An officer—in this case Officer Runkle—is assigned to patrol the second floor. To protect your private quarters after midnight, the far west elevator is switched off, and the stairway doors, top and bottom, are locked. There are the other elevators, nevertheless, and other stairs; and he spends much of his time watching those. If we had two men on the second floor—"

"But we don't," she said.

"Precisely. And like any other guard, Officer Runkle has developed a routine. It would be all but impossible for a man not to. Anyone who has observed his routine can slip by him."

"In other words—"

"In other words, his responsibility extends to the Stair Hall and East Hall, and when he goes to check those—"

"The President is not guarded," she said ominously.

Pickering nodded. "That is true."

Mrs. Roosevelt considered for a long moment. "Some changes must be made, Mr. Pickering."

"I am among those who has been so recommending for some years," he said.

"In any event," she said, "we need not concern ourselves much with what great bold ingenuity it required for Judge

Blackwell's murderer to gain access to his room. Anyone could have done it."

"Not anyone, madam," said Pickering. "Anyone who knows the White House, its routines, its deficiencies."

"It wouldn't take long to learn, would it?"

Pickering shook his head. "Especially if you were around here at night."

When Mrs. Roosevelt arrived at Barbara Higgins's desk in the Executive Wing, the young woman was in the process of cleaning it out.

"But I said you would have a job here, even though Judge Blackwell is dead."

Barbara wiped her eyes with the back of her hand. "I think I'll go home to New York, Mrs. Roosevelt," she said.

"Even if you eventually decide to do so," said Mrs. Roosevelt, "I should be grateful to you if you would remain in Washington until the investigation into the judge's murder is complete. That will be no more than a few days. You can remain on the White House payroll temporarily . . . uh, perhaps as an assistant to me."

Barbara frowned, then smiled. "You are very kind," she said.

"This is no time to make significant decisions," said Mrs. Roosevelt. "When something terribly distressing has happened."

The young woman nodded. "I suppose so," she whispered.

"Now," said Mrs. Roosevelt. "You said you have some bills of the judge's, from flower shops."

"As a matter of fact, yes," said Barbara. "I have two bills for flowers, from the same store."

"Good. How would you like to take a small role in the investigation? Could you go to that flower shop and see if you can learn anything more about those orders for flowers?"

Barbara nodded. "In confidentiality, of course."

"Yes, that's essential."

"I'll be glad to, Mrs. Roosevelt. Something useful to do. And if it helps find out who murdered the judge . . ."

"I can do better than we thought," said Detective Sergeant Wilbur Rainey. He had come to the White House, contacted Pickering, and arranged to be received by Mrs. Roosevelt before noon in her study. He and Pickering sat in chairs facing her desk. "When this, uh, undergarment was examined in the lab, under a magnifying lens, we found something interesting."

"Good," said she. "And what did you find?"

Rainey held up the pair of silk panties found in Judge Blackwell's bureau drawer. "Items like this," he said, "may be sold in the Washington area. But this pair wasn't. Do you have a magnifying glass handy?"

Mrs. Roosevelt opened a drawer in her desk and took out a lens.

"Look at the tag," said Rainey. "The manufacturer: Longanesi. You can see that, hmm? Italian. That pair of panties was imported from Italy. Then the number. See the little number?"

She squinted through the glass. "Yes. Five . . . three . . . three . . . oh . . . four."

"Correct," said Rainey. "Batch number. Not found on ordinary items, but sometimes found on silk things. If something silk, which is expensive, some way fails, like rips or gets holes, the customer will come back yelling. The manufacturer wants to know what batch of silk was flawed. He will yell for compensation from the supplier. So . . ."

"So?"

"We have made quite a few telephone calls," said Rainey. He was in a conspicuously self-congratulatory mood. "All the undergarments bearing batch number 53304 were sold to an importer in Boston. With one exception, all his retailers for

Longanesi brand lingerie are in the Boston area. The exception is in Newport, Rhode Island. That pair of panties was bought in Boston, or a suburb, or in Newport. Not in Washington. Not even in New York."

"And in shops," she said. "Exclusive shops."

"Expensive shops," he said.

"Not Sara Carter's, then?"

He shook his head. "Not Sara Carter's."

"Since the investigation has taken this turn," said Pickering, focusing heavy-lidded, contemptuous eyes on the pair of panties, which now lay on the table between him and Mrs. Roosevelt, "I am going to ask Sergeant Rainey to tell you what else was found in Judge Blackwell's room, when a thorough search was conducted."

"Have you withheld information from me, Mr. Pickering?"

"Not at all, madam. But certain items need not have been discussed until they gained significance."

"Significance?"

"Yes. Sergeant Rainey—"

"I think you should tell her yourself, sir."

Pickering looked annoyed, but he stiffened and shrugged. "Very well. You will recall, my dear lady, that we observed a condom in Judge Blackwell's ashtray."

"A *used* condom, Mr. Pickering."

"Indeed. Used. Well, there was a substantial supply of unused ones among his personal possessions. A carton that had once contained four dozen, in four smaller boxes. One box was missing. Another was half empty."

"Proving what, Mr. Pickering?"

"Proving, we may suppose, that the judge was . . . was an *active* man."

"Very well. Did you find anything else that I should know about?"

Pickering and Rainey exchanged glances. "He had a suitcase in the closet," said Pickering. "It was locked, but we re-garded it as our duty to open it. The judge . . . He seems to have enjoyed some bizarre practices. The suitcase contained two pairs of handcuffs, with keys, some lengths of rope, and a dog whip."

Mrs. Roosevelt flushed. "I . . . I don't know how to— Oh, *dear!*"

"I am sorry the matter had to be mentioned," said Pickering.

Mrs. Roosevelt sighed. "What fingerprints were on the handcuffs?" she asked.

"Wiped clean," said Rainey glumly. "Which means—"

"Which means they have some significance in the murder," said the First Lady. "Which also means we cannot overlook so distasteful a subject."

"The matron at the jail," said Rainey, "says there are no marks on Sara Carter. No welts."

"We can hardly go around examining young women for welts," said Mrs. Roosevelt. "Although I . . . I'd like to know if there are any on Barbara Higgins."

"I am not quite sure how we would find out," said Lawrence Pickering.

Mrs. Roosevelt shook her head. "In any event, is this *evidence?*" she asked. "Perhaps it is, of *something*. But I think it is an unlikely line of inquiry, so far as discovering who murdered Judge Blackwell. Whoever suffered that sort of . . . indignity, obviously did so voluntarily. It is hardly likely, then, to have been the motive for murdering the man."

"A false lead," said Pickering quickly, as though relieved to be excused from further discussion of a disagreeable topic.

"Still . . ." said Rainey. "Who wiped the prints off those handcuffs? And why? Who was with Judge Blackwell when he used that condom? If whoever it was didn't kill him, still she was with him not long before he was killed, and I'd like to know who she was."

Mrs. Roosevelt shook her head. "I am afraid we can't ignore such questions," she admitted. "Much as I'd like to."

Mrs. Roosevelt ate her lunch alone, at her desk, looking over some clippings and reading the day's newspapers. She had just pushed her tray aside when the telephone rang and she was told that Barbara Higgins would like to see her. She said Barbara should be sent up immediately.

"I went to the flower shop," Barbara told her. "The florist was very upset. The bill hadn't been paid; and hearing that the judge was dead, he decided he would never be paid, which made him decide not to cooperate with me. So I muscled him."

"Muscled him? How did you do that?"

Barbara Higgins frowned. "The story is out, you know. I had bought a newspaper to read on the bus. It carries a story saying the judge was murdered. I showed that to the man in the flower shop and told him he had better cooperate in the investigation. So he wrote down the name and address. The flowers were sent to the same woman. Both orders. And two orders before that."

"To whom were they sent?" asked Mrs. Roosevelt.

Barbara opened her purse and pulled out the slip of paper on which the florist had written the information. "The flowers were sent to a Blanche Tracy," she said. She handed the paper to Mrs. Roosevelt. "Blanche Tracy."

"Tracy . . . Tracy, of course. Mrs. William Tracy. Yes. Professor Tracy is another member of what the newspapers call the "brain trust." He and Judge Blackwell worked together, I imagine. Maybe the judge dined at the Tracys. The flowers would be his gift to the hostess."

"Maybe," said Barbara hesitantly. "But the florist told me something more. His instructions were very strict. The flowers were to be delivered immediately: immediately after the order was phoned in."

"What do you suppose is the significance of that?" asked Mrs. Roosevelt.

"He had them delivered when he knew her husband was not at home, when he knew her husband was here at the White House."

The First Lady smiled and shook her head. "I think that assumes a good deal, Barbara," she said. "What difference would it make? When her husband came home, the flowers would be there."

"Yes. But without his notes," said Barbara. "And she could say she bought them herself."

"Notes?"

"Notes," said Barbara. "He had notes delivered with the flowers. You know . . . Just a word or two written on a card. He told the florist what to write."

"And the florist told you what he said?"

"Yes. They were love notes. Always signed 'H.' 'All my love, H.' 'A million kisses, H.' And so on."

Mrs. Roosevelt knew William and Blanche Tracy, but only barely, and she tried to picture Mrs. Tracy in her mind. A blonde. With beautiful gray eyes. Plump. A somewhat haughty young woman. Always well dressed. Given to drinking a bit much when drink was available. She was perhaps ten years younger than her husband.

And the professor. A Harvard economist who looked like a Boston-Irish carpenter.

Blanche Tracy and Judge Horace Blackwell? It just didn't seem likely.

"Barbara," she said. "I would appreciate it if you would assume responsibility for assembling and packing the judge's papers. You've worked for him long enough to know what are government documents and what are personal. As you do this work, be on the lookout, please, for anything that might help us in the investigation."

Barbara nodded. "Of course," she said quietly. "It seems

like an intrusion, doesn't it? Uh . . . what about the bedroom suite?"

"That must be packed too. Since he had no family, no one is better qualified to pack his personal things than you are."

"I would be grateful," said Barbara, "if a Secret Service agent were with me when I'm in the suite. I feel a little uncomfortable about—"

"I understand. It will be arranged. Speak to Mr. Pickering about it."

V

IN MIDAFTERNOON THE PRESIDENT bestowed on Lou Gehrig the 1932 Man of the Year Award of the National Sports Reporters Association.

Half a dozen wooden armchairs had been placed in a tight semicircle on the lawn in the rose garden, just outside the Oval Office. The President sat in the center chair, with Mrs. Roosevelt to his left and Louis McHenry Howe to his right. As the President's wheelchair was taken away and disappeared inside the Executive Wing, the guests were led out, followed by a dozen reporters and half a dozen cameramen.

"Mr. President and Mrs. Roosevelt," said Jim Farley. "Let me introduce a pair of real American heroes. Step up, fellows, and shake the hand of the President of the United States. Mr. President—Lou Gehrig and Babe Ruth."

The President reached up and took Gehrig's hand first, then Ruth's. "If there's any place in the world I'd rather be than in the Oval Office," he said, beaming, "it would be at Yankee Stadium watching you fellows at work. It's nice of you to take the time to come and see me."

"Always glad to meet a President," said Ruth.

As everyone laughed, Mrs. Roosevelt and Louis Howe stood to shake the hands of the two famous ball players.

"Let's see," said the President to Gehrig. "You batted .349 last season, right?"

"Not as good as you, Mr. President," said Gehrig. "You batted a thousand."

"But no home runs," laughed the President. "And, Babe, you hit forty-one homers, as I recall. Right?"

"Not bad for an ol' feller, I s'pose," said Ruth. " 'Course, Jimmie Foxx, he hit fifty-eight."

At the call of the photographers, Ruth stood behind the President's chair and Gehrig stood behind the First Lady's. Ruth, looking rumpled as always, in spite of the expensive tailoring that had gone into his cream-colored double-breasted suit, mugged for the cameras, with a mouth-closed boyish grin that distorted his cherubic face. Gehrig stood with characteristic grace and dignity, smiling benignly on his impish teammate.

As pictures were taken, Louis Howe lit another Sweet Caporal, though he was already coughing shallowly. He stood, turned his back on the cameramen, and reached for Gehrig's hand. "The only disadvantage of moving to Washington," he said, "is not being able to duck out to the stadium now and then."

Ruth completed breaking up the photographers' pose. He sat down and turned his chair toward the President and Mrs. Roosevelt. He smiled shyly. "Say, I sure do admire the way you got to be President," he said.

"I admired the way you called your shot in Chicago," said the President.

In the 1932 World Series, last fall, the Chicago players had heckled Ruth unmercifully, calling him old and fat and slow on his feet. Ruth turned and stared at the Cubs' dugout for a moment, then pointed to the center field bleachers. He hit the next pitch into those bleachers, for a home run.

"Were you really calling your shot, Mr. Ruth?" asked Mrs. Roosevelt. Many people denied he had done anything of the kind.

"Why, ma'am, course I wuz," said Ruth with another grin.

"The Babe wants to run for Congress when he retires from baseball," Gehrig joked.

"Would that be as a Republican or as a Democrat?" asked Howe.

The Babe frowned for a moment. Then he mumbled, "As a Yankee, I guess."

As the afternoon papers began to come in, Mrs. Roosevelt had to be preoccupied with what they said about the death of Judge Blackwell. The story from the Baltimore *Evening Sun* was typical. After reciting the facts, the account went on:

> Judge Blackwell established his reputation as a crusading Manhattan District Attorney. Many of the friends of former New York mayor Jimmy Walker, as well as some friends of Governor Al Smith, found themselves unceremoniously arrested, tried, and sent to Sing Sing. In fact, a number of prominent members of the Walker and Smith administrations remain in prison, serving long terms for such crimes as embezzlement, fraud, and extortion.
>
> Wealthy contractors, accustomed to collusion in bidding on public contracts and other kinds of chicanery that made every public building project in New York cost far more than it should have, also wound up behind bars.
>
> Unquestionably, Judge Blackwell had many enemies. If he has been murdered, it seems not unlikely that he has been the victim of some Gotham thug's obsession with revenge.
>
> In reply to the question of why he never married, Judge Blackwell once said he could not, in good conscience, ask a woman to share the risks he took.
>
> As a judge, appointed by then-Governor

Franklin D. Roosevelt, Judge Blackwell augmented
his reputation as a man tough on crime and corruption. Even as a braintruster, it is reported, his assignment has been the drafting of tough laws to
combat fraud in the buying and selling of stock and
in the investment of bank depositors' funds.

Whoever investigates the murder of Judge Horace Blackwell has his job cut out for him. There
may be a thousand men who hated the judge
enough to want him dead.

While she was reading the newspapers, Mrs. Roosevelt
received a call from Sergeant Rainey at D.C. police headquarters. He said Sara Carter was asking to see her and asked
if she wanted to come to the jail. An hour later the First Lady
was once more led into the dim bricked-in room that contained the cell where the Negro girl was imprisoned.

Sara leaned on the thick steel bars. She looked tired, defeated, even wasted. "They tell me," she said quietly, "they
can't hold me more than forty-eight hours before they got to
charge me with somethin'—and that somethin' goin' to be
murder. They tell me that even if they have to let me go later,
I'll always have a police record sayin' I was once charged with
murder. Is that true?"

Mrs. Roosevelt shook her head. "I'm not a lawyer. I can't
advise you."

"If they let me out, I can't come back to work at the
White House, 'cause I been charged with *murder*."

"I have something to say about that. If you are exoner-
ated, you will come back to the White House."

"What choice they givin' me?" Sara asked in quiet de-
spondency. "They want me to confess I killed Judge Blackwell.
If I don't confess, they charge me with murdering him. An' if
I do, that mean they *not* goin' to charge me?" She shook her
head. "I git the worst of it either way."

Mrs. Roosevelt nodded. "If those are all your choices, you do. So why did you ask to see me?"

"I can explain some things. What I'm goin' tell you is goin' to make it worse for me, not better. But I don't come out good, no matter what. Maybe you won't have to tell . . . everybody . . . what I'm goin' to tell you."

"Are you about to tell the truth, Sara?"

"The *truth,*" the girl muttered.

She turned away from the bars and walked the three paces to the rear wall of the cell. For a moment she leaned against the brick wall. Then she returned to the bars.

"Why wuz I at Judge Blackwell's room at one in the mornin'?" She lowered her eyes. "I'd been there many times. Never that late at night before, but sometimes ten o'clock, eleven. Wednesday night, I work late, till half past twelve, later. Judge, he pay me $5.00 every time I come to his room at night, so I figure I might's well go up and see if I can make me $5.00 'fore I go home."

"Is that where your money came from—the money that was found in your room?"

"Yes. They was some others besides him. Jus' $2.00, was all the others paid. Not White House men, the others. Not government men."

"Did Judge Blackwell use his whip on you?" Mrs. Roosevelt asked.

Sara shook her head. "No. He showed it to me and said it wouldn't really hurt much. He offered me $10.00 if I'd let him. But I couldn't let him do that, no matter what he paid. You understand why I couldn't let him do that? You *understand?*"

"Perfectly," said Mrs. Roosevelt.

Sara nodded. "They ain't find the knife, have they?" she asked.

"No."

"Which proves I didn't kill him. For all the good that's gonna do me."

"Sara . . . I assume you didn't see anyone else about in the halls that night?"

"If I could say I did, I sure would."

"How did you get to Judge Blackwell's room without being seen? If you did it so many nights, how did you manage to avoid the officers in the halls all those times?"

Sara shrugged. "From the kitchen—where the coloreds are allowed—you can come up into what you call your private rooms. In the night, you just come up them narrow little stairs that goes beside the elevator. At the top, you wait and watch a little, to see if the police is in the private Sittin' Hall. They not, you sneak quick through there and to the door to the big Center Hall. Judge Blackwell's room just a little way from there. Sometimes I see the officer. I just wait. I know he won't be comin' back very soon, once he makes his turn some other way."

"That easy . . ." murmured Mrs. Roosevelt.

Sara frowned hard. "I want to kill the President, I could kill him," she said. "Or you. You think you guarded? You ain't."

"I think we will be, in future," said Mrs. Roosevelt grimly.

"I had to wait my chance downstairs, to get to the stairs without nobody seein' me. Then there was ushers in the hall on the first floor, and I had to wait, quiet, for a long time. When I got to the second floor and your sittin' room, I waited until that policeman come through. After he come through, I knew he wouldn't be back for a long time. So then's when I hurried along to Judge Blackwell's room. I mean, I maybe could have made some excuse about bein' up there at ten o'clock or eleven . . . but *one?* No. Had to wait."

"Didn't you expect the judge would be asleep?"

Sara shrugged. "I woke him up before."

"He was always glad to see you?"

Sara shook her head. "Sometimes his door was locked. Then I'd just sneak back downstairs and out."

"How did you get out of the White House without checking through a guard station?"

"Not too late, I *did* check through. Just say I'd been workin' late. They never asked questions. If it was kinda late, like after eleven, I'd go out through the East Hall. Down into the tunnel."

"Tunnel?"

"Tunnel to the Treasury Building. Goes under the street. You come out in the basement of the Treasury Building. Ain' nobody *there* in the middle of the night. Be a little careful not to come on a watchman, you go out. You can't get back in. Just out."

"Do lots of people know about this? Do you think many people know how to get around and out of the White House at any hour of the day or night?"

Sara pondered the question for a moment. "The colored people that work in the White House know," she said quietly. "I s'pose other people know, too. Why not?"

"So, Sara, all you were doing was ... trying to earn $5.00."

Sara's deep, dark eyes met Mrs. Roosevelt's eyes. She nodded solemnly.

The First Lady sighed and shook her head. "Sara ..." she said quietly. "I believe you. I don't think you killed Judge Blackwell. But ... If there is anything else you can tell me ..."

Abruptly Sara choked, then sobbed and began to cry. "*I didn't kill the man!*" she moaned. "I'm *'fraid!* I don't like it in here! I want out! I don' wan' go to the 'lectric chair! I don' wan' to—"

Mrs. Roosevelt put her hand around Sara's hand that was wrapped around a steel bar. "I believe you," she said. "I'll do what I can for you. I'll do *anything* I can for you."

Sara stared at the First Lady from between the heavy steel bars, her dark cheeks glistening with streaks of tears. "Colored gal got Miz Roosevelt for a friend, couldn't have no better," she whispered hoarsely.

Lawrence Pickering accepted Mrs. Roosevelt's invitation to tea in the West Sitting Hall. A little later the President would come there and call in his friends for cocktails, but at tea time the West Sitting Hall was the First Lady's. Because Barbara Higgins had just come with a report of what she had found in Judge Blackwell's suite, the First Lady asked her to remain and have tea with them—she could tell Pickering what she had found.

"You had already found what might be considered the evidence the room contained," said Barbara. "I mean the fingerprints and the . . . items the judge kept in ample supply. As I packed his clothes, I really didn't find anything much more. Except—"

"Except something that may be quite significant," said Mrs. Roosevelt.

"Well . . ." said Barbara diffidently. "It was wrapped up in a sock. Maybe it wouldn't mean anything if it had been just lying in a drawer. But in the toe of a sock!"

Mrs. Roosevelt reached to her desk and picked up a black sock. She handed it to Pickering. "You can see," she said. "Neither of us has touched it. If there are fingerprints on it, they will not be Barbara's or mine."

Pickering stretched the sock and peered down inside. "The key to a safe-deposit box," he said.

Mrs. Roosevelt nodded. "That's what *we* think it is. An odd sort of key. A sophisticated sort of key."

Handling the key gently and only with the fabric of the sock, Pickering stared hard at it and read, " 'First Fidelity Bank of Washington.' " He sighed. "We'll have to open that box. I suppose that requires a court order. It's too late to get an order before Monday."

"We shall be curious to see what is in that box," said the First Lady.

For a while then, as Barbara and Pickering sipped tea and munched on tiny sandwiches, the First Lady described what she had learned since she last talked with Pickering: that Judge Blackwell had sent flowers to Blanche Tracy and that

Sara Carter had confessed she went to the judge's room to sell him sex.

"I've been prowling around a bit myself," said Pickering. "I have two difficulties with the theory that Sara Carter killed Judge Blackwell. They are the same difficulties you have, of course."

"First, where is the knife?" she said.

"Yes. And second, what was her motive? I am willing to accept—for the moment anyway—her explanation as to what she was doing in the judge's room at one in the morning. Though, let me point out, it *is* a bit facile. But never mind that for the moment. I still cannot imagine *why* Sara Carter should want to murder Judge Horace Blackwell."

"So . . . ?"

"So I have been looking into the judge's career to see if I can find anyone who did have motive."

"The newspapers suggest there are perhaps hundreds of such people in New York and probably some in Washington," said Mrs. Roosevelt.

"I am quite sure there are more than a few," said Pickering. "But you eliminate most of them when you remember that whoever killed the judge did so in the White House in the middle of the night. A great many people know how to get in and out, I suppose. And a certain number had motive to kill the judge. The murderer has to be a member of both groups."

"Until now," she said, "we have made no list of suspects. Because we couldn't identify any, other than Sara Carter. Now . . . though it troubles me to do so, I am prepared to put Professor William Tracy on the list. If he knows about his wife's apparent love relationship with Judge Blackwell, he has motive: jealousy. And he has been working around the White House since March—during which time an intelligent and observant man could well learn the ways of getting in and out at all hours."

"He was in the White House for dinner the night of the

murder," said Pickering. "He could have hidden somewhere and waited for his chance."

"Sending his wife home alone," said Mrs. Roosevelt. She shook her head. "Not probable. I am afraid he doesn't make a very likely suspect."

"One worth keeping in mind," said Pickering.

"I interrupted you," she said. "You were saying you were looking for other suspects."

"In 1929," said Pickering, "District Attorney Blackwell prosecuted a man named Wilmer Cassell. Cassell was a sort of jolly bootlegger. He had a speakeasy on Lexington Avenue, where you could place a bet as well as buy a drink; and in order to keep the place open, he was bribing the captain and some sergeants at the precinct station. Blackwell didn't care about the sale of liquor, apparently, but he could be a fanatic about the corruption of police officers. He secured a series of indictments against Cassell. Two weeks before the case was to be tried, one of the witnesses was found at the bottom of the East River. Blackwell then secured against Cassell an indictment for murder. He won a guilty verdict, and eight weeks later Cassell was electrocuted."

"The judge told me about that," said Barbara. "And about what happened next."

"Yes," said Pickering. "That was not the end of the matter. The day after the execution, an attempt was made on the life of District Attorney Blackwell. A blast of submachine-gun fire barely missed him on a Manhattan street. An informant told an F.B.I. investigator that Cassell's partners, who lost a great deal of money in his fall, had—as the term is—'put out a contract' on D.A. Blackwell. The informant called the gunman by the name of 'Chickie' Pepino—formally, Achille Pepino. The informant said that was who it was, but there was no real evidence of it, so the matter had to be dropped."

"But they tried again," said Barbara. "I remember the judge talking about it. He said the Cassell gang had sort of declared war on him, like there was a blood feud between the gang and him. He was shot at again, last year, just before he resigned from the court."

"Did they suppose they forced him to resign his judgeship?" asked Mrs. Roosevelt.

"He told me they may have thought that," said Barbara.

"So what does all this add to the evidence we are trying to accumulate?"

"Just one thing," said Pickering grimly. "This man Chickie Pepino—who almost never in his life, except for a term in prison, has ventured outside the five boroughs—is now missing. He could be in the East River. Or he could be in Washington."

"A somewhat far-fetched thesis, is it not, Mr. Pickering?"

Pickering shrugged. "Are we so well supplied with suspects and evidence that we can reject it?"

Mrs. Roosevelt usually carried a notepad, in her purse or somewhere handy, and today she had a big yellow legal tablet. She laid it on her lap and drew a box and wrote names:

> Sara Carter
> Professor Tracy
> "Chickie" Pepino

"So," she said. "Three suspects—though one, this Mr. Pepino, is a *most* unlikely one."

"So far identified," said Pickering with his characteristic lofty scowl. "I am certain there will be more."

"Have you any further ideas, Mr. Pickering?"

"I have one," he said.

"I would be glad to write another name here."

"I am not certain I can offer a name. The judge—"

"Made many enemies?"

Pickering nodded. "Another case . . . A building contractor named David McKibben was indicted on charges of rigging the bids on construction contracts, by bribing city officials. He was a well-connected man: a personal friend of Mayor Jimmy Walker and of Governor Al Smith. District Attorney Blackwell secured an indictment of McKibben in November, 1930. He prosecuted vigorously, and McKibben was sentenced to a five-year term. He entered prison in April, 1931. Unfortunately, he was murdered in prison a few months after he arrived there. It was one of those sudden things that happen in prisons: a dispute over some small thing, a flare of temper, fists . . . His antagonist struck McKibben on the head with a length of pipe. McKibben died."

"And his family—"

"Swore revenge," said Pickering.

"What family had he? Are any of them in Washington?"

"He had a brother, two sons, and a daughter. The brother is a truck driver. He could be in Washington any time. One of the sons works as a carpenter in White Plains, New York. The other son is a criminal, unfortunately. He is known to sell illicit liquor, but he is something worse than a bootlegger. He is what men in the rackets call an enforcer. He has served time in prison for assault. The daughter . . . Well, her whereabouts are unknown. She declared herself humiliated and left New York shortly after her father was convicted. I suppose her family may know where she is, but she has never returned to New York, so far as the police know."

"What did Judge Blackwell say of this?" Mrs. Roosevelt asked Barbara.

"Nothing," said Barbara, frowning and shaking her head. "He never mentioned it."

"Well . . ." mused the First Lady. "I will write the name McKibben here: meaning any member of the family. Once again, it is a long shot."

"I suppose everything we know is a long shot," said Pickering glumly.

"Yes . . . Tell me, Mr. Pickering, do you think the case against Sara Carter is strong enough to convict her? Have you asked Sergeant Rainey about that?"

Pickering put his tea cup aside. "I really don't know," he said. "She was in his room—at least in the doorway to his room. Her fingerprints were on the lamp beside the bed, on the mirror above the dresser, and on a bathroom drinking glass. That means, of course, she was *in* the room. It means she didn't just discover the body and run out."

"The presence of her fingerprints does not disprove her story that she saw the body and immediately left the room," said Mrs. Roosevelt. "She could very well have left the fingerprints on the occasion of one of her previous visits."

"Her story that she went to Judge Blackwell's room in the character of a prostitute affords her a very neat rationalization for facts she cannot otherwise explain," said Pickering. "The young woman is not very articulate, but she is not stupid. Sitting alone in a jail cell, she has had time to review every ramification of the facts, and time—if she elected to do so—to fabricate a story that accuses her of a minor crime and exculpates her of murder."

"Judge Blackwell seems to have been a rather libidinous man," said Mrs. Roosevelt. "Barbara says he made advances to her. Did he not, dear? Obviously he had some sort of relationship with Mrs. Tracy. The several items found in his room suggest that he probably received one or more women there, for immoral purposes. So perhaps he did employ Sara Carter as a prostitute."

Pickering nodded. "Perhaps," he said quietly.

"My impression," said Barbara, "is that he was quite well able to find satisfying relationships without hiring prostitutes."

"In any event," said Mrs. Roosevelt, "they cannot hold Sara any longer without formally charging her with murder. I am sorry that must happen."

"Oh. I meant to tell you. Sara Carter signed a waiver."

"I beg your pardon?"

"She signed a waiver. She agreed to be held another forty-eight hours without being charged."

Mrs. Roosevelt shook her head and frowned. "I had so hoped," she said, "that we could close this case one way or another within the first forty-eight hours. How long will it be before we find a solution?"

"We have to confront the fact, dear lady," said Pickering, "that some murder mysteries are never solved, some murderers are never caught."

Half an hour after Mrs. Roosevelt's tea things were taken back down to the pantry, two White House ushers brought up the liquor and ice for the President's afternoon cocktails. His guests that afternoon were General Hugh Johnson, Undersecretary of the Treasury Dean Acheson, and Secretary of Agriculture Henry Wallace. Missy was there too. Mrs. Roosevelt had work to do before she began to dress for the dinner she and the President were to attend later.

"Tomorrow," said the President, tapping the hefty document that lay on the table to his left. "It will be introduced in Congress tomorrow. It may be the most important piece of legislation we have yet proposed."

The document was the National Industrial Recovery Bill. It would create the National Recovery Administration, which would have authority to centralize control over nearly every business and industry in the United States, for the purpose of working the country out of the Depression.

He had already chosen Johnson to head the N.R.A.; and Johnson, as was typical of him, was already acting like administrator of the N.R.A., as if enactment by Congress were only a minor formality.

"Looka this," said Johnson. He held up a sheet of artwork. "See. The emblem of the N.R.A.—the blue eagle. We'll make that as familiar a symbol as the Stars and Stripes."

Hugh Johnson, given the nickname "Ironpants" by his old cavalry buddies, was a thickset, rumpled man with a lined, leathery face and the puffy eyes of a heavy drinker, which he was. A successful businessman in the twenties, he had been recruited as a braintruster; and he was one of the most outspoken and prominent of the braintrusters.

"God help us," said Henry Wallace quietly.

Wallace was a gloomy, pessimistic man. His father had been Secretary of Agriculture under President Harding. Both father and son had been farmers in Iowa. They owned a magazine, *Wallace's Farmer*, and the younger Henry had also published books and articles on agriculture. He was regarded as the most liberal member of the Cabinet.

"God helps those who help themselves," said Hugh Johnson, "and I figure He'll owe us some help after we show him how much we can help ourselves."

"What will you do, General," asked Dean Acheson, "if an industry refuses to go along with one of the industrial codes you are proposing?"

"I'll pop 'em in the nose," laughed Johnson.

Dean Acheson was a handsome young man with blue eyes, dark curly hair, and a big bristly mustache. He was from Connecticut and was a graduate of Yale, plus Harvard Law. He had served as law clerk to Justice Louis Brandeis. Though he was officially Undersecretary of the Treasury, he was in effect Secretary of the Treasury, because Secretary Woodin was too ill to handle the office.

"I notice," said Acheson, "that Henry Ford has already announced he will not comply with any industrial code established for the automobile industry. What will you do about that?"

"Simple," said Johnson. "The government won't buy any Ford cars."

The President laughed heartily. "Pop him on the nose, Hugh," he said. "I hope it works out that easily."

"The Civilian Conservation Corps seems to be working out just fine," said Acheson. "What will we have, shortly? A quarter of a million young men working on C.C.C. projects? That's good, but I wonder how many of you have read the Nels Anderson report on young transients?"

"We don't need to read it, Dean," said Johnson. "We know you'll read it for us, and tell us about it. Anyway, you know what Henry Ford says about it. I quote: 'Why, it's the best education in the world for those boys, traveling around! They get more experience in a few months than they would in a year at school.' "

Acheson accepted that with a small smile at Johnson. "Anderson made a survey and estimates that there are 265,000 young Americans—I mean people under the age of twenty-one—who are simply on the roads. They have no homes. Some have left homes. Others were pushed out because their families couldn't support them."

"Hoboes," said Johnson. "The N.R.A. will create jobs for 'em—if they want jobs."

"Most of them are high school graduates," said Acheson. "And . . . almost half of them are girls."

"*Girls?*" asked Wallace. "Girl hoboes?"

Acheson nodded. "Hitchhiking. Riding freight trains. Living in hobo jungles. A serious problem, don't you think?"

The President looked up at Missy, who stood beside him, ready to help him mix his drinks. "Make sure Harry Hopkins knows about this report," he said.

* * *

That evening the President and Mrs. Roosevelt were guests of the California Democratic Party, at a dinner held in the Mayflower Hotel. The President spoke, and he departed from his prepared text to talk about the homeless young people wandering the roads. It was something the Californians needed to hear, since many of these young people headed for California, where they figured they would at least be warm.

When the Roosevelts returned to the White House, after ten o'clock, the President was pleased: pleased with the dinner and with the warm reception his speech had received. Mrs. Roosevelt was pleased. She had heard the President address concerns that were concerns of her own. She had read the Anderson report even before Dean Acheson saw it.

Coincidence. Mrs. Roosevelt would have been fascinated by the coincidence of two events taking place in other parts of the city at about the hour when she sat on her bed, brushing out her hair.

The first element of the coincidence:

In a modest but comfortable room, a young woman lay naked on her stomach on her bed. In her left hand she held a small round mirror, which she twisted this way and that to give her a view of her buttocks. With her right hand she smeared salve over the thin red welts that crisscrossed her flesh. They were not particularly painful, not in fact even very uncomfortable, but she was anxious that they disappear before anyone saw them. Not that anyone was likely to. Still . . . she didn't want them there. They were evidence of something she did not want anyone ever to know.

The second element of the coincidence:

A man stood at the kitchen sink in his home, in darkness except for a dim red safelight he had screwed into the socket over the table. He rocked a cake pan and watched the chemicals in the pan bring out the image on a 3 $\frac{1}{4}$ × 4 $\frac{1}{4}$ sheet of photographic paper. When he was satisfied with the image he pulled the paper from the pan and plunged it quickly into the chemicals in a second cake pan.

He had no enlarger. He was exposing the paper by laying his paper and negatives under a sheet of glass and switching the kitchen light on and off. The prints would be small, but they were big enough. They showed what he wanted them to show.

She had wept and pleaded with him not to take the pictures, but he had insisted. Angrily insisted. So she had lifted her skirt and pulled down her bloomers, and he had photographed the welts on her backside. Close up. Then at a distance—making her turn her face over her shoulder, so her identity would be clear.

Evidence. Evidence, if he ever needed it.

VI

A TREMBLING YOUNG WOMAN stood in the Center Hall—
dismissed and yet afraid to move. She kept shaking her head.
Her face was flushed. And she wiped tears from her cheeks.

"I don't know anything about it," she said.

She seemed to take comfort in the arrival of Mrs.
Roosevelt. At least, the First Lady's sympathetic smile was a
relief from the grim faces of the Secret Service men.

Lawrence Pickering stood just outside the door into the
book storage closet. His face was a picture of calm hauteur.
"Madam," he said to Mrs. Roosevelt. "It seems we have found
the missing knife."

"Oh . . ."

"Which, I suspect," he went on, "rather settles the matter of who killed Judge Blackwell."

"Who found it, and how?" she asked.

"That young woman discovered it," he said, nodding toward the short, chubby, bespectacled, tearful young woman
who had begun to wring her hands.

Mrs. Roosevelt turned toward the young woman. "What
is your name, dear?" she asked.

"Myrtle Lang. *Mrs.* Myrtle Lang," she whispered.

"How did you happen to find the knife?" asked the First Lady.

"I work for Mr. Tugwell. He sent me up here to find a volume of the *Congressional Record.* And when I began to look through the shelves . . . There it was! It's a horrible thing!"

Mrs. Roosevelt glanced inquiringly at Pickering.

"We haven't touched it," he said. "It remains where it is until fingerprints are taken."

Mrs. Roosevelt walked into the long, narrow room that extended from the Center Hall to the north front of the White House. It was lined on both sides with wooden shelves, on which several thousand volumes were stored—mostly, as she now saw, old records of congressional debates, old committee reports. The room had apparently been intended for some other purpose when the White House was built. It could be entered from the hall and from either of the guest suites.

A young Secret Service agent stood just beyond the door that led into the suite Judge Blackwell had occupied. She didn't know his name, though she had seen him around the premises ever since she moved in here. Without a word, he pointed to the knife.

It lay on top of a row of old, dusty, leather-bound books—a wicked-looking weapon, corroded, with cracks in the leather of the handle. The blade was stained, as was the book on which it lay—apparently with blood.

Pickering had followed. "So," he said. "Does that or does it not conclude the case?"

Slightly piqued by his self-assurance, with I-told-you-so implied, Mrs. Roosevelt shrugged and said, "It is evidence. Let us learn what fingerprints are on it. And if that is blood, it may be possible to learn if it is Judge Blackwell's type."

Pickering nodded curtly. "Quite so," he said.

Mrs. Roosevelt glanced around the room. She kept her

thought to herself, which was that these dusty old books were infrequently referred to, so the knife could well have lain there unnoticed for two whole days.

"I do have a question, Mr. Pickering," she said. "Assuming that Sara Carter ran in here from the judge's bedroom, where she had just murdered him with that knife, to hide the knife before she ran into the hall and screamed at Officer Runkle that the judge— Well . . . Assuming all that, why do you suppose she just left the knife lying on top of those books, rather than shoving it on back, where it would have fallen down behind the books, out of sight? Is that not a peculiar circumstance?"

Pickering glanced at the knife. "There seems to be no end of peculiar circumstances in this case," he said. He drew a breath. "I have arranged to interrogate Mrs. Tracy this morning," he said. "I suggest, with all respect, that you do not accompany me. I will report fully on what she tells us."

"Us?"

"Sergeant Rainey and I. We are going to the Tracy residence, as soon as Professor Tracy is here, at work."

Mrs. Roosevelt regarded him with a degree of skepticism. "Confronted with a District police detective and an agent of the Secret Service, she—"

"We will carry along no rubber hose, madam," he said dryly. "Nor indeed any other implements of what is sometimes called the third degree."

The First Lady let him see the glimmer of a smile. "I count on it," she said.

"She counts on it," said Pickering as Rainey pulled the unmarked little blue Ford Model A to the curb in front of the small house rented by Professor and Mrs. William Tracy.

Rainey laughed.

Two men could hardly have been more in contrast than

Agent Lawrence Pickering and Sergeant Wilbur Rainey: Pickering thin and carrying himself stiffly, wearing a handsomely tailored brown tweed suit, and Rainey, sloppy of posture as well as dress, huffing as he got out of the car, shrugging repeatedly to settle his loose checkered suit over his shoulders. Except that the dapper Oliver would never have appeared so garishly dressed, they bore a faint resemblance to Laurel and Hardy.

"She might not be at home," said Pickering as Rainey knocked on the door.

But she was. She answered the knock.

Rainey was instantly charmed by Blanche Tracy. She was pretty: pleasingly plump, as the saying went, in dishabille—another cliché that came to Rainey's mind—and, just maybe, containing a shot or two of hooch so early in the morning. She was wearing a tea-rose silk nightgown, covered—a little—by a sheer peignoir. Her blond hair hung around her shoulders, only casually brushed this morning.

"Yes?"

It was obvious she thought she was facing a pair of salesmen, selling Fuller brushes or Electrolux cleaners door to door. She cocked her hips and challenged the two men to state their business in a few words.

Rainey fumbled in his jacket pocket and brought forth his badge. "District police," he said weakly. "I'm Detective Sergeant Rainey. This is Agent Lawrence Pickering of the United States Secret Service."

"Investigating the murder of Judge Blackwell," she said with a resigned sigh. "Come in."

The little house had no foyer. The living room was directly inside the front door. It was quite modestly furnished and had the look of a house that had been rented furnished. She shrugged and indicated they should sit wherever they chose: in one of the two armchairs or on the couch.

"We have but a few questions," said Pickering.

She spread her hands and glanced around the room. "The palatial quarters of a braintruster," she said.

"A dollar-a-year man?" asked Rainey.

"Not *that* bad," she said. "That's for the wealthy, not for a professor of economics. Anyway . . . What questions?"

"You last saw Judge Blackwell alive . . . when?" asked Pickering.

"At the White House dinner Wednesday evening," she said. She put up her feet and made herself languidly comfortable on the couch, facing the two men, both of whom had chosen the chairs. "Are you asking the same question of all the guests?"

"At what time did you leave the White House?" asked Pickering.

"When the dinner was over," she said. "When we could escape the oppressive company of the Roosevelts and get out to where a drink was to be had."

"Did you and your husband leave alone?"

"Alone," she said. "In a cab. Other than for leaving with Justice Holmes, which would have been a pleasure, our options were to go with Julius Caesar, who needed a cab, too—"

"General MacArthur, you mean?"

She shrugged. "God Jr.," she sneered. "Or his Boy Scout aide and wife. Or some senator, whoever he was: the one with the perfume accent."

"Carter Glass."

"Whatever. Anyway, we left alone, in a cab. We went to a speakeasy. You won't ask where, will you? Bill telephoned from there, and we went on, in another cab, to play a late round of bridge with the Nelsons—that is, Harper and Bridget Nelson: the only other people in Washington we think of as real friends."

"And how late were you there?"

"What do you want? Until after Judge Blackwell was

killed? I hear that happened about one in the morning. At one
A.M. we were sitting in the Nelsons' living room, pretty thoroughly sloshed, and laughing over what was left of a game of
bridge."

"This man Nelson is . . . ?"

"He's a lawyer. He works for Ferdinand Pecora and the
Senate Banking and Currency Committee, investigating chi-
canery in the banking and securities businesses."

Pickering's significant glance at Rainey did not go unnoticed, and Blanche Tracy tossed her head and added, "So,
you see, I didn't kill Judge Blackwell, and neither did my husband—God knows why we would want to."

Pickering could not be so easily subdued. "I am afraid,"
he said loftily, "we have evidence of a quite sufficient reason
why one or both of you would want to."

Rainey broke in. He reached into his pocket and tossed
toward her the pair of white silk panties found in Judge Blackwell's bureau drawer. "Those yours?" he grunted.

She picked up the panties and looked at them disdain-
fully. "Of course not! She stopped. She flushed. She had read
the label. "No . . . Not mine."

Pickering raised his hand and cut off something Rainey
was about to say. "Madam," he said calmly, a little scornfully.
"As I told you, we have sufficient evidence that you and Judge
Blackwell were engaged in— How shall we say? Shall we call
it an affair of the heart? Obviously, that undergarment cannot
be traced to you. But it was purchased in Boston, not in Washington, and—"

"*All right!* We . . . did. And this is mine. But I can prove
where I was when he was killed. Ask the Nelsons. You might
even be able to find the cab driver who took us home at two
o'clock."

"An ironclad alibi," said Rainey.

Blanche Tracy rose from the couch and walked to a cabinet, where she picked up a bottle of Scotch. "Drink?" she

asked. When they shook their heads, she poured herself a shotglass of straight Scotch. "One thing . . ." she said. "If it is an ironclad alibi . . . then you won't need to question my husband about it. Will you?"

"Are you saying," Pickering asked, "that he doesn't know about the relationship between you and the judge?"

"He does know. That's the point. And if it involves us personally, maybe publicly, in the investigation of Judge Blackwell's murder, that just rubs salt in Bill's wounds. It could be the end of the marriage. I have reason to believe he's seriously considering doing something dramatic, anyway. I don't want to see him shoved over the edge."

"Something . . . dramatic," said Pickering. "Something less dramatic than murdering your paramour. Or is it murdering *you?*"

"No," she said, shaking her head. "Nothing that bad. But I think he may be planning to leave me."

"Not hard to understand," said Rainey.

"Do you have evidence of any such plan?" asked Pickering.

She tossed back her Scotch and slammed the shotglass down on the coffee table. "Two weeks ago he withdrew almost every cent we had in a savings account in a Boston bank," she said. "I saw the statement and asked him why. He just shrugged."

"How much money was that?" asked Rainey.

"A little less than $2,000," she said. "We were going to buy a house in Cambridge, Massachusetts. On the other hand, why should he put money in a house? He knew—"

"You are sure he knew?"

She smiled wryly. "We had some shouting matches over it. Oh, yes. He knew."

"I see no reason," said Pickering, "why we should interrogate your husband for the present."

"Then maybe that's all for the present," she said, rising

and stepping toward the door. She opened the door. "Isn't it?"

Pickering rose and nodded toward the door. "I suppose it is," he said.

Rainey got up, too. But he paused and tipped his head to one side and asked Blanche Tracy one last question. "Tell us, Mrs. Tracy, have you got any . . . *welts* anywhere on you?"

She flared. "You go to hell!"

In the car on the way back to the White House, Rainey lit a cigar. "Figure this, Brother Pickering," he said. "You could buy a lot of murdering for $2,000. There's almost nobody you couldn't get knocked off for money like that. Even inside the White House. A hit man—"

"You assume," said Pickering with his usual reserve and precision, his eyebrows well raised, "there exists a hit man, as you call him, with knowledge of the inside of the White House, plus its security arrangements."

"Yeah. Anyway, now that we got the knife, it looks like the case is about wrapped up."

A few blocks from the house, Rainey pulled the car to the curb. He glanced at Pickering, smiled wryly, then pulled the handkerchief from his breast pocket and used it to extract something from his jacket pocket. He showed it to Pickering, then wrapped it carefully in the handkerchief.

"The shotglass she drank from just now," he said. "Whether the case is wrapped up or not wrapped up, I wanted a set of her fingerprints."

Mrs. Roosevelt had a luncheon appointment that Saturday. It was with Samuel Leibowitz.

Leibowitz was a famous New York City criminal lawyer, and he had been hired by International Labor Defense to appeal and retry the case of nine young Negro men who had been convicted of the rape of two white women in a railroad car in Alabama. They were known as the Scottsboro Boys, and their case was an international *cause célèbre*. Their convictions had been reversed last year by the Supreme Court of the United States; and Leibowitz had just finished defending one of them in a second trial, which had resulted in a second conviction.

Several Negro organizations, supported by liberal organizations, planned a protest march in Washington next week, and Leibowitz had come to explain the cause to Mrs. Roosevelt and to assure her that, though the protesters would picket the White House, they had no wish to embarrass the President.

Samuel Leibowitz was a small, bald man, with liver spots on his brownish pate. He was intense but not without a sense of humor.

"Not a single Negro on the jury," he said to Mrs. Roosevelt. "Not at either trial. Couldn't have been. There was not a single colored man or woman on the jury roll. I asked why, and the answer was given that not a single Negro in Morgan County had enough 'education, integrity, good character, and sound judgment' to serve on a jury. That jury commissioner, testifying under oath, sat there and looked at me with a sober face and said not a single Negro— Why, Mrs. Roosevelt! I called colored men to the witness stand: physicians, college professors . . . graduates of famous universities. Still— Not a single Negro in Morgan County could qualify to be a juror!"

"I've read detailed accounts of the trial, Mr. Leibowitz. I was particularly distressed by the violent anti-Semitic remarks of the prosecutor."

Leibowitz chuckled. "Did you read what he said to the jury? 'Show them that Alabama justice cannot be bought by Jew money from New York!' " He shook his head and grinned. " 'Alabama justice . . .' Now there's an oxymoron."

"Mr. Leibowitz," she said somberly. "Can we be sure it would be any more fair in the District of Columbia?"

He frowned. "I cannot give you any assurance it would

be entirely fair anywhere in the United States," he said. "In a place like Alabama, the situation is of course far worse; but I cannot assure you that a Negro could get a fair trial in New York or Illinois."

"Would you mind if I discuss with you a bit a case that has come to my attention?"

The Buchanan had once been an elegant hotel. Time and Prohibition had changed it. The guests now were almost exclusively traveling salesmen, men looking for a clean, inelegant room they could rent for a little money, where they could sleep without fear of being robbed or being bitten by bedbugs. Evidence of its old splendor remained only in the size of the rooms and, in some rooms, in the size and weight of the furnishings. The veneer was chipped, and they stood on threadbare carpeting, but some of the old bedsteads were Victorian; and an occasional salesman, with the education to know about it and the curiosity to wonder, might speculate on what famous men and women had maybe once slept in his bed.

George McKibben was not thinking of famous men as he lay on the big bed in his room. His mind turned a different way, and he was thinking of the alluring women of half a century ago: fuller-figured than women today, and more compliant, and dressed in elaborate and intriguing lingerie. He was thinking, in fact, of a woman unpinning her hair and letting it fall down her back. Ahh . . .

Damn! A knock on the door. He'd paid the damned rent. Annoyed, he rolled off the bed and went to the door.

"Who?"

"Police! Open the door!"

He glanced toward his suitcase, lying open on the folding luggage rack in front of the tattered drapes—and decided he didn't have time to do anything about what was in it. He slid the chain out of the catch and turned the knob.

He faced a short, squat, red-faced, out-of-breath man in a checkered suit and a broad-brimmed, pinched-crown gray hat, backed by two uniformed policemen.

Trouble.

"Rainey," said the short man. "District police. You Mc-Kibben?"

George nodded. For himself, he was a taller-than-average young man, thin, with caved-in cheeks and furtive, hollow eyes. He wore a white shirt, open at the collar, and black pants held up by suspenders. He had been lying on the bed, and his feet were bare. He had been drinking gin and was a little muddled.

Rainey and his two policemen walked past him, into the room, glancing around, aggressively suspicious.

"From New York, right, George?"

"What'd you say your name is?" George asked.

"Detective Rainey."

"I mean your first name."

"What the hell's my first name got to do with anything?"

"Well . . ." said George. "If you're going to call me by my first name a minute after we meet, I guess I'll call you by yours."

Rainey let a smile spread slowly across his face. "Been hustled by the cops before, haven't you?"

George shrugged. "I suppose I have. What can I do for you today?"

"Well, I—"

Rainey was interrupted by one of the uniformed officers, who had raised a hand to catch his attention. The officer was looking into George McKibben's suitcase. There was a quart of Beefeater's, besides the one on the nightstand by the bed, and a quart of Cutty Sark.

"Heavy drinker, are you, George?" Rainey asked.

"I'm away from home the whole week," said George.

"Yeah . . . Well, you made my problem simpler. I can take you in on the basis of that."

George McKibben nodded. "In and out pretty quick," he said. "Prohibition's got a short life ahead of it. No judge is going to ask much bail for possession of that stuff. Not anymore."

Rainey walked around the room, pushing back the drapes to look out the window for a moment, opening the drawers in the bureau. "Right," he said. "But to spare you the inconvenience, suppose you answer some questions."

"Suppose I do," said George. He shook out a Lucky and lit it. "Whatever you want to hear."

Rainey sat down on the bed. "What do you do for a living?" he asked.

"Straight answer? Or official answer?"

Rainey shot a glance at the suitcase and the bottles. "I don't give a damn about that, McKibben," he said. "In fact, I'm thirsty myself. And I know you don't sell the stuff in my jurisdiction. You'd be face down in the gutter in four hours if you tried that. So it's your personal supply. Or presents for somebody."

"Right."

"You sell it in New York?"

"Gotta find another job," said George. "Repeal's gonna put me out of business."

"How long you been in Washington, George?"

"What'd they tell you down at the desk?"

"They say you checked in here Monday."

George nodded. " 'Kay. Monday."

"So what you doin' in Washington a whole week?"

"Seeing the sights," said George.

"The sights. I, uh—"

Again, Rainey was interrupted by one of the policemen. The officer had been picking up the liquor bottles one by one, with a handkerchief so as not to leave his fingerprints. He was holding up a bottle of gin when he tossed his head to one side to alert Rainey.

"You like gin?" George asked. "Take it. My compliments. Always like to cooperate with the police."

"Sergeant . . ."

Rainey stood and looked at what the officer was nodding at—

A knife. A long, ugly blade. It was hidden, partly, under bottles and under an undershirt.

"Oh, George," murmured Rainey. "You should have got rid of it."

"I swear, sir! I swear, ma'am. I *did* look. I am not—"

"Ballenger . . ." said Pickering, his chin rising.

Stuart Ballenger was a young and junior agent of the Secret Service. He stood facing Pickering in the First Lady's office. She sat at her desk, looking up into his troubled face and trying to show him sympathy.

Ballenger stiffened. "I *am not* incompetent, Mr. Pickering," he said resolutely.

"But the knife—"

"Was *not there*, Mr. Pickering, Mrs. Roosevelt! It was not lying on that shelf Wednesday night . . . Thursday morning. A perfectly obvious place to hide it. It was not there."

"Then it must have been placed there subsequently," said Mrs. Roosevelt.

"Hardly . . . likely," said Pickering.

"Likely or not, sir," said Ballenger.

"Mr. Ballenger," said Mrs. Roosevelt in a kindly voice she meant should afford the young man some measure of confidence. "You are, I take it, sure of what you have just told us?"

"I swear it," said Ballenger.

"Very well. Thank you."

When Ballenger was outside the room, Pickering sighed

loudly and shook his head. "If what he says is true, we are back—as the cliché saying is—to square one. But do realize, dear lady, that he could be lying to protect himself from a suggestion of incompetence."

"The whole thing doesn't *fit*, Mr. Pickering," said Mrs. Roosevelt. "As I said this morning, why would the murderer leave the knife lying atop the books, when he or she could just as easily have pushed it back and let it fall behind the books on the shelf? In that case, we might not have discovered the weapon for months. I am much inclined to believe the young man."

Pickering compressed his lips and seemed to focus his eyes down the two sides of his nose. "Square . . . one," he said.

"Has there been a fingerprint report?"

"Fingerprints on the knife? There were none. The weapon, like everything else was clean—wiped clean."

"The blood type?" she asked.

"Oh . . . I haven't heard. I can telephone, if you like."

"Please do."

Pickering picked up the telephone; and while the First Lady scanned half a dozen letters and signed them, he spoke to someone at District police headquarters.

"What? You are certain of that? The test was repeated? Didn't . . . Yes, I suppose a careful analyst could. So . . . Very well. Thank you."

Mrs. Roosevelt looked up. "Astonishing news, Mr. Pickering?" she asked.

His eyes bulged with anger and frustration. "Square one?" he asked thinly. "Square minus *six!* This investigation is going *nowhere!*"

"Allow me to form a judgment of my own."

Pickering slumped. He shook his head. "The blood on the knife," he said. "It was *chicken* blood. Chicken . . . Chicken!"

"May I suggest that, in the circumstances, it would be appropriate to release Sara Carter?"

Pickering drew his lips back between his teeth. "That may be premature," he said. "She might—"

Mrs. Roosevelt drew herself back and up. "Are you saying, Mr. Pickering, that it would be *convenient* to keep Sara Carter confined to a squalid cage?"

"She waived—"

"I don't care what she waived. She did not place that knife on that bookshelf, and what is more she did not stain it with chicken blood. Whoever did killed Judge Blackwell. I think we should ask Sergeant Rainey to arrange for her immediate release."

"I cannot argue otherwise, dear lady," said Pickering.

That Saturday evening the Marine Band played on the South Lawn. The President and the First Lady, beaming, sat in chairs facing the band, listening to the music, greeting guests.

Among the first guests brought to them was a chubby young singer, who was presented by Congressman Carl Vinson. Her name was Kate Smith. A part of her stage character was her line "Hello, everybody!" and she had just made a movie with that title. In a little while she would sing with the band—the closing number. She sang "God Bless America" in her own special way, belting it out in a voice that was undistinguished but powerful—out of her ample chest—and projecting a down-home sincerity that was oddly appealing to middle America in those years. She would close the concert with that song.

"Oh," she said to the Roosevelts, "it is *such* a pleasure!"

She said it so they knew she meant it; and Mrs. Roosevelt stood to take her hand and tell her how welcome she was to the White House, while the President looked up and smiled and nodded until the rotund young woman knelt before him and took his hand.

"Mr. President—"

"Miss Smith . . . Please—"

He struggled as if to rise, and she rose and bent over him and kissed him on the forehead.

Something about her was latently tragic. Mrs. Roosevelt sensed it, and the President did, too. He held her hand longer than he might have done and told her he was grateful to her for singing this evening. When she backed away, still smiling, tears glistened in her eyes.

A later guest was the famous comic actor W. C. Fields.

"Mr. President," he said, half through his nose. "That is . . . if I may be so informal as to call you 'Mr. President' . . . It is a pleasure to meet a President who stands for the return of booze. Not that it has ever been away."

"The President doesn't exactly stand for that," said Mrs. Roosevelt.

"Oh, I do, I do," the President laughed. "If you had been here an hour ago, Mr. Fields, I would have been honored to have a drink with a man who is *famous* for drinking."

"Heh-heh-heh," said Fields; and he withdrew from his bulging jacket pocket five small rubber balls, which he proceeded to juggle deftly, some behind his back. "See what I mean?" he said as he tossed and caught balls in all directions. "Dexterity depends on gin. Without it, pilots couldn't fly, to give just one example. Why . . . *birds* couldn't fly! Ever see a crocked robin, Mr. President? Fact is, you never saw an *uncrocked* robin. They talk about the 'cock' robin. It's a misnomer. 'Crocked' robin is the correct term."

"It will be legal again soon," said the President gaily.

"Yeah, but the prices! I hear gin is going to go for $1.00 a quart, decent whiskey for $1.50! Mr. President . . . see what you can do about those prices! What's it going to cost to get crocked?"

"It takes seven years to make a decent whiskey," said the President.

"Yeah, but seven hours to make a decent gin," said Fields.

"So— Well . . . *Is* there such a thing as a decent gin, come to think of it? Seven hours to make an *indecent* gin. Keep those prices down, Mr. President. Keep 'em down. We do want to share the wealth, don't we?"

VII

"I'M GOIN' HOME AND take a damn bath," said Sara Carter bitterly.

"Don't get the idea you're off the hook," said Sergeant Rainey. "If it was up to me, I'd hold you. So you *go* home. Don't go anywhere else. You be for sure available, girl, in case I want to talk to you again."

Dressed again in the uniform of a White House maid—the clothes she'd had on when she was brought to the jail—Sara stood with her hips cocked, a scornful expression on her face. "You wouldn't let me go if you didn't have to," she said.

"I don't *have* to," he said. "I had a request to. I'm goin' along with that, but you still have some answerin' to do. So don't get too smart, gal. You're not off the hook yet."

Sara turned and sauntered out of his office; and Rainey left the room, too, turning the opposite way in the hall.

Threading his way through the halls and then down a flight of stairs, he came to a room closed and guarded by a uniformed officer. The man stepped aside, and Rainey opened the door and went in.

George McKibben sat on a wooden chair in the center

of the room, in the light of a lamp that hung directly above his head. He was stark naked. His pallid skin gleamed with sweat, and his nakedness revealed the elaborate tattoos on both his arms.

The chair was fastened to the floor, and the front legs had been sawed off three inches or so, tipping the seat forward just enough for nagging discomfort. Two detectives sat in armchairs behind a desk that faced McKibben. Short lengths of heavy rubber hose lay on the desk. They hadn't used them—and in fact wouldn't—but a subject being interrogated knew what they were for.

"Excuse the interruption," said Rainey. One of the other detectives got up from one of the chairs, and Rainey sat down. "Did you explain everything while I was gone, George?"

George did not respond. He just glared resentfully at Rainey.

"Okay, so let's get back to the questions, kiddo," said Rainey. "First. What have you been doing in Washington all week? That's a question I gotta have an answer for. For sure. So . . . ?"

George closed his eyes and sighed. "I told you. I came down to look around, to see the sights. I'd never been in Washington before, so I—"

"Just a tourist, hey?"

George nodded. "Just a tourist. That's all."

"See the White House?"

"Sure. Also the Capitol. Went to the zoo . . ."

"You ever been in trouble, George?"

"Yeah."

"What kind of trouble?"

"You want to know if I've done time, don't you? So okay, I've done time."

"In New York," said Rainey.

"In New York," George agreed. "I did a year in the city lockup."

"And what was that for, George?"

"Assault."

"What kind of assault, George?"

George McKibben turned down the corners of his mouth. "I put a couple of nicks in a guy," he said.

"As a matter of fact," said Rainey, his voice turning grim and threatening, "you're an enforcer for one of the New York mobs. Bootleggers, what else. You're a bagman; you collect money; and when you don't get it you use a knife on people. You've only been convicted once, but you've used that knife on a dozen guys, at least. You—"

"If you say so, Rainey," George sneered.

"We've got your F.B.I. sheet. I talked a while ago to a reporter for the New York *Herald,* and he read me the story he wrote about you when you were convicted. You're an artist with the knife, George. You didn't write your name on that guy, but you sliced him where it hurt and where it left scars, so he'll always remember. If Blackwell had still been prosecuting, you'd have got ten years."

"If *he'd* been prosecuting, I'd have got twenty."

"Yes. He prosecuted your father and got him five."

"Got him killed," said George McKibben. "And the old man hadn't done anything, either. Just a businessman who happened to be a friend of guys Blackwell didn't like. A political prosecution, that's all it was; and my father died for it."

Rainey nodded. "So you hated Judge Blackwell. And the judge got killed with a knife. And you're in Washington with no explanation of what you're doing here. Odd bunch of coincidences, hey, George?"

George McKibben's face hardened. The cords in his neck hardened. "Coincidence . . ." he muttered. "You can't hang that on me, Rainey."

"We'll see," said Detective Sergeant Wilbur Rainey.

* * *

"The evidence is, indeed, even more suggestive than those co-incidences," said Lawrence Pickering to Mrs. Roosevelt.

The Marine Band concert was over, and she had returned to her office to look over some drafts. Pickering had come up.

"I should be really glad to find someone other than Sara Carter—"

"She, incidentally, has been released," said Pickering. "Sergeant Rainey believes it was premature to release her, but she has been released."

"I am glad to hear it."

"Anyway . . . The evidence is yet more suggestive. After Mr. McKibben was taken from the hotel, officers made a very thorough search of his room. They found money. Cash. Two thousand dollars."

"Suggestive evidence . . ." Mrs. Roosevelt mused with a frown. "Suggesting what?"

"Allow us not to forget that Professor Tracy withdrew almost two thousand from his savings, only a week or so ago. What did he do with that money? Is it not possible that he paid what is called a hit man to kill a man who was destroying his marriage?"

"It is entirely possible," said the First Lady, "that Professor Tracy can explain exactly what he did with that money."

"If we suppose so, we'll have to ask him," said Pickering. "And when he is asked, he will know he is suspected of murder."

"Professor Tracy," she said, "is no more valuable than Judge Blackwell. If an unpleasant fact has to be brought to his attention in the course of our investigation into the murder of the judge, so be it."

"The police are pursuing another line of inquiry at the moment," said Pickering.

* * *

Sergeant Rainey sat in the shabby little office behind the desk in the Buchanan Hotel. The fat, bald, sweating manager, compelled to leave the desk and come back here to talk to the police, was hostile.

His name was Allan Morrow. "This is no hot-sheet hotel, Sergeant Rainey," he said angrily. "We don't let hookers work here. We don't—"

"Frankly, I don't care if you do or not," said Rainey. "I'm a homicide detective, not vice squad. I don't care if hookers work your hotel or not."

"I can't promise that none ever come in here," said Morrow. "But when we detect one, we throw her out."

"Good for you. What I want to know is who if anybody visited this guy McKibben."

Morrow turned down the corners of his mouth, turned up the palms of his hands, and shrugged. "Should I know who comes to see every guest?"

"George McKibben," said Rainey, "is a gangster. His business is selling liquor and cutting people with knives. I want to know why he's in Washington."

"Gangster . . ."

"Maybe a killer. So talk. Everything you know about him. Everything you noticed."

Allan Morrow picked up the fat cigar butt he had laid aside in an ashtray. He frowned over it for a moment, then struck a match. "I don't know much," he said as he sucked fire into the ragged end of the cigar. "He paid in advance, two days at a time. One of the maids told me he had liquor in his room. But who doesn't? He had a girlfriend or two, visited him. I suppose hookers, but I didn't recognize them."

"White or colored?" asked Rainey.

"Oh, white, for sure. No colored allowed in this hotel, hookers or not."

"If I showed you a picture of one of these girls, would you know her?"

Morrow considered for a moment, then nodded. "I s'pose I might," he said.

"Can you describe them?"

"Little fat girl, one of them. Black hair. And the other one—" He shook his head. "Luscious! Light brown hair. Great figure. Hey! You couldn't believe it."

"Never saw either one of them before, I suppose."

Morrow shook his head. "I swear," he said. "Not street hookers. I never saw either one of 'em before."

"If I showed you pictures of some girls, could you pick them out?"

"Figure I could. Yeah . . . Figure I could."

"Anybody come during the day?"

"Hey, these gals came during the day. Did I say they came at night? No. Came . . . Well, one of them was in here in the morning. The other came, like, early evening."

"They came once? Or more than once?"

Morrow shrugged. "I don't work *every* goddamn hour," he said. "I don't see *everybody* comes in and out. I saw the little fat broad once and the other one twice. They could have been here other times."

"Any guys come to see him?"

"Not that I ever saw. I figured the guy was a tourist and the broads were his fun and games."

"What makes you say you figured him for a tourist?"

"No special hours for goin' out and comin' in," said Morrow. "Your salesman, he goes out of here in the morning with his shoes shined and drags his weary ass back in in the evening. McKibben, he sometimes went out at noon. Sometimes he was back in the middle of the afternoon, sometimes in the wee hours. That's like a guy that's just takin' in the sights of the town, huh? Or—"

"Or came to town to kill somebody," said Rainey.

"*Jeez!*"

"Anybody asks for him, I want to know about it."

Morrow nodded. " 'Kay. I'll call."

"This is a homicide investigation, my friend. Be damned *sure* you call."

George McKibben lay on his back on the cot in his cell. The cops had not used their rubber hoses on him, but he had been slapped around, and his face was red and swollen; and he had been thrown into this cell—literally thrown—and had slammed hard against the floor and the rear wall.

He ached. He hated.

They could do this to you. Yeah, in their respectability, that they put on and took off like the cheap suit that detective wore. They could do it to him. That was easy. But they'd got away with it against the old man, too, in spite of all he paid them.

There was the trouble. You could pay them, but they didn't *stay* paid. And when they decided to cheat on you, they turned up their noses at you. They were so *moral*.

You had just one way to fight back.

Sara Carter lay in a tub of hot water, soaking the ache and cold out of her bones. Her mother sat on a stool by the tub, keeping Sara's glass filled with sweet white wine, scrubbing her back with a big round sponge.

"You fancy," her mother said. " 'At's the problem."

Sara fixed cold eyes on her mother. "I fancy," she said. "But even the money they took from my room, they givin' back. This thing is over. I din' kill that son-a-bitch. They know I din', now. I'm goin' be Miz Roosevelt's special darlin', 'cause I was locked up three days. That woman got a *painful* conscience, Mama."

"Sara— You he'p the man that *did* kill Judge Blackwell?"

"Mama, don' ask questions like that there. You under-stan' me? Don' you ever ask me no question like that ag'in."

"Non è ciò che avevo ordinato. Ho chiesto uno Scotch."

The bartender glared angrily at the swarthy little man at the bar. "Speak English, wop," he said. "And that's two bits. Pay up."

The little man shook his head.

The bartender snapped his fingers. A big man appeared at the side of the little man.

"What's the trouble?"

"This wop, or spic, or whatever he is, don't wanna pay for his whiskey."

"Oho," said the big man.

He grabbed the little man by the lapels and shook him. The little man struck out with a fist, grazing the side of the big man's head. The big man dropped him with a short left to the chin. Then he picked him up; and, as about half the customers laughed, he carried him by the collar of his jacket and the seat of his pants to the alley door. And there he tossed the little man into the gravel and the dirty water of a rain puddle.

"An' don't never come back— *Hey! No! No!*"

The little man, lying on his back in the dirt and water, had drawn a black snub-nosed revolver. As the big man screamed, the little man took deliberate aim and fired two shots. The big man toppled back, hit the door, then toppled forward and landed face down in the same water and gravel where the lit-tle man lay on his back.

The little man rose on his hands and knees, then stood. For a moment he looked down on the dying bouncer, and very carefully he replaced the revolver in the holster inside his wet jacket. So— Maybe it hadn't been a good idea. But it was done.

He turned and walked out of the alley. He snapped his

head around, then slapped dirt off his clothes. Scotch. He'd ordered Scotch.

Damn! He had work to do in Washington. He could not leave town until it was finished. He didn't need to become the subject of a manhunt over the shooting of a speakeasy muscle man.

On the other hand . . . he had his dignity. Nobody manhandled him and threw *him* in an alley. Nobody. Nobody *lived* who did that to Achille Pepino.

Mrs. Carter heard the knock. She had just sat down, having placed before Sara a heaping platter of ham and beans and greens, with a big glass of beer, and now she had to rise and carry herself wearily to the front door.

The man at the door was tall and thin, with coffee-with-cream skin and a shiny bald head. Prematurely bald, she judged. Most prematurely, for she took him to be not much older than Sara.

"Is this the residence of Sara Carter?" he asked.

Mrs. Carter nodded but maintained the stiff reserve born of skepticism.

"My name is Beauford Jones," he said. "I work at the White House. I would like to speak with Miss Sara, if I may."

"What makes you think she's here?" asked Mrs. Carter.

"Rumor spreads fast in the White House," said Beauford Jones. "The rumor is that she was released from the District jail this afternoon."

"Okay. You wait. I ask if she wants to see you."

Sara shrugged. "What you s'pose he want? Okay. Let him in."

For an awkward moment, Beauford Jones stood in the kitchen and watched Sara eat. Then, concluding apparently that no one was going to offer him a chair, he pulled one back from the table and sat down uninvited.

"What you want, Beauford?" asked Sara.

"I know somethin' about what happened Wednesday night," he said. "I decided to tell you."

"If it's somethin' helpful, why didn't you tell it while I was in jail?" she asked.

He shook his head. "Two reasons," he said. "In the first place, I didn't want to get mixed up in something that could only make trouble for me. That is, I didn't want to get mixed up unless it would help you, for sure. And, besides that, you were in jail, and no one was allowed to talk to you. If you'd been charged and had got a lawyer, I—"

"What you talkin' about, Beauford?"

"I know you didn't kill Judge Blackwell, Sara," he said.

"You know that? You *know* that, an' you didn't come tell the cops while I was rottin' in—"

"Do you think they would have listened to me?" he asked. "Anyway, you were only in jail Thursday and Friday, and—"

"And most of Saturday," she sneered. "Not long, you figure? You try it sometime, Beauford, and see how long that seems to *you.*"

"The rumor is that Mrs. Roosevelt has taken a personal interest in your case," he said. "If you hadn't been released by Monday, I'd have gone to talk to her. She, I think, would listen."

Sara nodded. "She came to the jail to see me, twice."

"Yes. She listens. So—"

"How you know I didn't kill the judge?" asked Sara.

"You were in the pantry on the ground floor until about twelve-thirty," he said. "You were there when I came back down from the second floor, where I'd gone up to pick up a tray that had been left in the President's study. While I was up there, I heard sounds from the guest suite where Judge Blackwell was staying. I think now those were the sounds of the judge being attacked and dying. And if they were, he was dead before you went up."

"What sounds?"

"As I came out of the President's study, I could hear sounds through the door across the hall. Like . . . Like grunts. Muffled, you know, by the door. But was like: 'Ughh! Ooh! Ughh!' Grunts, you know? Like . . . Like the sounds a man might make when he's being stabbed with a knife."

"Beauford, your imagination—"

"Not imagination. I *heard*. You know, I . . . I didn't think too much of it right then. But when I learned he was murdered with a knife about that time . . . Well, it fit together. You know? It fit together. So, I've been trying to figure out when to tell. And who. And when I heard you were out of jail, I figured I'd come and tell you."

Mrs. Roosevelt took the telephone call from Sara Carter, even though the hour was almost eleven o'clock. Yes, she said, Sara could come to the White House tonight. Yes, she could bring Beauford Jones. Yes, she knew who Beauford Jones was: one of the White House ushers. He had information that—? All right, bring it now.

The First Lady was puzzled, but she decided to telephone Lawrence Pickering. He lived only a few blocks from the White House—lived alone, as a widower—and he said it was no inconvenience for him to return and hear what Beauford Jones had to say.

Because the President was probably asleep and because her office was adjacent to his bedroom, Mrs. Roosevelt told the gate guard to have Sara Carter and Beauford Jones escorted to the Red Room. Pickering arrived before the two young people, and he and the First Lady were seated in the Red Room sipping coffee when Sara and Beauford came in.

"Pour yourselves some coffee," said Mrs. Roosevelt, "and have a seat."

She pointed to a settee that faced the two chairs where she and Pickering were sitting.

Sara poured herself a cup of coffee. Beauford sat down nervously, without coffee. He was wearing a tan double-breasted suit with white buttons, an olive-green shirt, and a yellow necktie. Sara wore a calf-length light yellow dress with a floppy white ruffle at her throat. She also wore a small, flat, round hat that matched her dress.

"Beauford heard the judge bein' killed," said Sara.

"And didn't tell anybody?" asked Pickering indignantly.

"I wasn't sure that was what I was hearing," said Beauford timidly. "It could have been the sound of something else."

"Well, just what did you hear?" asked Pickering. "Describe it."

"First," said Mrs. Roosevelt, "tell us when you heard it."

Beauford repeated what he had told Sara, amplifying the detail a little. In the pantry on the ground floor, someone had noticed the absence of a tray and coffee set. The President had ordered coffee brought to his study after the state dinner, and in the bustle of cleaning up the dining room and getting all the services back downstairs, the coffee tray had been forgotten. Beauford Jones had been sent up to get it—between 12:00 and 12:30, and in any case while Sara Carter was still in the pantry on the ground floor.

"I came out the door," he said quietly. "Out of the President's study. Carrying the tray. The entrance to the suite Judge Blackwell was occupying is just across the hall. As I passed by, I heard the sound of grunting in the suite. The sound was muffled, of course, but it was the sound of someone . . . Well . . . Grunting. Sharply, as if in pain. And repeatedly. I—"

"What did you think you were hearing?" Pickering asked. "What did you think *then?* Don't tell us what you later decided it might be. Tell us what you thought at the moment."

Beauford lowered his chin and stared at his feet. "I thought I was hearing something that was none of my business."

"Be more specific," said Pickering.

Beauford glanced up, then lowered his eyes again. "Well . . . All of us . . . the night staff . . . knew Judge Blackwell had visitors in his room some nights. And— Well . . . You know . . ."

"You thought," said Pickering sarcastically, "you were hearing someone in the transports of ecstasy."

Beauford nodded.

"And maybe you were."

"Well . . . the grunts were kind of sharp. Sharp, and kind of loud, for me to hear them through the door. When I heard the judge had been killed with a knife, I thought maybe I'd heard—"

"And maybe you did," said Mrs. Roosevelt.

"Doubtful," said Pickering. "Did you hear any other sounds, like the sound of a struggle?"

"No, sir."

"But these . . . grunts, you now suggest, may have been the sound of the judge receiving blows from a knife."

"Mr. Pickering," said Beauford Jones, "what I heard was not the sounds of a man in what you call the transports of ecstasy. I *know* what that sounds like, and that's not what I heard."

"You have heard many men in—"

"*Mr. Pickering!*" Mrs. Roosevelt protested. "Whatever Beauford heard, what he heard proves something very significant."

Pickering raised his chin high and looked down his nose. "What do you suggest it proves, dear lady?" he asked.

"The sounds Beauford heard," she said. "Whatever they were, I believe you will agree they were hardly likely to issue from a man who was alone. If they were not the sounds of a man taking the blows of a knife, and even if they were not the sounds of a man 'in the transports of ecstasy,' they were hardly the sounds a man would make whilst lying in bed alone."

"Which proves—"

"If it does not conclusively prove," she said, "that Judge Blackwell was not alone when Beauford went up to retrieve the coffee service, it proves it very little short of conclusively. Whether those were the sounds of a man being stabbed or the sounds he made as the result of . . . doing something else, they—"

"Beauford . . ." Sara interrupted. "How was those grunts spaced out?"

"What do you mean?"

"Well, did he go 'grunt-grunt-grunt' or 'grunt . . . grunt . . . grunt?"

Beauford nodded. "I understand," he said. "The grunts were kind of spaced out. Not right after another. A little time between them."

"How much time?" Pickering demanded.

"Well . . . How can I say? Like 'grunt!' Then maybe two or three seconds pass. Then 'grunt!' Two or three seconds."

"A person stabbing another to death would strike repeated blows, as fast as possible, would he not?" asked Mrs. Roosevelt.

"Let's play it out," Sara suggested. "Beauford, you lay down on the floor. I'll make like I'm stabbin' you."

Beauford Jones stared at Mrs. Roosevelt, then at Pickering, as if he hoped one of them would object to this. When neither did, he slipped off the settee and lay face down on the floor.

"Now . . ." said Sara. She raised her hand and brought it down on his back. "The knife sticks a little," she said. "I have to pull to get it out. But I do, and I stab again. Now again. Now again. How much time this takin'?"

"Not enough," said Beauford into the carpet. "That is too fast for what I heard."

Beauford got up and again took his place beside Sara on the settee.

"It could have been done slower," muttered Pickering thoughtfully.

"No!" cried Sara. "S'pose I stabbin' him. While he asleep. Or anyways, when he ain't lookin' for it. S'pose he asleep, or just not lookin' in my direction. That first stab don't kill him. Hardly nobody dies of being' stabbed once. Right? So he's just hurt, and I gotta do it to him ag'in, 'fore he rolls over and comes after me. Am I gonna wait two, three seconds? Not likely! No, sir! I hit him as quick as I can, one stab and then another. Fast as I can!"

Pickering nodded. "A valid point."

Mrs. Roosevelt ran her hand down her cheek. "Beauford," she said. "Are you . . . Are you absolutely certain the voice you heard was that of Judge Blackwell?"

Beauford Jones shook his head. "No. The sound came through the door. It was . . . what I called sharp grunts. Like 'Ughh! Ooh! Ughh!' You couldn't tell whose voice it was."

"You couldn't even tell, could you, Beauford," asked Mrs. Roosevelt, "whether the voice was a man's . . . *or a woman's?*"

Lawrence Pickering jerked erect. His mouth dropped open, and he extended a hand toward the First Lady. Their thoughts were the same, identical.

"Could . . . Could have been a woman's voice, come to think of it," said Beauford. "Yes. Could have been."

"A woman bein' *whipped!*" yelled Sara.

"Do not leap to that conclusion, young woman," said Pickering. "But it is my own thought, too—as a possibility. A possibility . . ."

"And, of course, my thought as well," said Mrs. Roosevelt.

"While I was still downstairs," said Sara, tossing her head back and forth, triumphant.

"You could still have come upstairs and killed him," said Pickering.

"You ain' *never* goin' let me off, are you? So handy, to have a colored gal to—"

"You will be freed of suspicion on the basis of the evidence," said Mrs. Roosevelt. "Just as you would have been convicted if the evidence was against you. As I told you, there will be no lynching in this case."

The First Lady stood. "Now," she said. "We thank you. And please do notice, Sara . . . you were released from jail even before this new evidence was brought to us."

In the First Lady's study a few minutes later, speaking quietly so as not to risk wakening the President, Mrs. Roosevelt and Lawrence Pickering discussed this new development.

"It could be a fabrication," said Pickering.

"Yes, but you don't think so, do you?"

"No, I think what you were thinking when you asked Beauford if it could have been a woman's voice. I think what Sara thought when she shouted that what he heard were the cries of a woman being whipped."

"Yes," said Mrs. Roosevelt. "I very much suspect that is what the young man heard."

"So—"

"It was almost certainly not Mrs. Tracy. Her alibi seems good. Obviously it was not Sara. I . . . I would suspect it was Barbara Higgins. She acknowledges that Judge Blackwell made her propositions, but she says she didn't accept his attentions. Of course, we don't know that the panties really were Mrs. Tracy's. We—"

"There was a woman with him half an hour or so before he died," said Pickering. "Either she killed him . . . or she let in the man who did."

Mrs. Roosevelt picked up from her desk the pad on

which she'd drawn her list of suspects. "I am not prepared to cross out Sara Carter entirely," she said. "So—"

Sara Carter
Professor Tracy
"Chickie" Pepino
A McKibben
Miss X
Man Working with Miss X

For a long moment, Mrs. Roosevelt stared at the sheet. "How dissatisfying," she said. "How very frustrating and dissatisfying."

VIII

ON SUNDAY MORNING, THE President slept late. He called for Missy and his breakfast at the same time, about nine, and Missy came down to join him. She sat on his bed, sharing eggs and ham and coffee and scanning the Sunday newspapers. In an hour or so he would call for his valet to help him dress, and he would go down to the Oval Office for half a day or so of work. Meanwhile he enjoyed his breakfast and Missy's company and the view from his bedroom window of a lovely spring morning and the view toward the Washington Monument and the Tidal Basin.

Mrs. Roosevelt rose early. Joined by her friend Elinor Morgenthau, she rode horseback for an hour in Rock Creek Park, after which they went to church. Her schedule for the day included luncheon with the Persian ambassador and his wife; after which she was to conduct a seminar for women interested in political campaigns.

Lawrence Pickering left his apartment at dawn and joined three friends for a drive to Annapolis, where they would board a boat for a day's fishing in Chesapeake Bay. Although he did not take exception to the First Lady's calls, he had decided that this day he would avoid them. Wearing a shabby old black suit that he had retired from workaday life, with a gray fedora that had accumulated stains since 1927 when he bought it, he carried his rod and his tackle box and happily climbed into his friend's Model-A Ford.

Detective Wilbur Rainey took Sunday off, too. In the afternoon, he would go see the Senators play. So he slept till almost ten and got up for a big breakfast with his wife and fourteen-year-old son. They would go with him to the ball park. He was glad the skies looked clear.

George McKibben didn't know if the skies were clear. Lying on the bunk in his cell in the District jail, he could not see outside and didn't care anyway. He was stiff and sore. He needed a drink. He was sullen, and he had begun to feel a little fear.

Sara Carter slept until noon. When she got up, she drank gin from her mother's kitchen cabinet before she ate anything. Mrs. Roosevelt had told her last night to come to work again on Monday. She looked at the neat maid's uniform hanging in her room, for a little while thought about giving up the White House job, then remembered she was proud of this job. She would go to work tomorrow, but she was glad she didn't have to go today.

Barbara Higgins lived in a residence hall for young women, funded by a charitable trust to afford young secretaries and clerks a clean and moral place to live. She had her own small room, but early each morning, including Sunday, the place filled with the laughter and bustle of a score of girls standing in line for the bathrooms and scurrying down to the buffet breakfast. Barbara did not readily fit in with the crowd and usually did not eat breakfast from the buffet. Nor did she today. She dressed and went out. She ate alone in a cafeteria on H Street, then walked down to the Mall, where she sat on a bench in the sunshine and read the morning paper.

In her mind she kept reviewing the things she had packed from Judge Blackwell's suite and office. She worried that she might have overlooked something that would suggest a solution to the mystery of his murder.

The Tracys, husband and wife, suffered headache and nausea, the result of too much drinking on Saturday night. The professor was not sympathetic about Blanche's discomfort and nudged her out of bed to make coffee and bring him aspirin. She did, but not until after she vomited in the bathroom.

Achille Pepino left his hotel early and went out for breakfast. It annoyed him a little to see people reading the newspapers at all the tables around him. He did not read English well enough to labor his way through a newspaper, and he wondered what the papers said about the death of the speakeasy bouncer last night. He wondered if there was any kind of a description of him in the papers. Well . . . No one stared at him. No one even seemed to notice him. So maybe it was all right.

It would be all right, if he could get his job done and get out of town. It wasn't so easy. Washington was a dumb town. It wasn't New York.

A casket was put on an eleven o'clock train for New York. A cousin had claimed the body of Judge Horace Blackwell. He couldn't pay for the casket or for the funeral and burial, but a group of lawyers and judges in New York had collected the necessary funds. No one accompanied the casket to the station. It sat alone in the baggage car. It would be taken from the train at Penn Station by the employees of a funeral home.

Mrs. Roosevelt's luncheon with the Persian ambassador, Mr. Zahedi, and his wife, was a memorable experience. The newly accredited ambassador spoke almost no English, and his wife spoke none at all. Even so, they were anxious to make a good impression, in a chatty, informal way; and their interpreter struggled to translate what was apparently slangy and idiomatic Persian into some form of English.

The Emperor of Persia was Padishah Reza Khan. The interpreter explained that Padishah was the official title, usually shortened in the west to just Shah.

"His people call him Shahinshah," said the interpreter. "That means 'King of Kings,' the possessor of the Peacock Throne."

Mrs. Roosevelt, who had been brought up to think of someone quite different as King of Kings, wondered if Reza Khan—a general who had seized power only eight years ago—had any idea how Westerners would react to any claim by a Persian monarch to call himself King of Kings.

The ambassador explained that his master—another term that struck Mrs. Roosevelt as inappropriate—was interested in modernizing his kingdom and instructed all his servants—meaning diplomats—to investigate Western ways and report on them.

"My master," the ambassador said through the interpreter, "has heard of an American athletic activity called football. He wonders if it is not good training for soldiers and has ordered me to learn as much as I can about it. Alas, I find no one is engaging in this activity."

"You must wait until the autumn," said Mrs. Roosevelt. "It is only played at that time of year."

"But how do the young men train during the balance of the year? Shooting? Riding?"

"No, they play other games. Baseball. Basketball . . . Tennis . . ."

"These are . . . contests? They *compete?*"

"Yes."

"We must learn about all of these contests," said the ambassador. "My master will want to know complete details of every one of them."

Mrs. Roosevelt smiled gently. "You may find baseball a bit difficult to understand," she said.

* * *

Two young women checked their bare backsides on Sunday afternoon. Well and good . . . Healing. Healed. But not invisible. In fact, in the case of one the thin white stripes might never disappear; but healed and barely visible.

That Sunday afternoon, Achille Pepino sat a long time in Lafayette Park, studying the façade of the White House with intense interest. After that he walked all the way around it twice. Too many gates. Too many ways in and out. A low fence that was no great barrier. He smiled. Sure. No great barrier.

The President, in midafternoon, spent most of an hour writing a letter to his mother. In no other documents from his hand did he ever adopt quite the same tone. He and she understood each other as no one else understood either of them. She was proud of him, of course, but she had also made a great sacrifice in giving her son to the nation.

Wouldn't it have been better for both of them, she obviously wondered, if he had come home after the horrible destruction of his health, to live in the family home, to enjoy life? Both of them could have enjoyed that.

But no— He knew she acknowledged it. It would have been comfortable and only comfortable. And she had reared him to be something better.

She had not been surprised, she was quoted as having said, that her son became President of the United States. Why not? Why shouldn't he be President? What was beyond his grasp?

He might have wanted to open a little distance between himself and her. But . . . how could he? How could a man distance himself from a mother so innocently devoted?

How, in cynical terms, could he distance himself from a mother who still paid him an allowance, like a child? During the bad years, Sara Roosevelt had paid him money she could not readily afford. The nation's press was accustomed to thinking of Franklin D. Roosevelt as the son of wealth and position. When his wife dropped the remark that the White House kitchen was not well equipped, a newspaper editorialized that "The Roosevelt, after all, could re-equip the White House kitchen from pocket change." Which was not true. They could not.

The Roosevelts of Hyde Park—contrasted to the Roosevelt of Oyster Bay—were prosperous, not rich. The President's father, James, had left a handsome estate, one sufficient to allow his young widow to live comfortably and to support their son in comfortable circumstances; but he had not left them wealthy. Over the years Sara had spent the income of the estate each year, plus a little of the capital, as was necessary, so that each year the capital was a little diminished.

At her urging, Franklin had devoted himself to public service—as befitted a Roosevelt and a Delano. He had been a state legislator, Assistant Secretary of the Navy, candidate for Vice President of the United States . . . And then . . . And then the crushing attack of polio had left him unable to earn a living.

Not entirely. He had practiced law, as his health would allow. And then . . . Then the Democrats had prevailed on him to become a candidate for Governor of New York. He had lost, then won. And now, he was President of the United States!

And his salary did not meet the expenses. President Hoover could have lived on the salary—and didn't have to, because he had earned a fortune during his business years. President Roosevelt could not live on it, either—but had not earned his own fortune and so supplemented the salary with money from his father's estate, generously paid over each year by his mother, as the estate dwindled.

Franklin Roosevelt did not write affectionate letters to his mother because she sent him checks. He would have written them, with complete sincerity, in any case.

"Dearest Mama—"

In the evening Mrs. Roosevelt took a light dinner early and alone; and, after going in to chat a few minutes with the President, who was listening to symphonic music on his radio and working on his stamp collection, she retired to her bedroom, bathed, and sat up in bed to read something light and relaxing.

The President was not lonely. He enjoyed his hours alone. He enjoyed working with his stamp collection. It was always touching to see how a man who had once found so much pleasure in good health and constant energetic hubbub now took his pleasure sitting in bed, examining his stamps. Besides, there was a another reason he would not suffer loneliness. Missy was upstairs, in her third-floor suite. If the President felt the need of company, he would call her. She would come down. At any hour.

Barbara Higgins glanced at her loudly ticking alarm clock. Almost midnight. She sat propped up in bed, propped up by pillows, nude. She had been reading a book that was so funny she had stayed with it long after she had meant to switch off her light and go to sleep.

James Thurber, *My Life and Hard Times*. She had sat there shaking with laughter, tears fogging her vision, as she read the story called "The Night the Bed Fell."

Well . . . She had to be at the White House by eight in the morning, to report to Mrs. Roosevelt for whatever assignment the First Lady might have for her.

Barbara wound the alarm clock and set it for 6:45. As she put it aside on her night table, her eye stopped on the watch fob.

The watch fob . . . She had taken it from Judge Blackwell's things, as she was packing them. She had not taken the watch or the chain. But on impulse she had pried open the link that suspended the watch from the chain and dropped it in her purse.

Which made her a thief.

But no one would notice.

The fob was probably valuable. It was gleaming solid gold, and heavy, in the form of a Maltese cross. It was not the emblem of any fraternity or club, so far as she knew. It was engraved on the front with a pattern, not with any lettering. But on the back it was engraved—

J.J.W.

That puzzled Barbara. Why J.J.W.? Who was J.J.W.? Why were those initials there? *Why?*

George McKibben woke in a cell that stank of cigarette smoke and stale urine, feeling dirty and unshaven, the way a man always felt when he was behind bars—felt that way because he was.

They didn't take long to do their Monday-morning thing. He'd expected something like the paper the screw handed to him just after he'd shoved down the garbage they called breakfast. It was— Sure, the notice that he was charged with criminal possession of alcoholic beverages, in violation of this law and the that law, et cetera, et cetera. So they could hold him. A little possession charge, but they'd get his bail set high enough to keep him here.

Okay. Bastards! They couldn't make a case that he'd killed Judge Horace Blackwell. They knew that, and they knew he knew it. So they'd sweat him.

So let 'em. He knew something they wanted to know, but he'd never tell them. Not in a thousand years. Not in ten thousand years. Hell with 'em.

* * *

Lawrence Pickering was efficient. By 10:00 A.M. he had the order required to open Judge Blackwell's safe-deposit box at First Fidelity Bank. The matter was relatively simple. All he had to do was open the box in the presence of an officer of the bank, who would make an inventory of its contents. Once the inventory was made, he could, as an agent of the Secret Service, take anything from the box—provided only that he give a receipt for what he took.

Mrs. Roosevelt agreed that she could not accompany him. Her presence at the opening of the box would have to be made a matter of record, which might later have to be explained. Instead, Pickering asked Wilbur Rainey to go. It was well, he thought, to have another witness.

The bank was cavernous. The great banking room was three stories high. The floors, parts of the walls, and even the tables where people wrote deposit and withdrawal slips had tops of thick white marble. Voices echoed off the hard surfaces. As Pickering and Rainey walked toward the rear of the room, Pickering could distinguish the echoes of their footsteps.

The banker who met them was dressed in morning clothes: cutaway coat, striped trousers, waistcoat. He glanced at their identification but was obviously far more interested to see that they had the key.

He led them into the vault, past the immense and immensely heavy, thick, round, stainless steel door. Inside, the vault was lined with hundreds of small flat doors, each with two keyholes. Pickering offered the judge's key, and the banker pushed it into a keyhole and turned it. Then he took another key from the small leather folder he was carrying and used it to work the second lock.

The banker pulled out the box and carried it to a table. There the three men sat down.

Pickering opened the box and looked in. "Not much here," he said. "Letters. Pictures."

The letters were obviously personal, handwritten notes on blue and pink notepaper. The pictures were snapshots of young women: some of them faded, some cracked.

"Evidence," said Rainey.

"Letters and photos," said the banker. "We shall inventory them as 'documents and photographs. No value, except as they may constitute evidence.' Correct?"

"No value except as evidence," Pickering agreed. "No stocks, no bonds, no insurance policies, no money. Just letters and snapshots."

The banker signed the inventory form, which he then handed to Pickering and Rainey for their signatures.

"Will you be taking these letters and photos with you?"

"Yes, we will," said Pickering, "but I'd like to read the letters here first."

The banker wrote, "Documents—personal letters, also photos," on the receipt form. Pickering signed it.

"I shall, then, leave you for the time being," said the banker.

"Uh . . . One more thing," said Rainey. "Judge Blackwell's account balances. The order included—"

"Yes, of course," said the banker. He withdrew a slip of paper from his pocket. "Judge Horace Blackwell had just one account with us: a checking account. His balance is $1,876.54."

"A lot of money for a government employee to have in a checking account," said Rainey.

"I couldn't comment on that," said the banker. "So, if that will be all—"

"That will be all," said Rainey.

Pickering scanned a letter he chose at random: the one that happened to be on the top of the stack. "Sickening . . ." he muttered after he had read for a moment.

My darling— To be your love slave is the most wonderful thing that has ever happened to me in my

life! To lie in *your* chains, to feel *your* strong hands
doing with me whatever you will, is a fulfillment I
could never have believed possible!

The letter, which was signed "Becky," continued in the
same vein for two pages, becoming more and more explicit
in describing Becky's relationship with Judge Horace Blackwell and just how she felt about it. The envelope was postmarked New York, May 21, 1929.

Except for one of the snapshots, which was autographed
"Junie," the two men could not match the photographs and the
letters.

"This one's juicy," said Rainey, frowning over a note written in blue ink on paper printed with violets.

I thought I knew all there is to know about
doing it. But, Daddy, you taught this little girl some
tricks I never heard of, never dreamed of! Where'd
you learn, Honey?

Then she, too, became more explicit. She was Junie: a
bleached-out shopworn young woman with a faint resemblance to Jean Harlow. Her letter was postmarked New York
City, August 11, 1928.

"The judge's trophy case," said Rainey.

"Imagine this," said Pickering. "He has carried these letters with him from New York to Washington. And keeps them
in a safety deposit box!"

"Figure that," said Rainey. "Look at this one."

Dearest Darling. He knows. Thank God he doesn't
know who, doesn't dream who, or God knows what
he'd do. I don't think anything is beyond what he
might do. And he's solving the problem his way.
He's going to get me pregnant. With that, he says, I

won't be so attractive to another man. Anyway, he
says he knows me well enough to know I won't
have any more adventures once I have a child. He's
right about that, of course. So— Well, you can imagine how it goes. Every night. I think I am pregnant.
If I'm not yet, I soon will be. So I'm afraid it's goodbye between you and me, Dearest Darling. I will
never forget. Don't you, either.

Signed "Marjorie" and postmarked Greenwich, Connecticut, January 4, 1933.

"Just before he left New York for Washington," said Pickering. "It is difficult, is it not, Rainey, to attach too much regret to the fact the man is dead?"

Detective Sergeant Wilbur Rainey shrugged. "My business is investigating homicides," he said. "If I didn't work just
as hard on the murders of rink-stinks as I do on the murders
of solid citizens, I'd have an easier time of it and leave half the
cases unsolved. You can't think about it, friend. Truth is, the
solid-citizen types usually don't get murdered. Oh, they do
sometimes, sure. But you look at the statistics, if there are any,
and you'll see what I mean. A lot of cases, it's a tossup between
who gets killed and who does the killing. Especially in the
mysterious cases. When you can run right out and arrest your
killer right off, usually that's a solid-citizen murder. The cases
that are hard are where half a dozen guys had good enough
motive to kill. Then you've got to sort 'em out."

Pickering scanned another letter and put it aside. Then—
"Oho!" He read quickly. "Well . . . For what it's worth."

I am reluctant, as you can imagine, to set my
feelings down in writing. I do it because you have
so urgently pleaded. It is difficult for the further
reason that I am totally confused, the most confused I have ever been in my life.

In one sense, Horace, you are a monster and knowing you has been the most grievous misfortune of my life. In another sense, I must confess my life could hardly be called complete without what I have been for you.

How I have been for you. That's how I say it, because I understand you have made me something that suits you and have done nothing to yourself to make you more acceptable to me. This relationship has been one-sided.

I have learned from it. From you. I am grateful for that. My life is more colored, more varied, for this tragic experience. I have learned that what I have—a life defined in tones of gray, as you put it—is far more to be cherished than the garish life you offer a woman.

Oh, I'm *glad* to have known you, Horace. Certainly I will never forget those half-dozen nights. Indeed, as you know, I may be compelled to remember them, vividly and regretfully, for the rest of my life, since obviously our secret has seen the light of day.

So, it's over, you superb and superbly flawed man. Thank you, and goodbye.

This letter was not signed. It was postmarked Washington, May 12, 1933—three days before the death of Judge Blackwell.

"There is no doubt about who wrote that, I suppose," said Pickering.

Rainey flipped through the snapshots. "None of these are her, right?"

Pickering shook his head.

"The handwriting will prove who wrote it. Plus maybe fingerprints."

"No doubt," said Pickering. "They will prove the letter was written by Blanche Tracy."

Rainey shook his head as he read the letter. "The judge was a real rink-stink," he said.

"In my very limited experience, gained mostly by reading mystery novels," said Mrs. Roosevelt, "it is often useful to— Tell me, Mr. Pickering, have you ever read *The Big Bow Mystery* by Israel Zangwill? A marvelous writer. His story is a puzzle that— Well . . . I was about to say that it is useful from time to time to summarize what one knows."

"How would you summarize, my dear lady?" asked Pickering.

"Well . . . Sergeant Rainey, you are an experienced homicide investigator. Will you follow this and point out any errors?"

Rainey nodded.

"Let's begin with pinpointing the time of the judge's death. The autopsy report, which is the least specific of our possible sources of information, fixes the time of death as between midnight and 1:00 A.M. Officer Runkle saw the body at approximately 1:15. Beauford Jones heard sounds from the judge's room no later than 12:30. Those grunts, as Beauford Jones described them, may possibly have been sounds the judge made as the knife struck him. But—"

"But unlikely," said Pickering.

"Well, you have another idea as to what Beauford heard," said Mrs. Roosevelt with a measured smile. "And Sara Carter offered still another idea, you remember."

"That he heard a woman being whipped," said Pickering.

"In either event, the judge was still alive when Beauford Jones heard those sounds—no later than 12:30."

"Or possibly heard him being murdered," said Rainey.

"I don't think so," said Mrs. Roosevelt. "I've performed my little whiskey test time and again. Tipping back and draining a glass of whiskey, a man leaves a tiny quantity in the glass: what clung to the surface of the glass and ran back down to the bottom. That tiny quantity of whiskey will evaporate in half an hour to forty minutes, leaving the glass dry. The glass I saw in Judge Blackwell's room at 1:20 or a few minutes after was still wet, and the liquid was clear. And from that I conclude the judge had drunk from that glass no later than, say, 12:45."

"You're overlooking a possibility," said Rainey. "Maybe the last drink from that glass was taken by the murderer."

"You assume, then, that the murderer remained in the suite for some little time after killing Judge Blackwell?"

"For some little time, yes," said Pickering. "Long enough to have wiped the fingerprints off that glass and off the bottle. Long enough to have opened the locked suitcase that contained the handcuffs and whip and wiped the fingerprints off the handcuffs."

"Yeah, and whoever wiped the prints off those cuffs had the key to that suitcase," said Rainey. "We had to cut the suitcase open."

"A cold-blooded killer," said Pickering. "While the judge's bloody body lay there on the bed, the murderer went about the suite, unlocking and opening a suitcase, wiping fingerprints from two pairs of handcuffs, then wiping fingerprints from a glass and bottle. It must have taken a few minutes."

Tommy Thompson slipped in to tell Mrs. Roosevelt there was an urgent telephone call for Detective Rainey. She asked him if he wanted to take the call there, in her office. He did, and for a minute or so he listened to something, apparently from headquarters. Then he put down the phone and returned to his seat.

"Another interesting point," said Mrs. Roosevelt, who had used the interruption to reflect on their chain of logic. "Why would anyone want to wipe the fingerprints off handcuffs? I can think of only one reason: that the wiped-off fingerprints were those of the murderer. In other words, Judge Blackwell was murdered by one of the young women he abused."

"I can think of a small variation on that," said Pickering. "If the murderer was someone hired by Professor Tracy, a part of his job would have been to wipe Mrs. Tracy's fingerprints off the handcuffs—which she could have touched only if she were one of the judge's lovers and had worn them."

"That doesn't square with the judge having sex with whoever was in his room before 12:30. Or whipping her. A professional hit man—"

"Is it possible," asked Mrs. Roosevelt, "that there were *two* murderers?"

"Fanciful, I'm afraid," said Pickering.

"Maybe," said Rainey. "But think of this— We've got George McKibben in jail. He's what my call was about. I'll tell you about it in a minute. He's got no explanation about why he's in Washington. He's got a criminal record for using a knife. He's the son of a man who died because Judge Blackwell prosecuted him. All George doesn't have is experience in moving around the White House at night. But any one of the judge's lovers—the ones he's had since he's been in Washington, that is—probably knows how to get to his room and get out of the White House after it's officially closed."

"The woman is with the judge," speculated the First Lady. "She encourages him to drink, to become intoxicated. He drifts off to sleep, and she admits the man—maybe this George McKibben—to the suite. He stabs—"

"I still say it's fanciful," murmured Pickering, though obviously he was thinking about it.

"Yes," Mrs. Roosevelt admitted. "Even so, maybe this man George McKibben is the key. You say you've just received new information about him?"

"Right," said Rainey. "I put it pretty tough to the manager of the Buchanan Hotel that he was to call if he got any kind of new dope on McKibben. Well, he called. He says a woman called and asked to talk to George McKibben. He says she got upset when he told her McKibben wasn't there anymore."

"Did he tell her the man had been arrested?" asked Mrs. Roosevelt.

"Yeah. Which wasn't too smart. That's what got her upset."

"I suppose you have interrogated McKibben," said Mrs. Roosevelt. "Rigorously, in fact."

Rainey smiled. "As rigorously as the law allows," he said. "And he's defiant. He's a tough boy, McKibben. I know how to get answers out of him, but I don't think you want me to."

"Oh, no," she said. "Only as the law allows."

Rainey laughed. "Okay," he said. "Only as the law allows."

Pickering pursed his lips and raised his chin.

Mrs. Roosevelt smiled. "As the law, *strictly interpreted*, allows," she said. "And . . . Well, I am afraid we have been overlooking a piece of evidence."

"And what is that?" asked Pickering.

"Those . . . those *hairs* that were found on the judge's body. Uh . . . pubic hairs. They were, you recall, in an envelope marked 'B.' I never looked at them. Did either of you?"

"I did," said Rainey. "Half a dozen hairs. You could maybe try to match them with those from a suspect, if you had a suspect. But—"

"I have that envelope," said Pickering, opening his briefcase. He took out the envelope and handed it to Mrs. Roosevelt. "I, uh, glanced inside it once."

Mrs. Roosevelt opened the envelope, gingerly, and stared at the few short, coarse hairs lying inside. She looked up and shook her head, frowning. "Gentlemen . . ." she said quietly. "Really!"

Rainey shrugged. "Something wrong?" he asked.

She handed the envelope to Pickering. "These . . . *blond*

hairs," she said crisply, "did not come from the body of Sara Carter."

Pickering peered into the envelope. "My God!" he mumbled.

"I am scratching her name off the list of suspects," said Mrs. Roosevelt firmly.

"Yes," said Pickering.

Rainey grinned. "Okay," he said. "But don't strike off Professor Tracy. These hairs could have come from his wife."

"I believe it is possible, is it not, Sergeant Rainey, for a scientific analysis to be made of human hair. Is a person's hair not distinctive, so that a match can be made between hair found as evidence and a sample taken from a suspect?"

"Right," said Rainey. "You can match it. But you've first gotta have a suspect. Which we don't have. Obviously we can't go around pulling young women's pubic hair, looking for a match. First we've gotta have a suspect."

IX

MRS. ROOSEVELT'S MONDAY LUNCHEON appointment was with representatives of the Advertising Council. They came in: a jolly, mostly youthful group, little interested in a White House lunch, much more interested in showing the First Lady some samples of their work, samples of what they called advertising campaigns that they said would be recognized everywhere in the nation in the next few months.

They showed her magazine pages, some of which would be printed in color. One full-page ad, in color, would advertise Prince Albert Tobacco: loose tobacco meant to be rolled into cigarettes. The slogan was "Finest 'makin's' ever!" Another magazine ad was for Camel Cigarettes and featured a woman smoking and proclaiming "Camels set you right!" Still another, to be run in black and white, showed a man pouring boiling water from a tea kettle—onto the shiny surface of a dining table, as his wife and child watched in shock. If the varnish used on that table had been Valspar, the ad promised, it would not be scarred by the boiling water.

As the First Lady well knew, one of the most-used forms of advertising was signs on barns and other roadside buildings. The makers of Mail Pouch chewing tobacco would actually paint one or two sides of a farmer's barn—if the farmer did not mind its being painted with a huge black-white-yellow-blue ad: MAIL POUCH TOBACCO. TREAT YOURSELF TO THE BEST. It was very practical. The farmer got part of his barn painted, and Mail Pouch got its sign prominently displayed.

More modestly, farmers allowed advertisers to glue posters to barns and other buildings. The heavy posters covered the cracks and kept out the wind, sometimes for a whole season or two—by which time the advertiser would be back with a fresh poster. Mrs. Roosevelt's visitors had brought samples of posters. They said tens of thousands of these would be printed and would be seen by every motorist on every highway. The motorists would read:

—666. COLDS, FEVER

—PAZO FOR PILES

—GROVE'S TESTED CHILL TONIC. MALARIAL FEVER
  CHILLS COLDS

—GROVE'S BROMO QUININE. STOPS COLDS

—RED DOT. THE REGULAR 5¢ CIGAR

Some of these posters, Mrs. Roosevelt understood, would be pasted on shacks where people lived, the more layers the better, to keep out the cold.

When Rainey pulled his car up before the Buchanan, he was surprised to see a marked District cruiser—one of the new ones, a '33 Ford V-8 coupe with a shiny, nickel-plated siren and warning light mounted on top—pulled to the curb. He went in.

"Ho, Sarge."

"Ho, Wendelken. What's up?"

"Assault. Somebody roughed up the manager. Don't know why yet."

"You mean Morrow? He hurt bad?"

"He'll live. Got a busted nose. Newton's in the office with him."

Rainey went back. Sure enough, Allan Morrow sat slumped weakly in a chair, still covering his face with a bloody handkerchief. Newton was scribbling something in a notebook.

"Rainey," the manager muttered. "You're damned fast. How'd you know so quick?"

"I didn't," said Rainey. "I came here to talk to you about something else."

"This is something else," said Morrow. "It's got to do with the same damned thing. McKibben. I wish to God I'd never seen McKibben."

"So, what's getting your nose busted got to do with McKibben?"

"The guy that busted my nose came in here looking for McKibben. When I told him McKibben wasn't here anymore and I didn't know where, her grabbed me by the coat and slammed his fist in my nose."

Rainey turned to the uniformed cop. "Newton," he said. "This has got to do with murder. Get on your radio, call for my team of guys, and tell 'em to bust ass over here."

The surprised policeman hurried out, and Rainey sat down facing Morrow.

"You need a doctor?" he asked.

"Damn right . . ."

"Newton! Tell 'em to bring along a first-aid kit."

"First-aid kit . . . Thanks," Morrow sneered through his handkerchief.

Rainey turned around, toward a young man who was apparently a hotel clerk, in rolled-up sleeves and loose collar. "Get a bucket of ice in here, fella," he said curtly. "And a couple of towels. Toot sweet."

Morrow was a pale, bald, overweight man whose only

distinctive feature was penetrating little brown eyes that peered out at the world like the eyes of a small, wary animal. His suit and shirt were splattered with blood.

"So who hit ya, Morrow?" asked Rainey.

"Wish I knew. Well . . . I *guess* I wish I knew. If I knew— If I told you, I'd want to think you'd lock the guy up till he's too old to hurt anybody. 'Cause this guy, Rainey . . . this guy is *deadly!* I don't ever want to see him again."

"From the beginning," said Rainey.

"Okay. I'm behind the desk. Morning. Late morning. When guests check out, and I present their bills and collect. I have to pass on all checks, and most of them want to pay with checks. So, okay . . . I'm working the desk, and this guy comes in. Little guy. Dressed natty. You know? A little . . . what you might call *over*styled, huh? Anyway, he's a little guy. Dark complexion. Black hair. Kind of a sharp nose. Hey! The guy's *Italian.* Y' know?"

"Okay."

Morrow grunted through the handkerchief that was now soaked. Rainey looked around for the flunky, who hadn't returned. He took his own handkerchief from his pocket and offered it to Morrow. Morrow took it and pressed it to his face, dropping the first handkerchief on the floor.

Morrow grunted again. "This *hurts*, y' know."

Rainey walked out to the desk and shouted across the lobby. "Somebody get that dummy back here with the ice! Tell him if I have to come after him, we'll need *two* buckets!"

Morrow looked up at him and managed a wry smile as Rainey sat down again. "You can get away with it," he said.

Rainey nodded. "Okay, so this guy came in. So what happens?"

"Didn't speak English," said Morrow. "Well . . . A little, but mostly not. He wanted to see McKibben. I wasn't about to tell him McKibben was in jail, unless he asked, like that girl did. He said something about how he had 'information'— That was his favorite word: 'information,' *an-for-mah-chone*, the way he said it. He had 'information' that McKibben was staying here. I said he had been but wasn't anymore."

" 'Kay. So what next?"

"He didn't like that answer. Where had McKibben gone? I had to work on this one, try to figure out what the hell he was asking—but I got it that he wanted a forwarding address. Obviously, I didn't have one. So I told him—no forwarding address. Just left. Didn't say where he was going. And . . . hey . . . I could see I was irritating the hell out of the guy."

"You got a gun under the desk," said Rainey.

"Okay. A sawed-off shotgun. You wanta arrest me for that? You run a joint like this, you wish you had a machine gun. Maybe a hand grenade or two."

"Never mind. I'm looking for a murderer, not gun violators," said Rainey.

"Reach for a gun? It was like facing the goddamn lightning. I mean, hell, I hadn't said anything worse. Just gave him the bad news that I didn't know where McKibben was. Hey, Rainey . . . I think he *knew* . . ."

"So? He swung on you—"

"And how! Looka this!" Morrow pulled away his handkerchief and exposed a bloody nose that had been for sure flattened by a hard punch.

"Your guy—"

Rainey meant that if the hotel flunky did not appear immediately with the ice— But the young man ran, literally ran, in, carrying a bucket of ice and a wad of towels.

"Don't touch any goddamn thing around the desk," Rainey said to him. "It may be our tough Italian friend touched something. And if the members of the D.C. police have not pawed all over, we might—just might—have fingerprints that will identify the murderous little bastard."

"Be sure you send armed men to get him, when you know who he is," said Morrow as he made a wad of towel and ice and pressed it to his face. "Heavily armed."

"Feel like looking at some photos?" Rainey asked. "Of good-lookin' girls?"

Morrow shrugged. "Why not? What great thing am I doin' here?"

Rainey took an envelope from his pocket and offered Morrow, one by one, the photographs from Judge Blackwell's safe-deposit box: the judge's collection of young women. "Handle 'em all you want," he said. "We've got the prints off 'em."

Morrow looked at each photograph. He kept shaking his head. "I never saw one of these girls," he said. "An' if one of 'em had come in here last week to see McKibben, I'd remember."

"What about the broad who called to ask for him?"

"Telephone voice," said Morrow. "I heard it again, I'd recognize it, probably."

"So all I gotta do is find her and have her call you again."

"You want me to identify her, you do."

"Fingerprints," said Lawrence Pickering to Mrs. Roosevelt. "Those taken from the shotglass Sergeant Rainey so conveniently appropriated from Mrs. Tracy—that is to say, Mrs. Tracy's fingerprints—match one of the unidentified sets found in Judge Blackwell's room. They match the prints found on the windowsill and window glass. Also, they match the fingerprints found on the unsigned letter we suspected Mrs. Tracy wrote."

"I am not certain it does us any good to know all this," said Mrs. Roosevelt. "Mrs. Tracy has already acknowledged she had an affair with Judge Blackwell. In any event, she and Professor Tracy seem able to prove beyond question where they were when Judge Blackwell was murdered—visiting their friends the Nelsons, miles from the White House."

"We have so far accepted that story," said Pickering. "I

am beginning to wonder if it would not be a good idea if I were to visit the Nelsons and make sure."

"I had hoped that could be avoided, Mr. Pickering."

"Well, so had I. But we are making very little progress toward identifying the murderer of Judge Blackwell, and I think we are obliged to check out every thread of the fabric."

"I can't argue," said Mrs. Roosevelt. "But be most discreet, please."

"Mrs. Roosevelt," said Barbara Higgins. "I am sorry to impose myself into your busy schedule, but I really have no work to do, and I feel strange just sitting around. I . . . I really think I should be assigned to another job or I should go back to New York."

"Oh, dear," said Mrs. Roosevelt. "I know how distressing it is to be idle. Tell me, what is your preference for the future? I mean, what do you think you want to do after the investigation into the death of Judge Blackwell is complete? Will you really want to return to New York? Or would you like to stay in Washington? I can readily find you an assignment here in Washington."

"I came to Washington only because I worked for Judge Blackwell," said Barbara. "I really have no friends in Washington."

"Thousands of girls work for the government and make friends here," said the First Lady. "You have been here only— What? Three months?"

Barbara nodded.

"It is less than a week since the judge died," said Mrs. Roosevelt. "I really would be grateful if you would stay on a little longer. You may have something to contribute to the investigation. You've finished packing his papers and personal things, I gather. And I suppose you found nothing significant."

Barbara shook her head. "No, not really. Beyond the fact

that Judge Blackwell was something of a satyr, with a taste for sadism, he was a rather ordinary man. A brilliant man, but otherwise rather ordinary. I knew him well enough to see that."

"In New York, where did he live?"

"He had an apartment in Greenwich Village."

"Did he live alone?"

Barbara smiled. "He had many friends," she said.

"And some enemies, apparently," said Mrs. Roosevelt. "What more, if anything, can you tell me about this man Chickie Pepino?"

"The judge was afraid of him," said Barbara.

"He may well be in Washington," said Mrs. Roosevelt. "There is new evidence that suggests he is."

"What!"

The young woman was staggered. Mrs. Roosevelt studied her flushed face for a moment, trying to read from it more than it conveyed.

"What . . . ? What makes you think so?" Barbara asked, her voice strained.

"A man who rather closely matches his police description has been seen in Washington," said the First Lady. "He broke the nose of a hotel clerk. The District police are getting pictures of him from the New York police, so we may soon know if it is in fact this Pepino."

"Why? What hotel?"

"The Buchanan Hotel. He came in asking for a guest, and when the clerk told him that guest was gone, no forwarding address, the small Italian-looking man attacked him."

"Pepino . . ." said Barbara. "Did he think Judge Blackwell lived in that hotel?"

"No. He was looking for someone else."

"Anyone whose name I might know?"

Mrs. Roosevelt shrugged. "A name we've mentioned before. A Mr. George McKibben."

"McKibben . . . ? The brother of the man who was killed at Sing Sing?"

"His son," said Mrs. Roosevelt. "He's being held in the District Jail."

"Oh? What kind of trouble is he in?"

"He's being held on charges involving illegal possession of liquor. But he's a suspect—a rather unlikely suspect, I should say—in the murder of Judge Blackwell."

"Pepino . . ." Barbara muttered. "McKibben. I hope the case can be proved against one of them. Both of them wanted the judge dead."

"A hard case," said Mrs. Roosevelt. "One of them had to get inside the White House at midnight. I am told it is easy enough if you know how. But how did one of them learn how?"

"Frank, I told you. Frank, I goddamn told you."

The President shook his martinis and returned Al Smith only a skeptical glance.

The "Happy Warrior," 1928's Democratic candidate for President—Franklin D. Roosevelt had given the nominating speech—had immensely degenerated in five years. He still smoked big cigars, and he still talked like the Lower East Side character he was—still called radio "raddio" ("Friends of the raddio audience")—but he was a grotesque caricature of the man he had once been. Bitterness had destroyed him. Now he sold his name to the highest bidder. As the New York *Times* had put it, he had traded the brown derby for the silk hat. He wore more expensive suits than he had ever worn before—today a double-breasted beige linen, with a pink-striped silk shirt, and he looked like the keeper of an uptown speakeasy.

With Al Smith there, the President had invited only Missy to join them. She sat close to the President, as if he might need a defense against this bitter old man, and held a whiskey in her hand, waiting while the President ritually shook his mar-

tinis. Smith, too, had a whiskey and drank without waiting for
the President to finish mixing his own drink.

"Somebody was gonna wipe out that son of a bitch
sooner or later," said Smith.

"Al—"

"Sooner or later," said Smith with more emphasis. "He
wanted to be the next Mayor of New York. Listen, there was
no limit to that guy. You ever heard the story about Jimmy
Walker's watch fob?"

"Watch fob . . ." said the President.

"Yeah. Jimmy Walker wore an antique gold watch fob. I
don't know where he got it. I don't think it was a family heir-
loom. Anyway, he and Dave McKibben were a pair of drinkers
and jokers. Besides which, Dave McKibben had a mean streak
in him. One night they were clowning around, and Dave
grabbed for Jimmy's watch chain and snatched it off, tearing
his vest. Jimmy didn't think it was too funny, and he said
something tough and lunged at Dave to grab his watch and
chain back. That made Dave mad. He was a big guy, and he
shoved Jimmy back and said he'd be damned if any two-bit
politician would lay a hand on him; and he jerked the fob off
the chain and said he'd keep that, as a souvenir. And Jimmy
never did get it back. Dave McKibben wore it and flaunted it
at him all the time."

"Which has got what to do with Horace Blackwell?"
asked the President.

"Plenty," said Al Smith. "Blackwell knew all about it.
And when they checked Dave McKibben in at Sing Sing, the
guards took his watch and chain, and the fob, and put them
in the property room, where cons' personal stuff is kept
while they're there. Somehow District Attorney Blackwell
got into that stuff and claimed the fob. It wasn't McKibben's,
he said, so he'd take it. And he did. And since then he's worn
it, showing it off to Jimmy Walker and daring him to try to
get it back, the same way Dave McKibben did. Oh, he was a

fine fellow, Judge Horace Blackwell. A real fine fellow."

"Well, he won't be Mayor of New York," said Missy. "Who will be, Mr. Smith?"

Al Smith grinned. "John P. O'Brien," he said. "The Democrat."

"I'm not so sure," said the President.

"Anybody but that goddamned sawed-off wop, La-Guardia," muttered Al Smith. "Any . . . body."

"Are you suggesting," asked the President, "that someone had political motive to murder Judge Blackwell?"

"Lots of people had lots of motive," said Al Smith. "Do you think he went after businessmen because he wanted to make business honest in New York? C'mon, Frank! He was making a reputation. You fell for it and made him a judge. Then he came down here and added to his reputation by working for you as a braintruster. But he'd have been back in New York in time to make a big campaign for the primary in September and—"

"Which party?" the President asked.

"Some kind of reform thing he was going to put together. Anything to make a bigger man of himself. I tell ya. He may have had it in mind to run for governor later on. Even for President, maybe. As a Communist, like as not."

The President smiled at Missy. "Okay," he said. "Who killed him, Al?"

Smith tossed back his whiskey and handed his glass to Missy to refill. He shook his head. "The people I associate with," he said, "aren't sorry the s.o.b. is dead, but people like that don't kill people. He made bitter enemies of a lot of eminent men: wealthy and respectable. And . . . he made enemies of some tough guys, too."

"Two names, Al," said the President. "George McKibben and Achille Pepino."

Smith's head jerked back. "McKibben . . . and Chickie Pepino! I wouldn't want one of those guys after *me!*"

"Pepino works for the Cassell gang, right?"

Al Smith nodded. "And for anybody else who pays him enough."

"McKibben?"

"McKibben would put a knife between anybody's ribs, for the right money. But he had a special reason to want Judge Blackwell dead."

"His father."

"You said it."

"Okay, Al. One more question. Where's the daughter? Angela McKibben."

Al Smith shrugged. "Disappeared."

"Nobody disappears," said the President. "If she's alive—"

"If she's alive, she lives in Boise, Idaho, married to an electrician."

"Did you ever see her, Al? Do you remember the girl?"

"You bet," said Al Smith. "A blonde. Luscious. The kind of girl you don't soon forget."

"I suppose there were newspaper pictures of her," said Missy.

"Sure. You bet. You want some? I'll have some sent down. Soon as I get home."

"Cooperate, Bruno. Cooperate. Or I'll shut you down."

Rainey had come to the speakeasy where the bouncer had been shot Saturday night. He'd read the description of the gunman.

"Hey, why me, Rainey? There's plenty of speaks in Washington. What you got against me?"

"You got violence here," said Rainey. He took a sip of the whiskey the bartender had poured. "And you sell bad whiskey. But the violence . . . Can't stand for that."

"My bouncer gets killed, and you call it violence?"

"Well, I'd call a murder violence. You had a murder on the premises."

"Ahh. So what cooperation is it you want?"

"I want to know who shot the bouncer," said Rainey.

"I don't know. I've told three other detectives I never saw the guy before. He was never in here before."

"Then how'd he *get* in here? You don't let just anybody through the door."

The bartender sighed loudly. "We been through this," he said. "But okay. Cooperation. He came to the door. My guy at the door—Harry—checked him out. Harry says the guy mentioned some name, but he says he don't remember who. So Harry let the guy in. You wanna know the truth? The guy slipped Harry a fin. Harry knocks down on me that way. I'm not s'posed to know it. Harry says he never saw the guy before. *I* never saw the guy before."

"Describe him."

"Cooperation. I've described the guy a hundred times. So, okay— He's a little guy, a sawed-off runt, with kind of a dark complexion. Dressed sharp. I mean *too* sharp. Y' know what I mean? And he didn't speak English."

"What did he speak?"

The bartender shrugged. "At first he didn't speak nothin'. Just pointed. So I poured him a whiskey. He took a sip, and then he started to raise hell. Wasn't what he wanted, I guess. What was he speakin'? I guess it was Italian. I couldn't understand him. I told him to pay up. He wouldn't. So I called out my muscle guy."

"Sam."

"Right, Sam. Sam grabbed him to give him a little shake, and the guy swung on him. Popped Sam alongside the mouth, with a fist. And that's when Sam gave him the bum's rush. Out in the alley. And the next thing I know, I hear two shots. Bang, bang. Y' know, real quick."

"Would you know the guy if you saw him again?"

"Yeah. Right off. But God forbid I ever see the guy again."

Rainey glanced around the speakeasy. There were few customers in the place in late afternoon, and it looked sad and dingy. A sorrowful cigarette girl sat at the bar, her tray of merchandise lying to one side. She glanced at him. He knew her. He'd hauled in her for prostitution a dozen times, years ago, when he was a uniformed cop.

Rainey took a photograph from his inside jacket pocket. It was a New York mug shot of Achille Pepino. "That the guy, Bruno?"

The bartender stared at the picture for a moment. Then he nodded. "That's the guy. Who the hell is he?"

"His name is Chickie Pepino. A New Yorker. A hit man. Or that's what they say he is, anyway. He's got no convictions."

"Like I said, I hope I never see him again. Even to testify against him. The guy could kill you with the evil eye."

Rainey nodded. "I wanta talk with Harry. Alone."

He sat down at a table with the emaciated, gray-haired doorman—and immediately recognized him as an ex-con, a onetime burglar who had made some spectacular scores about twelve years ago. Harry remembered him, too. Rainey showed him the photo, and Harry confirmed Bruno's judgment that the mug shot was a picture of the man who'd shot the bouncer.

"Off the record, Harry," said Rainey. "Strictly not for Bruno."

"You were square with me in the old days, Rainey," said Harry quietly, keeping an eye on Bruno behind the bar.

"I'll be square with you now. Bruno figures you palmed a fin to let that guy in. From what I know about the guy you let in, I figure he'd have cut your throat before he slipped you anything. So—"

"He never slipped me no fin," said Harry.

"So why'd you let him in?"

"He used a name. He couldn't speak English, I don't think. He just said the name."

"You've been asked for that name half a dozen times," said Rainey. "Why the big secret?"

"The kind of guys we're talkin' about," said Harry, "are like you said: the kind who'd cut your throat before slippin' you a fin to get through a door. So what you figure they'd do to the guy that helped the cops identify one of them?" He shook his head. "I been around, as you well know. I did time. A lot of time. I saw guys dropped with a shank in the back, in the joint. For talkin' outta turn. Hey— You sure you can be straight about this?"

Rainey nodded. "What name did he use, Harry?"

Harry paused for a moment, hesitant. Then in a low voice he said, "McKibben."

"McKibben? How come that name cut ice?"

"McKibben had been in here a couple of times. Talk about guys slippin' a fin? He slipped me a sawbuck. To let him in. Quiet guy. Drank at the bar. Talked to Bruno, and— Hey, if you ask Bruno—"

Rainey nodded. "I get ya. Damn. I'd like to ask Bruno what he said. But I told you I'd be square with you, so . . . Anyway . . ."

"Well. He told me this guy'd be comin' in and would ask for him. He handed me another sawbuck and said to let the guy in. They were goin' to meet here."

"I'll be damned . . ." muttered Rainey.

Lawrence Pickering knocked on the door of an apartment in an ivy-covered brick building on the edge of Georgetown.

A woman opened the door: an attractive blonde, in her late twenties, as Pickering judged.

"Mrs. Nelson?"

"Yes."

"I am Lawrence Pickering of the Secret Service. Here is my identification. Is your husband at home?"

She shook her head as she frowned over the identification.

"I'd appreciate a few minutes of your time," he said. "I am investigating the murder of Judge Horace Blackwell."

"*I know nothing about it!* Neither does my husband."

"I'm afraid you do know something about it, Mrs. Nelson," he said. "I—"

She slammed the door in his face.

Mrs. Roosevelt joined the President when he came down for dinner at 7:30. This was not a state dinner but a dinner for a few guests in the private dining room.

The guests for dinner this evening were James Farley, the Postmaster General, Louis Howe, the Notre Dame football coach Knute Rockne, and the famous aviator Wiley Post and his pretty wife, May.

Post would leave shortly to attempt to fly around the world, solo. If he succeeded, he would be the first person ever to do it. Howe, who had suggested he be invited, had joked that it would be well to have him to dinner now, if the Roosevelts wanted to meet him, because, "Who knows if he'll come back alive?"

Post was a handsome man. He wore a neat mustache and a white patch over the empty socket of his left eye.

"Tell us about your airplane, Mr. Post," said Mrs. Roosevelt.

"We call it the *Winnie May*," said Post. "It's a single-engine monoplane."

"It's a beautiful airplane," said Mrs. Post. "Purple and white."

"It carries six hundred gallons of gasoline," said Post.

"What will be your route of flight?" asked Mrs. Roosevelt.

"Well, I'll follow pretty much Lindbergh's route across the Atlantic," said Post. "Then to Berlin, on to Moscow, across Siberia, then to Alaska and down the West Coast and back across the States."

"Do you have good maps for all of that?" asked the President.

Post smiled. "For the European part, I have Michelin road maps. For Siberia I have a *National Geographic* map. The Soviet government doesn't allow the publication of road maps or air charts, you know. They're afraid an 'enemy' might use them. Then, getting back to the States, I'll use real charts, plus oil-company road maps."

"How long do you expect the flight to take?" asked Knute Rockne.

"One week," said Post. "If it takes more than seven days, I'll be disappointed."

A little later the conversation shifted to the topic of the Chicago World's Fair—the Century of Progress Exposition—which was scheduled to open the following week. James Farley had taken great interest in the fair and would represent the President at the opening.

"They're going to use the light of a star to switch on the lights at the fair," said Farley. "Some kind of deal the astronomers have set up. They'll catch light from the star Arcturus, which they say left the star forty years ago, and shoot it through their telescope onto some sort of photoelectric cell, which will put the current through some relays and turn on the lights all over the fairgrounds."

"Going to be a great thing for this country's morale," said Howe. "I've read that you'll be able to go into the General Motors building in the morning, order yourself a Chevrolet, and they will build it while you watch. In the afternoon you can drive away the car you ordered in the morning."

"I understand that Mussolini is sending airplanes," said Post.

"That's true," said Farley. "General Italo Balbo is bringing over a fleet of twenty-four seaplanes. They'll fly over the opening, in formation."

"They are going to display George Washington's false teeth," said Mrs. Roosevelt with an amused smile.

"Those won't be the chief attraction," said the President, and he laughed. "I am told that in an exhibition hall on the midway a girl is going to keep alive the tradition started by Little Egypt at the Columbian Exposition in 1893."

"Another belly dancer?" asked Knute Rockne.

"Not quite," laughed the President. "A young woman who dances altogether nude, twirling a pair of ostrich-feather fans to prevent complete uncoverage. Now, *that* will be the highlight of the fair!"

"Her name is Sally Rand," said Farley. "A group of church people is threatening to sue. They'll try to get a court order to prevent her appearing."

The President laughed again. "You must bring me back a full report, Jim."

When she went back upstairs after dinner, Mrs. Roosevelt found a note to the effect that Lawrence Pickering would like to see her as soon as possible. She called the Secret Service office, and Pickering came up.

"I went to talk to Mrs. Nelson," he said. "She slammed the door in my face."

"I can't imagine why," said Mrs. Roosevelt.

"I can," said Pickering. "I only saw her for a minute, but it was long enough to recognize her. Bridget Nelson is one of the young women in Judge Blackwell's collection of snapshots."

He reached into his inside jacket pocket and took out a

photograph, which he handed to Mrs. Roosevelt. She stared at it and shook her head. The picture was of a pretty blonde: pretty in an unimaginative, currently stylish way. She had written a simple inscription:

X

MRS. ROOSEVELT HAD BREAKFAST with a small group of Negro women. They were joined by Frances Perkins and Elinor Morgenthau. It was a cordial meeting, with some discussion of the Scottsboro case but mostly talk about the extent to which various new programs would be available to American Negroes.

At his press conference that morning in the Oval Office, the President was asked several questions about the apparent lack of progress in finding the murderer of Judge Horace Blackwell. He said the Secret Service and District police were following some promising leads but that he did not ask for or receive detailed reports.

He did not tell them what he knew: that Mrs. Roosevelt would be meeting with Agent Lawrence Pickering and Detective Sergeant Wilbur Rainey as soon as her breakfast meeting was over, to talk about bothersome new disclosures in the case.

The First Lady stared again at the snapshot of Bridget Nelson. She shook her head. "Do you suppose," she asked, "that this young woman wrote one of those letters the judge had collected?"

"I don't think so," said Pickering. "There was only one unsigned letter, and that one was written by Blanche Tracy."

"Unless she signed herself 'Becky' or some other name," said Rainey.

"The 'Becky' letter is postmarked 1929," said Pickering. "Mrs. Nelson impresses me as not old enough to have been involved in an affair with Judge Blackwell as long ago as 1929."

"On the other hand, the Nelsons are from New York," said Mrs. Roosevelt.

"The 'Becky' letter is rather silly and also rather explicit," said Pickering. "She did not impress me as the type of person to have written it."

"In any event," said Mrs. Roosevelt, "this changes the complexion of the case, does it not? The Nelsons are the Tracys' alibi for last Wednesday night. Could it possibly be that all four of them conspired to kill Judge Blackwell?"

"The two husbands had motive enough," said Rainey. "Both of them would know how to get inside the White House and move around at night. That is, they would know if they *wanted* to know. And maybe one of the wives, or both even, were with the judge when—"

"Speculative," said Pickering.

"When you're investigating one of these cases, lots of things are speculative," said Rainey.

"What can we do, besides confront Mrs. Nelson?" asked Mrs. Roosevelt.

"I tried to confront her," said Pickering.

"Let me try," said the First Lady.

She picked up the telephone and placed a call to the Nelson apartment. Bridget Nelson answered.

"We've met, I believe," said Mrs. Roosevelt. "If not, I regret the omission. I am wondering if you would do me the kindness to come to see me at the White House this afternoon?"

"You want to talk to me about the Blackwell murder?" asked Bridget Nelson, her voice coming across the telephone in a strained, anxious tone.

"I am afraid there are a few questions that must be asked and answered," said Mrs. Roosevelt. "I thought it might be easier for you—perhaps less embarrassing—if we two women talked together, alone."

"I can't avoid the questions, can I?"

"My dear, I am afraid you can't."

"Very well. What time would you like to see me?"

"Shall we say two o'clock, if that is not inconvenient?"

"I will be there," said Bridget Nelson—but plainly she was coming only most reluctantly.

Mrs. Roosevelt put down the telephone. "And now," she said, "what significance do we place on the fact that George McKibben and Chickie Pepino know each other and were preparing to meet here in Washington?"

"Two guys with all kinds of reason to kill the judge," said Rainey. "A son of David McKibben and a hit man for the Cassell mob. A guy who's done time for using a knife on a man, and a guy reported to have shot at Judge Blackwell."

"Neither of them were particularly good suspects until we discover them associating with each other," said Mrs. Roosevelt. "But their being together is highly suggestive."

"Either one of them could well be the killer," said Pickering. "But neither of them would have known how to get into the White House at night. There has to be another person involved."

"The woman whose grunts were heard by Beauford Jones," said Mrs. Roosevelt.

"A woman with welts on her backside," said Rainey. "Or— Well, by now they'd be healed. Little white scars, maybe."

"I am going to speak with Bridget Nelson at two," said Mrs. Roosevelt. "I am afraid I see no alternative but for you,

Mr. Pickering, to speak with Professor Tracy."

Pickering nodded, without enthusiasm. "I am afraid," he said, "that I, too, see no alternative."

"And Sergeant Rainey—"

"I've got every man I can spare looking for that character Pepino. The charge is the murder of the speakeasy bouncer, and we've wired the New York police department that we want him for murder here in Washington. I'm gonna get him, ma'am; and when I do I'm gonna sweat him maybe just a little more than the law allows."

The First Lady stared at something on her desk, as if she had withdrawn from the conversation. "I didn't hear it, Sergeant Rainey," she said.

Pickering walked with Rainey to the gate where the detective's District police car was parked and watched over by the White House guards.

"Couple of things," said Rainey as they walked toward the gate. "The fingerprints on the collection of snapshots and on the letters besides Blanche Tracy's. Nothin'. None of those broads have criminal records. None work for the government."

"I didn't expect much from that source," said Pickering.

"I can't get a make on the gal that called the Buchanan Hotel and was upset to find out McKibben was gone. Can't get a make on the two who came to see him while he was staying there."

"The telephone call is important," said Pickering.

Rainey shrugged. "Yeah, but how you gonna find out who it was?"

"Keep trying, Brother Rainey," said Pickering with a small, wry smile. "Keep trying."

Professor William Tracy occupied a shabby temporary office in the Old Executive Office Building. Its shabbiness was accentuated by his professorial untidiness. He sat at a crippled wooden desk—one of its legs was broken off, and that corner was propped up on a small wooden box that was not exactly the right height, so that the desk slanted just a little. Except for a small area cleared in the middle, every square inch of the desktop was heaped with books and papers. Every other horizontal surface of the room, including much of the floor, was similarly heaped. In the middle of all this, the professor sat placidly puffing on a pipe, looking academic, if there is a way a man can look academic. He seemed disinterested in his appearance, so he needed a haircut, and his clothes looked as though he had slept in them more than one night.

"What can I do for you, Mr. Pickering?" he asked amiably.

Pickering cleared some papers off a chair and sat down. "Let's start with the answer to a direct and simple question," he said. "Did you kill Judge Blackwell? Or did you have anything to do with it? Or do you know who did?"

The square-jawed, yellow-haired professor was apparently not offended by the questions. He cocked his head to the right and regarded Pickering with calm curiosity. "That is *three* questions, Mr. Pickering," he said. So— Let's see. No . . . no . . . and no."

"Good," said Pickering. "Do you know why I ask?"

"I rather imagine I do," said Professor Tracy. "But suppose you tell me why."

"I dislike what I have to say," said Pickering. "I—"

"Don't be embarrassed. Don't be hesitant. I think I know what you are going to say."

"You have motive, Professor, to kill Judge Blackwell. He and your wife had an affair, a rather intense affair."

"I know," said Professor Tracy blandly. "I also know it was over before he died."

"It was over three days before he died," said Pickering. "It was over if we accept her word that it was over."

"You've talked to her about it?"

"I have, indeed. But, more than that, I have in evidence a letter she wrote him three days before he was murdered, telling him the affair was at an end. I am not at all sure, though, that Judge Blackwell would have accepted that, so—"

"So there was a motive for killing him," the professor interrupted. "You're *damned right* there was, Mr. Pickering. It was no ordinary love affair. It was cruel, unnatural. And I have lain in bed many a night, scheming about how I could rid myself and my wife of the malign influence of Judge Horace Blackwell."

Pickering smiled faintly. "The District homicide detective in charge of the investigation refers to the judge as a 'rink-stink.' "

"A term invented by General Hugh Johnson," said the professor. "I would use another term. He was a sadist."

"Uh . . . There is some intimation of that," said Pickering.

"Intimation? I can *prove* it to you! I— Well . . . You may think I am only showing you the basis for my loathing for that evil man—which will make you more likely to think I killed him—but I will risk that. Mr. Pickering . . . I will show you something. In confidence, if it may be."

"I cannot promise to hold anything in confidence, if it is evidence."

"That is understood," said the professor. "But you won't need evidence in my case, because I can clearly prove I didn't kill the man. So—"

Professor Tracy pulled up from under his desk a battered old leather briefcase, one with a missing strap. He opened it and pulled out a manila envelope. "So," he said, and he pulled out a photograph and handed it to Pickering.

The picture was of his wife. She stood facing a wall, with her head turned back over her shoulder, showing her face to the camera. She was a portrait of pain and humiliation. Though the photo was small, Pickering could see the tears on her cheeks. She was painfully humiliated because she was holding her skirt up around her waist. Her bloomers were shoved down to her knees. Her generously fleshed derrière— for she was a chubby little woman—was crisscrossed with dark stripes.

The professor handed Pickering another picture. This was a close-up of Blanche's buttocks, much more distinctly exhibiting the cruel welts on her flesh.

"I had suspected for some time that she was seeing someone," said Professor Tracy. "She is younger than I am, and vivacious. I could understand a . . . fling. Then I began to suspect who it was. *He* was no younger than I. No more virile. No more attractive. He—"

"I agree with your observations of Judge Blackwell," said Pickering. "But there was something . . . attractive about him, apparently. Your wife was only one of many young women he—"

The professor interrupted. "I discovered the welts. She had suffered them before, obviously, since she had done some rather grotesque things at times to prevent me from seeing her nude. But I saw her. In the bath. I burst in, for the very purpose of seeing, and compelled her to turn over and let me see."

"Perhaps you should not be telling me all this," said Pickering sympathetically.

"She wrote the letter because I required it," said the professor. "I let her say what she wanted. Let her . . . ? I encouraged her to express herself. *Demanded* she do. I wanted, myself, to know why she had submitted herself to . . ."

Suddenly Professor Tracy was overcome by his emotions. He reached for the photographs, which Pickering handed back to him; and his eyes flooded with tears.

For a long moment Professor Tracy sat looking at the pictures of his wife. Then, abruptly, he snatched from his head the yellow wig and revealed himself to be quite bald.

Pickering shook his head. His own emotions were a bounty of sympathy for this tortured man. He hesitated for a moment, then said quietly, "I have some further questions."

Professor Tracy nodded, and Pickering went on. "You withdrew a substantial amount of money from the bank not long ago," he said. "I am required to ask why."

The professor raised his chin, drew in a stiffening breath, and regarded Pickering with a new skepticism. "You *have* investigated," he said. "Why am I obligated to tell you anything? I can prove where I was when Judge Blackwell was murdered. I can prove it by the testimony of three witnesses."

"I know," said Pickering. "But the amount of money you withdrew was enough to employ the services of a professional killer. What is more, two professional killers—what the police call hit men—are in Washington from New York. The money . . . We believe it was about $2,000. That much money would buy you an attempt on the life of just about anyone, Professor. You can eliminate that source of suspicion by telling me where the money is."

"I can tell you," said Professor Tracy. "And will. I withdrew the money from the joint account my wife and I maintained in a Boston bank—the fund that was to buy us a home, eventually—because I knew she was involved in an affair with a charlatan, and I had reason to fear he would convince her she should withdraw the money and make it available to *him*. They could flee to Rio together. Or to Timbuktu. Except, as she would have been surprised to learn, it would have been Judge Blackwell who flew to Rio, with *our* money and that of others . . . and left her behind."

"You call him a charlatan—"

"He was a cheap, sleazy, slimy New York political hack—and, if you don't mind my saying so, President Roosevelt was a *fool* to trust him! Judge Blackwell would steal anything that wasn't nailed down. And seduce any woman not wearing a chastity belt. You say he was attractive to women? Yes, of course he was. He was a gigolo. He was a slick, lying debauchee!"

Pickering frowned and nodded. "Where is the $2,000, Professor?"

Professor Tracy had exhausted himself. For a moment he closed his eyes and slumped in his chair. "The money," he said, "in cash, is in the hands of a friend of mine, who can produce it for your inspection any time."

"Your friend's name?"

The professor swallowed loudly, and blew a breath. "Harper Nelson. He is on the staff of the Senate Committee on Banking and Currency, working with Pecora on the investigation of fraud in the banks and securities markets."

"And this is the same Harper Nelson who is your alibi witness for the night of Wednesday, May 17?"

Professor Tracy nodded. "As I suppose my wife told you. Harper Nelson and his wife Bridget. Harper Nelson holds my money. It is in a sealed envelope. He doesn't even know how much is there."

"You trust the man that much?"

The professor nodded. *"Some* of us are honorable men," he said.

Lawrence Pickering was moved by this whole interview. He stood and walked across the cluttered floor to the window, where he stood and looked at the Executive Wing of the White House.

"Professor," he said. "What do you suppose was the relationship between your friends the Nelsons and Judge Horace Blackwell?"

"None, I should think," said Professor Tracy. "Hardly the same kind of people."

"Yes, I should think so. But they seem to have known each other, just the same. I am sorry to tell you this, Professor Tracy, but there is all but incontrovertible evidence that

Mrs. Nelson was another of Judge Blackwell's inamorata."

The color washed out of the professor's face. "My God!" he whispered hoarsely. "Then everything— Am I to consider myself under arrest?"

"Not at all," said Pickering. "But it will be helpful to you in more ways than one if your $2,000 is intact in its sealed envelope in Harper Nelson's possession."

"Let us go together and find out," said Professor Tracy. He rose. "But . . . Does Harper know?"

Pickering sighed and shrugged. "I don't know," he said. "We will know in a little while, after Mrs. Roosevelt interviews Mrs. Nelson."

The First Lady looked forward with some trepidation to this day's lunch. She seldom felt nervous these days when meeting new people, but shortly after noon when she went down to the private dining room to greet her famous guest, she went apprehensively, unsure of how she would cope with the woman she was about to meet.

Her luncheon guest was Gertrude Stein.

Miss Stein disliked being called an expatriate, but she had lived in Paris for many years, leaving the city only when it was threatened by German attack in 1914. She insisted she was an American through and through, but she plainly did not like living in America. She was a famous collector of modern art, with an established reputation for recognizing talent and buying the works of artists long before they were generally recognized. She had, for example, been among the first actually to pay money for a work by Henri Matisse; and in later years she was known for her early sponsorship of Pablo Picasso and for collecting his works. She was, in her own right, an author—but of eccentric, obscure prose that many people knew about and few read.

This year, 1933, she was publishing her autobiography, cryptically titled *The Autobiography of Alice B. Toklas*—using the name of her longtime lover, who lived with her in her famous *atelier* in Paris. The autobiography, Mrs. Roosevelt had been told, was, in contrast to Miss Stein's previous body of work, an eminently readable book. It was being serialized in the *Atlantic Monthly*, was a Book-of-the-Month Club selection, and the early printings were sold out, though the official publication date was still a month or more away.

Gertrude Stein had returned to America for a promotion tour. She was accompanied—and she would be accompanied at this luncheon—by her friend Alice B. Toklas.

So the First Lady was about to meet the woman who had written, "A rose is a rose is a rose," and who had said of Oakland, California, "There is no there there." Not only that, she was to meet Miss Stein's lover. Mrs. Roosevelt was broadminded, but she was not quite sure how to do this.

She had asked Lorena Hickok to join her for this meeting. If anyone would know how to talk to these two women, it was her good friend Hick, who—she suspected but never knew for certain—shared their special eccentricity.

The formidable Gertrude Stein was sixty-three years old that year. She was, if appearance and manner were any guide, a woman altogether content with herself; but she proved also to be a warm and gracious personality, overtly anxious to win Mrs. Roosevelt's respect and affection. Her strong, mannish face was capped by graying hair cut exactly as a man's hair would be cut by his barber, only shorter. A wide-framed, imposing figure, she was also a little overweight.

Alice B. Toklas was a little younger than Gertrude Stein. She was tiny and fragile-looking. Her face was flat and bland. No one ever suggested she was beautiful. She deferred to her companion and seemed, in public anyway, to play a subservient role.

"You don't come home very often, Miss Stein," said Mrs. Roosevelt. "You must have developed a great deal of affection for Paris."

"Paris has developed an affection for me," said Gertrude Stein. "I am an American, but I am not sure I like the America of Warren Harding and Calvin Coolidge."

"I hope you will like the America of Franklin D. Roosevelt better," said the First Lady.

"That is possible," said Gertrude Stein. "Something new is stirring, at least in parts of America. Unfortunately, most of America is as provincial as some remote mountain village in China: proud of ignorance, unwilling even to attempt to cope with the world."

"Bravo," said Lorena Hickok.

"Don't you think there is something approaching nobility in the hard-working farmer or factory worker, struggling to support his home and family?" asked Mrs. Roosevelt.

"Perhaps," said Gertrude Stein. "But I prefer to observe him from a decent distance."

"The nobility of toil," mused Hick. "A romantic idea, but I believe there is some truth about it."

"Lovey works very hard," said Alice B. Toklas ingenuously, nodding toward Gertrude Stein.

Gertrude Stein laughed. "Thank you, Pussy," she said. Then she spoke more seriously to Mrs. Roosevelt. "It takes a lot of time to be a genius," she said. "You have to sit around so much doing nothing."

Barbara Higgins sat in Mrs. Roosevelt's office, typing final drafts of letters and memoranda someone else had typed earlier and the First Lady had marked. Missy LeHand came in.

"Do you know where Mrs. Roosevelt is?" Missy asked Barbara.

"At lunch with Gertrude Stein," said Barbara.

"My God, the people you get to meet around here!" said Missy. "Okay. Well, anyway, here's a package that came down on the train from New York. Tell Mrs. Roosevelt that Al Smith came through p.d.q. He called the *Mirror* in New York and asked for some old pictures, and the boys up there put them on an early morning train. Have a look if you want to. Curious."

Barbara opened the big envelope crammed with what turned out to be old newspaper pages. They were pages carrying the story of the conviction of the New York building contractor David McKibben. A picture newspaper, the *Mirror* had carried big front-page photos of McKibben in custody, leaving the courtroom after his conviction, others showing him in handcuffs being led aboard a train for Ossining, New York, and Sing Sing Prison.

Whoever had sent these newspaper pages had used a red pencil to circle the face of a young woman seen at the edge of the pictures, sometimes being jostled out of the way by reporters. She appeared in three pictures but was mentioned in one caption only:

> Seen to the left of the notorious grafter is his
> daughter, Angela McKibben, who sat in the court-
> room every day of his trial. She angrily pronounced
> her father's conviction "a travesty of justice" and "a
> political prosecution."

Barbara studied the face of the young woman in the pictures. She picked up a magnifying glass from Mrs. Roosevelt's desk and peered thoughtfully at the photos.

Angela McKibben was—or had been, two years ago—a beautiful and stylish young woman. In one of the pictures her marcelled blond hair was only a little covered by her tiny felt cap, though in the two others it was nearly hidden, in one by a cloche, in the other by a slouch hat that left just enough uncovered to show clearly that she wore her hair short, just to her ears, and rigidly styled. In the single picture that showed her close up, you could see that she wore dark lipstick, and stiff mascara on her lashes. In two of the pictures she wore a

fox fur around her neck. In one she wore a loose blouse, probably silk, with deep décolletage partly hidden by a floppy tied
scarf.

So— The daughter of David McKibben. Mrs. Roosevelt
would be interested. Barbara stuffed the newspaper pages
back into the envelope and put them aside for the First Lady's
return.

Bridget Nelson had arrived a little early for her appointment,
so she had been conducted to Mrs. Roosevelt's office and
served tea while she waited. For a moment, she encoun-
tered Barbara Higgins, who looked at her with bold cynicism
and compared her to the pictures she had seen of Angela
McKibben. She was not the same young woman, though
maybe Mrs. Roosevelt, too, would be struck by the resemblance.

Mrs. Roosevelt was only five minutes later, but she apol-
ogized. "I hope it has not been too great an inconvenience."

"No. Not at all," said Bridget Nelson.

For a long moment Mrs. Roosevelt sat and considered
what she would say to open this interview. Then she turned
to a cubbyhole in her desk and withdrew the snapshot of Bridget that had been found in Judge Blackwell's safe-deposit box.
She handed the picture to the young woman.

Bridget Nelson looked at it for a moment, then asked,
"Where did you get it?"

"It was among the possessions of the late Judge Horace
Blackwell," said Mrs. Roosevelt. "He had kept it in a safe-
deposit box in a bank, together with the photographs of several other attractive young women, and their love letters."

Bridget returned the picture. "What do you expect me to
say?" she asked.

"What do you want to say?"

"Ideally, nothing."

"Yes, I suppose so," said Mrs. Roosevelt gently. "But it will hardly do, will it? Someone—a woman—was with the judge within half an hour of his death. It could have been you."

Bridget shook her head. "It couldn't have been me. I was at home with my husband. The Tracy's came by to visit. We were playing bridge when the judge was murdered."

"Playing bridge," said Mrs. Roosevelt quietly. "Four of you. But I am afraid, Mrs. Nelson, that all four of you had strong motive to kill Judge Blackwell. All four of you . . ."

"It was over between Horace and me," said Bridget. "Had been for some time. It started in New York and continued here in Washington. I was in his room here in the White House just once. I was with him in a hotel room just once. And not since . . . since the first week in April."

"Does your husband know?" asked Mrs. Roosevelt.

Bridget shook her head sadly. "No. If he finds out—"

"He need not be told," said Mrs. Roosevelt. "That is, he need not if you are telling the truth."

"How can I prove that?"

"Tell me what you know. You know who else—"

"*Yes, I do.* But I swear she was with us that night. So was her husband. The four of us—"

"The four of you, unfortunately, constitute for each other what people who work in the field of criminal investigation call an alibi," said Mrs. Roosevelt. "Each of you vouches for the others. Each of you with powerful motive to—"

"But we didn't! We are not the kind of people who go around murdering other people. Whatever the motive. We are not that kind of people."

"Husbands," said Mrs. Roosevelt, "have been known to murder men who seduced their wives. Wives have killed to protect their reputations. Strong motives. In the case of Judge Blackwell, the motive may have been stronger, because the judge somehow persuaded women to permit him . . . to permit him unnatural liberties."

"I will not pretend I do not know what you mean," said Bridget Nelson.

"He saved your picture," said Mrs. Roosevelt. "Did you not write him a letter?"

"No. He wanted me to. By the time he demanded that, I knew what he would do: he would save it as a part of a collection. And furthermore, Mrs. Roosevelt, if you know what he demanded, then understand that I did not allow him the liberties he wanted."

"No liberties . . . ?"

"I didn't say *no* liberties. I am a modern girl. But not the kind of liberties he asked for. If you don't know what I mean, I can describe them."

"I am afraid I know what kind of liberties you mean," said the First Lady.

"So . . ."

"And you say your husband doesn't know."

Bridget Nelson nodded, then put her hands over her eyes to squeeze back tears. "He doesn't know . . ."

"If you are telling the truth, there is no reason why he should ever know. That is . . . not from me."

"Thank you . . ."

"But I should be pleased if you could explain to me, Mrs. Nelson, what it was about Judge Blackwell that made him so attractive to young women that they allowed him to intrude upon their marriages—and more than that to persuade them to permit him to—"

Bridget Nelson sighed loudly. "How can I explain? He was not a very handsome man. But he was . . . He was *charming*. There was about him a certain . . . What is the word? Charisma? Magnetism? My own relationship with him began in New York. An element of his attraction was his aura of power. Power . . . As a judge, he had power. As a D.A., he'd had power. He spoke with quiet authority, Mrs. Roosevelt . . .

yet with an underlying implication of . . . of *animal* power. Does this make any sense at all?"

"It is an education for me," said the First Lady. "Maybe. Maybe I should not say this, but my husband is the same kind of man: a man of great, persuasive personal charm. We don't often see it externally. It is something inside a man, that a woman has to learn from closer knowledge of him. I cannot condemn you, Mrs. Nelson. I only hope you did not, indeed, play any part in murdering Judge Blackwell."

XI

"I'LL BE DAMNED IF you do," said the President.

The valet, for some unfathomable reason, had not appeared when he was called. The cocktail hour was over, guests had left, the President had wheeled himself into his bedroom, and he was ready for his bath and to be helped to go to bed. Missy was with him, as was the secretary, Grace Tully, and they had offered to help him out of his wheelchair and onto the bed, without a bath.

"You can help with this," he said curtly. He had begun to pull up his trouser legs and to detach his braces.

The two women knelt at the two sides of his wheelchair and helped him to unbuckle and to remove the torturous braces he wore all day.

"And put my robe and pajamas in the bathroom," he said.

Grace Tully, half sickened by the sight of his braces—though she had always known about them—scrambled up and hurried into the bedroom, to find in the closet his robe and pajamas.

"EffDee . . . Please . . ." whispered Missy.

"Girl . . . leave a man some measure of—"

"Dignity has nothing to do with refusing help," she said.

"Dignity has nothing to do with— Girl . . ."

Standing with tears in her eyes, Missy watched help-
lessly as the President shoved himself out of his wheelchair,
dropped to the floor, and crawled into the bathroom.

Before he closed the door he looked up at her and said,
"Order a Chinese dinner for two. Threaten Mrs. Nesbitt with
immediate death if she will not part with a chilled bottle of
white wine. And see me in thirty minutes."

Achille Pepino had waited for dark. Now that the sky was
black, he walked north on 15th Street, huddled against the
rain, glancing back with almost no interest in the tall lighted
obelisk: the Washington Monument. In fact, he did not know
what it was. What was more, he did not care. This town was
contemptible, its monuments meaningless. He had *business*,
and he cared nothing for the obelisks these Americans of
Washington put up to their little tin heroes. The sooner he
could get out of here, the better. Grass . . . Marble shrines to
nothing that meant anything. People who spoke a barbaric di-
alect of a tongue that was barbaric at best. But— Unfinished
business.

On the concrete floor of a new cell in the District jail, George
McKibben lay in his own blood and urine. He couldn't understand why they had suddenly run out of patience and restraint.
What the hell did they want to know? Right now—since the
middle of the afternoon—he'd have told them anything they
wanted. They were ahead of the game. They were in charge.

He'd been inside before and knew something about what
they could do to a man. His chief worry right now was if they
had damaged his kidneys. Blood had run out in his urine, but
there could be other reasons for that. They . . .

They'd asked him why Chickie Pepino was supposed to
meet him in that speakeasy. And he'd told them why: that
Chickie had come looking for him at the hotel, had hung

around outside and found him finally, and he, George, had told Chickie to meet him at the speak.

That was the truth, but it wasn't good enough for them. They had some other idea about him and Chickie. Hell— He didn't work with nuts like Chickie! That guy was dangerous!

What the hell did they want to know? They hadn't asked the tough question. If they had . . . maybe he would have answered. There was a limit to what a man could take. But the stupid bastards hadn't asked the only question that counted. And since they didn't know what counted, volunteering something wouldn't have made any difference.

Sara Carter and Beauford Jones were together in a closet in the Executive Wing. Someone had told Beauford once that this was the closet where President Harding had sex with Nan Britton.

"It may be so," whispered Beauford. "It sure does accommodate."

Sara laughed.

She was working in the White House again. Mrs. Roosevelt had said she would overlook—but just once—what Sara had confessed to her about making love for money. She would have to choose, the First Lady had told her, between that and working in the White House.

"I still can't figger somethin'," said Sara. They were relaxing now, on the floor among the overshoes and umbrellas. "Who put that knife on the bookshelf? And who was dumb enough to put chicken blood on it?"

"What I want to know," said Beauford, "is, what did I hear? Anyway, *who* did I hear?"

"I been thinkin' about somethin'," said Sara. "You know how when you see somethin', sometimes it kind of burns a picture in your brain? Y' know? Well, I got a picture burned in my head of that room, with the judge layin' there dead and blood

all over. Most every time I think about it, that's what I see: the
judge and all that blood. But there's something more. I can't
get it out of my head."

"What more?" Beauford asked.

"You know how they are, those two guest suites: the one
Judge Blackwell had and the other one. You remember there's
two ways to get out of those bedrooms. You can go out into
the main hall, which is what you'd usually do. But you can also
go out through another door, into that big old closet where
they store all them books. You know?"

"I haven't been in either of those rooms," said Beauford.

"Well, it's the way I say. Take my word for it. And that picture I got in my mind. Every time I see it, I see that door open.
I mean the door to the book closet. Then Runkle drags me
back in there, with my hands cuffed behind my back, and I see
that door again. *Closed.* Closed for damn sure!"

"What are you saying, Sara?"

"I came up to that suite. I knocked on the door, sort of
gentle like. Then I turned the knob an'— An', *you know what?*
Whoever killed the judge was in there! They heard the knock.
They heard the doorknob turn. They ran! So fast they didn't
have time to close that door."

"Then you screamed and ran out," said Beauford. "And
whoever it was, he or she was in the book storage closet."

"Right. Trapped! Except that Runkle drags me back inside that bedroom, and when both of us are in there, whoever
it was . . . run! Down the hall and through the big doors into
the stair hall. And from there, downstairs! And out!"

"I'd say you came close to getting killed yourself," said
Beauford.

"Question is, do I tell Mrs. Roosevelt?"

"If you want my advice, I'd say you're lucky to be out of
jail and out of this mess. If I were you, Sara, I'd do my job quietly and do nothing to attract attention. You've had enough attention, girl."

"You're right, Beauford," she said, squeezing his hand affectionately. "You're absolutely right."

Lawrence Pickering sat alone in a car, watching the door of the apartment house across the street.

More and more he regretted that late in his career he found himself investigating a murder. His job was to protect the President, and he had done it all these years, only to find himself, a few years short of retirement, compelled to play Sherlock Holmes, a job for which he considered himself conspicuously ill suited.

For example, he had proved unable to avoid developing distinct prejudices. He identified with a man like Professor Tracy and hoped the facts would exonerate the professor. He sympathized with the plight of a man whose young wife had elected to betray him. He felt a kinship for an educated, cultivated man.

Mrs. Roosevelt was the same. Her womanly and humanitarian instincts had generated in her an unrealistic sympathy for the young Negro maid.

As detectives, they were amateurs, with all the faults of amateurs.

Still . . . the woman had an analytic mind. Maybe that was most important.

The door opened. Professor Tracy came out. He walked across the street to the car, opened the door and climbed in, and tossed a manila envelope on Pickering's lap.

"Count it," he said.

Pickering tore open the envelope. It contained money. Cash. Pickering did not count it. He riffled the bills and would not dispute the professor's contention that here was his withdrawn $2,000.

Mrs. Roosevelt drove her own car to dinner. The Midwestern Caucus of Democratic Women had come to Washington. At

their dinner they would hear a message from the President,
but it would be read by the First Lady. Then, having read that
message, she would address them herself.

The subject of the President's message was farm policy.
He spoke of the Agricultural Adjustment Act, which had been
passed by Congress only last week. "The new law," he said,
"has something in it for everybody. Something for everybody
to like. Something for everybody to hate. It is not a perfect law.
But . . . my friends, *something had to be done.* If the alternative to doing nothing is to enact an imperfect law, then we
must have the imperfect law . . . because it will help. It may
not solve all problems. Indeed, we may be sure it won't. But
it will solve some of them. *It will help.*"

Mrs. Roosevelt then talked about farm wives and farm
children. She talked about bringing electricity to rural homes,
then about improving the schools for rural children. "In the
end," she said, "the question is, what kind of lives will people lead? Our new administration is dedicated to the idea
that all of us, farm dwellers and city dwellers, shall live with
some degree of economic security, yes, but beyond that shall
be able to live in dignity: fed, clothed, and housed, yes, but
literate, too, and in touch with all the world and all the mar-
vels in it."

Her speech was broadcast on radio, and in the President's bedroom he and Missy listened to it. He sat propped up
against pillows. Missy sat on the foot of his bed, dressed in a
pink nightgown and white peignoir. The bed was covered with
newspapers from Pittsburgh and points west, that had come
in on afternoon trains.

"Let me see," said Missy. "What she said— Bertie
McCormick will call it socialism."

"Bill Hearst will call it fascism," laughed the President.

"And Huey Long will say she borrowed the lines from
him."

* * *

Achille Pepino stood on East Executive Avenue, across the street from the East Wing of the White House, in front of the Treasury Building. The rain had slacked off.

For a few minutes he stood and stared at the White House. Not a very dignified building. Not well guarded, either, he had been assured. Simple to go upstairs. Simple to reach the man. Simple to earn his money.

With this money he would go home. With this money he would be a rich man: esteemed, deferred to, maybe a little feared, and he would be offered some man's virginal daughter, and she would be honored to marry a wealthy man, a traveled man, a respected man. He would live in Palermo, or maybe in a town on a hillside overlooking the sea, and he and his once-virginal wife would become the parents of many children.

He turned and faced the Treasury Building. A few lights burned there. Not many. He glanced around, to be sure no one was watching, and he walked through the gate in the low fence and toward the building.

He did not go up to the main entrance. He had been told not to. Instead, he walked around to the right, that is, to the south, and found a ground-floor door. It was unlocked as he had been told it would be, and he walked into the ground floor of the Treasury Building.

No guards. Or, if there were any, they were asleep. Standing inside the door he glanced around and matched what he saw to the map he had been given. He didn't need to take it from his pocket; he had impressed it on his memory.

A tunnel . . . This way . . .

Down stairs. The tunnel. Just where the map showed. He stood for a long time, staring into the tunnel, unable to believe a passageway into the official residence of the President of the United States would not be guarded. A trap . . . A trap for

Chickie Pepino. But— No. He walked into the tunnel. And through.

Unbelievable. He climbed a set of narrow, winding stairs and stepped out into a long and dimly lighted hall. He was inside the presidential palace!

And now . . .

Ah! It *was* a trap! Cursing his stupidity, he grabbed for the pistol inside his jacket, knowing he would never reach it in time.

The first slug was ill aimed and caught him high, ripping through his topmost rib and blasting out through his back, missing everything vital, leaving him with burning, excruciating pain but still able to clutch at his own weapon.

But then the second slug! As soon as he felt the shock, he knew it was lethal. He knew death. He ceased to feel pain, even to know fear. He had no time for anger, none for anguish. He didn't even know that he was falling. He didn't know a third shot hit him.

"Chickie Pepino," Pickering said to Mrs. Roosevelt. "In the East Hall on the ground floor. There is no point in your going down. He's been taken out of there."

"Inside the White House!" she said, anger rising. "Mr. Pickering, is there *no* safety in this place?"

"He came in through the tunnel from the Treasury Building," said Pickering. "He was carrying a crudely drawn map, showing how to get to the White House from the ground floor of the Treasury Building. That's been taken for fingerprint work, so I can't show you. A door that is ordinarily locked was unlocked tonight. I would have to say that Mr. Pepino was led into a trap."

"In the White House?"

Pickering nodded. "In the White House. A gangster-type killing, my dear lady. Whoever killed him dropped the death weapon on the floor and left it for us to find. It, too, has been taken for fingerprint examination, but I have no expectation—

nor does Sergeant Rainey—that we will find any fingerprints on it."

"The killer escaped—"

"Almost certainly the same way that Pepino entered: through the tunnel to the Treasury Building. By the time officers arrived—"

"The killer was gone."

"Yes. The shots fired were extremely loud. They echoed through the whole building. I should be surprised if even the President didn't hear them. But half a minute or more passed before an officer entered the Center Hall. When he reached the body of Achille Pepino, he knelt over him. And in the minute or so that passed before he or anyone else thought to enter the tunnel—"

"The murderer was long gone," she said.

"Long gone," Pickering agreed.

Mrs. Roosevelt, still dressed in the beige silk dress and the flat felt hat she had worn when she went out to make her speech, turned down the corners of her mouth and shook her head.

"A farce," said Lawrence Pickering, guessing her thought and anticipating her words.

But Mrs. Roosevelt's thoughts were fixed not so much on her disgust with learning that another murder had been committed within the precincts of the White House as on the facts of the case and possible explanations.

"What weapon was used?" she asked.

"A Harrington and Richardson .38 caliber revolver," he said. "Snub-nose. Almost no barrel at all. Fired at no more than three feet from the subject. A pistol like that blows burned powder and wadding all over. Pepino was covered with debris. Whoever killed him stepped right up to him and fired at point-blank range."

"Meaning," said Mrs. Roosevelt, "that whoever shot him almost certainly knew him."

"Very likely," said Pickering. "Pepino himself was armed. He apparently grabbed for his own pistol at the last second, but he was too late."

Mrs. Roosevelt shook her head wearily. Only now did she pull off her white gloves. "Mr. Pickering," she said. "Achille 'Chickie' Pepino was, allegedly at least, a professional killer. Why on earth did he come to the White House—and by a secret entrance? Do we not have to assume he came here to kill someone? Was that someone the President?"

"He wouldn't have succeeded in that," said Pickering grimly. "We've augmented the force that guards the second floor. Have you not noticed?"

She nodded. "I have noticed. Still . . . He did come here to kill somebody. I can think of no other reason why he should have been in the White House—and armed with a revolver, too. And he was no Zangara, either. He was no fool, thinking he could just rush the President's quarters. He came—"

"He came to kill someone else," said Pickering.

"With the assistance of someone in the White House," she said. "And that someone killed him. Led him into a trap, I have to believe."

"I suspect you are right. Well . . . We know someone who *didn't* kill him."

"Which is?"

"George McKibben. He remains in jail. I regret I have to tell you that some of the men at headquarters interrogated him more severely than the law allows this afternoon."

"Is he injured?" she asked.

"I can only tell you what Sergeant Rainey said. As he put the matter, 'It didn't do him any good.' "

Mrs. Roosevelt frowned and sighed. "I cannot approve of that sort of thing. A confession of something, if they got it, would be worthless. *I* wouldn't believe a statement beaten out of someone. Would you?"

Pickering shook his head.

She sighed again. "So . . . did he tell them anything?"

"No. Either he's telling the truth, or he's a man of considerable courage."

"So who did he come to kill?" Mrs. Roosevelt asked again.

"Not Judge Blackwell, certainly," said Pickering. "But the judge was the only contact we know of, between Pepino and anyone in the White House. The matter of the Cassells . . ."

"A professional . . . How does Sergeant Rainey put it? A professional 'hit man.' Judge Blackwell murdered. And now a 'hit man' killed inside the White House. All the motives we've talked about, for murdering the judge, died with the man. Why, for example, would Professor Tracy want—?"

"Oh. Something else about Professor Tracy," said Pickering. "He was telling the truth about how he'd disposed of the money. I went with him to the Nelson's apartment, and he went in and came out with the money."

"I am glad," said Mrs. Roosevelt. "I should hate to think Professor Tracy killed Judge Blackwell."

"My own feelings, as well," said Pickering.

Detective Sergeant Rainey arrived at the White House a few minutes before midnight. Mrs. Roosevelt and Agent Lawrence Pickering met with him on the first floor, in the Red Room, where coffee and rolls waited on a tray. Rainey was hungry and chomped gratefully on the rolls, washing them down with gulps of coffee.

"Nothing much to tell you," he said. "Here is the map they found on him. No fingerprints on it. None, that is, but his own. The revolver. Well, I didn't bring it along, but I can tell you it's nothing special, something anybody might have."

"Fingerprints?" asked Mrs. Roosevelt.

Rainey shook his head. He had to chew and swallow before he could speak. The trigger and grips were all wrapped in tape—rough cloth tape. No fingerprints on that. No fingerprints on it anywhere. No fingerprints on the empty shell casings in the chambers. No fingerprints on the cartridges not yet fired. Whoever used that pistol knew what he was doing."

"A gangster-type killing, then," said Mrs. Roosevelt.

"Right. A gangster-type hit. Also, we checked the serial numbers on the gun. It had never been used in a crime in the District—not that we have any record of. It has not been reported stolen. It's an old fella. Been fired a lot. It's kind of loose, like it's ready to fall apart."

"Expendable," said Pickering.

Rainey nodded. "Nobody's favorite gun. Whoever used it doesn't want to see it again."

"Pepino . . ." mused Mrs. Roosevelt. "I understand you subjected George McKibben to rigorous interrogation but didn't learn anything. You didn't learn the connection between him and Pepino?"

"Well . . . He says Pepino came looking for him at the hotel. He says he told Pepino he'd talk to him at the speakeasy but he couldn't keep the appointment because we arrested him first. That's all he'd say about it."

"Obviously he didn't kill Chickie Pepino," she said. "Is it possible he ordered someone to do it?"

"He's had no visitors," said Rainey.

"If the Cassells didn't send him to the White House—and why would they, now that Judge Blackwell is dead?—then who did?" asked Mrs. Roosevelt. "It seems unlikely, does it not, that Pepino came here with any motive of his own?"

Pickering picked up the pot and poured himself half a cup of coffee. He looked at it distastefully for a moment. Rainey grinned mischievously, nudged him, and handed him a small flask from his pocket. Pickering raised his chin and eyebrows, but he accepted the flask and poured another cup half full of whiskey.

"Maybe we are overlooking something," he said to Mrs.

Roosevelt. "Looking for motives that might have caused someone to murder Judge Blackwell, we have posited three: first,
revenge for something he did as a district attorney or judge,
second, the fury of a woman outrageously abused by him,
and, thirdly, the obsessive jealousy of a wronged husband.
Allow me to suggest another motive."

"Please do," said Mrs. Roosevelt.

"Blackmail," said Pickering.

"Blackmail?"

"Think of it. Why did the judge keep his love letters and
his photographs in a safe-deposit box? Could it be that he
abused these young women, encouraged them to give him
photographs of themselves and letters expressing their feelings for him, and then threatened to expose these letters and
pictures if—"

"Some of those pictures and letters are from girls that
could hardly pay blackmail," said Rainey.

"The ones we have identified," said Pickering, "are the
young wives of successful men. We don't know who the others may be or to whom they may be married. Besides, let us
not forget that the judge left an extraordinarily high balance
in his checking account when he died. Half a year's salary. Is
not that unusual?"

"Very unusual, I suppose, but how does that shed any
light on the question of who killed Chickie Pepino?" asked
Mrs. Roosevelt.

"A blackmailer," said Rainey, "very often works with a
partner."

"Still—"

"A very great deal is left unexplained," said Pickering.

"Another idea," said Mrs. Roosevelt. "Much as I would
like to strike the name of Professor Tracy from the list of suspects, I'm afraid we can't just yet. Suppose he—"

"I get ya!" exclaimed Rainey. "Suppose Professor Tracy

hired Pepino to kill Judge Blackwell. Suppose he hadn't paid
him yet, which was what the $2,000 was for. And suppose—"

"I am thinking along those exact lines," said Mrs.
Roosevelt. "Suppose the professor lured Pepino into the tunnel and into the ground floor of the White House tonight, perhaps on promise of payment. And suppose he killed him, to
cover the fact he had hired Pepino. Suppose all that."

"A great many supposes, all laid one on top of another,"
said Pickering.

"Why did the professor have the money in cash?" asked
Rainey. "Isn't that unusual? That much money? In cash?"

"At what time did you leave the professor this evening?"
Mrs. Roosevelt asked Pickering.

"Oh . . . Half past six. Quarter to seven."

"And Pepino was killed at—"

"Nine," said Rainey. "And what you wanta bet somethin'
else? What you wanta bet the only witness that places him at
home at nine o'clock is his pretty little wife?"

"Suppose, suppose," said Pickering.

"Or maybe they were playing bridge with the Nelsons
again," said Rainey, a note of scorn in his voice. "Very convenient."

"I see no option but to inquire," said Mrs. Roosevelt.

"The only element of this that persuades me in the least,"
said Pickering, "is the matter of the $2,000 in cash. I must say,
it seems to me a man withdrawing that much money from a
bank would take a cashier's check or something of the kind."

"Blackmail," said Pickering.

"I should like to know the whereabouts of Professor and
Mrs. Tracy all this evening," said Mrs. Roosevelt. "And Mr. and
Mrs. Nelson. Also, just out of curiosity, Sara Carter. And, while
we are about it, the whereabouts of Barbara Higgins as well."

"A new suspect?" asked Pickering.

"It would be foolish to overlook anyone," said the First
Lady.

* * *

Coincidence. At the hour, almost at the minute, when Mrs. Roosevelt was telling Pickering and Rainey she wanted to know where the Nelsons, the Tracys, Sara Carter, and Barbara Higgins had been all that evening—

In the bathroom of their apartment in Georgetown, Harper Nelson stood facing his wife Bridget. He was entirely naked. She was dressed in a light blue nightgown. He had just risen from the bathtub and stood beside it, dripping water, his towel hanging from his hand. She had been sitting on the closed toilet, talking to him while he bathed.

Harper Nelson was a lawyer: a well-put-together young man of twenty-nine who had graduated from Columbia Law School, joined a good Manhattan firm, and was now in Washington working for Ferdinand Pecora, chief counsel for the Senate Banking and Currency Committee. Ordinarily, Harper Nelson was a conspicuously self-confident young lawyer, who had done well throughout his career. At the moment, tears streamed from his eyes. His face was red. He clenched and un-clenched his fists.

His wife had told him what she had decided to tell him, before he found out from some other source. Now, that past, she drew a breath, set her shoulders, and lifted her chin high.

It was an unfortunate signal for that moment. Harper Nelson did something he had never done before in his life and likely would never do again.

He dropped his towel and slapped his wife hard across the face. She slumped down on the toilet and wailed.

At almost the same moment, in their bedroom, Professor William Tracy and Blanche Tracy faced each other. With all but identical result. Professor Tracy tossed the pictures of Blanche's bare bottom on the bed beside her, one by one. Then he tossed down the envelope with the money in it. He pointed at the envelope, and she picked it up and pulled the money out, clutching the bills to her bosom.

At that instant he grabbed her hair in his left hand, jerked her face up toward him, and with his right hand slapped her cheek.

Sara Carter had already been slapped, by her mother, so hard her teeth had cut the inside of her cheek, and now she lay in bed, tearful and angry and a little frightened.

Barbara Higgins sat in the bathtub in the women's residence hall where she lived. She had waited until after midnight to take her bath, confident that at that hour no one would knock on the door.

She sat in hot water. A rough washcloth was wrapped around her left hand. With that rough cloth and soap and hot water she scrubbed the flesh of her right hand: the soft flesh at the junction of her thumb and her index finger. The scrubbing was painful, and she winced, but she worked hard at it, just the same. And as she scrubbed, the black color gradually disappeared, leaving only angry red.

XII

SEATED BEHIND HIS DESK in the Oval Office, the President pushed aside a thick report he had been trying to scan hastily while Harry Hopkins and Rexford Tugwell sat by, waiting to have his comments on it. He shook a Camel from a pack, stuck it in his long cigarette holder, and lit it. He had just told Missy to send Mrs. Roosevelt in, and he was taking a moment's break from the big report and the issues he had to discuss with his two aides.

"We must be careful not to push the Congress too far," he said to Hopkins and Tugwell. Then he looked up, smiled, and said, "Good morning, Babs! Sit down."

"Am I interrupting something?" she asked.

"Yes," he said. "Thank God you are. Can anything in this world be more boring than money? That is, not your own money and your troubles in paying your bills, but money as a subject all its own: international finance. Why can't business be done with bottle caps or wooden nickels or something?" He grinned. "Whatever any of you do, don't quote me on that."

"Why," she asked, "can't the milk the farmers propose to pour out on the ground to bolster milk prices be poured instead down the throats of poor children?"

"Harry or Rex can explain that to you," said the President. "It's a matter of economics, I understand: an iron law of economics."

"It is nothing to joke about, Franklin," she said. "If our farms produce a surplus, why can't the surplus be used to feed poor families? They can't afford to buy all the food they need, so it wouldn't change the—"

"That would be un-American, Mrs. Roosevelt," said Harry Hopkins. "Any number of experts on the American Way would testify to that."

She smiled thinly. "You are being facetious," she said. "I was not."

"I'm sorry, Babs," said the President. "We're working on the problem. But what Harry just said isn't really off base. A lot of outspoken men will tell you that any proposal to *give* anybody anything—that is, to hand them something they didn't work to earn—is un-American."

"There are only two American ways of getting things," said Tugwell. "Earn them or steal them."

"No wonder they call you a Communist," she said to Tugwell; and now she could not control herself and grinned, then chuckled.

"Babs . . ." said the President. "Do you happen to recall whether, among the things found in Judge Blackwell's room after his death, there was any sort of extraordinary watch fob?"

"Watch fob? Why no, I don't recall anything about a watch fob. What about it?"

"According to Al Smith," said the President, "Judge Blackwell wore a watch fob originally belonging to Mayor Jimmy Walker. It was stolen from him by David McKibben; when McKibben was processed into Sing Sing it was taken from him, and Judge Blackwell laid claim to it, apparently as a souvenir. Apparently both McKibben and Blackwell refused to return it to Jimmy Walker. I was just curious—"

"His personal things were packed in boxes by Miss Higgins," said the First Lady. "I shall ask her about a watch fob."

"Please do. I doubt it adds anything to the solution of your mystery, but—"

"I shall find out," said Mrs. Roosevelt.

Wilbur Rainey was taken with Blanche Tracy, so when the work of inquiring where various people were at the hour of the death of Achille Pepino, he volunteered to drive out and inquire of her.

Once more, he found her at home. As before, she had not yet dressed for the day. She pulled back the lace curtain and peered through the glass in the door, and when she saw who it was she opened the door and let him in, even though she was wearing just a knee-length flesh-colored silk slip, with a pair of high-heeled red satin slippers.

"Well . . . the cops again," she said. She had been drinking. "Am I under arrest? Can I put my clothes on before I go to jail?"

"Mrs. Tracy—"

"Blanche. Call me Blanche, Rainey. We're friends, aren't we?"

"Well . . . I— Sure, I s'pose so. Why not?"

"I haven't got very many friends," she said. "Want a drink?"

He frowned, considered. "A light one," he said.

She walked over to the cabinet where they kept their liquor and poured two shots of Scotch. The silk clung to her hips, and Rainey guessed she was wearing nothing under it.

She read his thought apparently. "Excuse my want of modesty," she said. "Course . . . what's the diff? You saw the snapshots of my bare backside."

"I didn't see them," he said. "I heard about them."

She handed him his drink. "Well, no reason you should be the only one who doesn't get a look," she said.

She turned her back to him, raised the slip, and exposed her buttocks.

"*Mrs. Tracy* . . . Blanche! You don't need to . . ."

The scars were thin and white, but he had no doubt the whip had made cuts, not just welts.

She dropped the slip and turned around. "An' how about this?" she asked. She put a finger on a small swelling under her eye. He had not noticed it before, probably because he had not been looking very closely at her face. "My men treat me real great, don't they, Rainey?"

Rainey could only shake his head sadly. He tossed back his Scotch.

She sat down facing him. Her eyes were wet. "So . . . You didn't come for the show. No, and not to bring me sympathy, either. What's up, Rainey?"

"I need to know where the professor was last evening. For that matter, I need to know where you were last evening."

"We strike out," she said. "I was here alone all evening. He came in a little before midnight and slapped me around."

"Did he say where he'd been?"

"Said he'd gone to a movie."

"A movie . . ."

"Like I say, we strike out. If something evil happened last evening, he could have done it, or I could, and we don't have any alibis."

Barbara Higgins sat with Mrs. Roosevelt in the First Lady's office on the second floor.

"Watch fob . . ." she said. "I don't remember seeing a watch fob."

"Have his things been shipped to New York yet?"

"No, not yet."

"How much trouble would it be to open the box where you packed the things from his dresser and see if there is a watch fob?"

"No trouble at all. I know which box it is."

"Then open it, please. Let's see his watch and chain. And the fob if there is one."

Barbara nodded. "Of course. If someone stole . . . That could be an important clue, couldn't it?"

"Perhaps," said Mrs. Roosevelt. "I am not sure."

"I'll look for it."

"Thank you. Oh, have you hurt your hand?"

Barbara raised and flexed her bandaged right hand. "Strangest thing," she said. "I slipped on a rainy sidewalk last night and fell. My hand was jammed into an old wrought-iron fence, and some of the flaking old black paint was actually driven under my skin. I had the very devil of a time washing it off."

"Be careful of infection," said Mrs. Roosevelt. "You know, you can contract a tetanus infection from rusty iron. You should go down to the White House physician's office and have that looked at."

"Well, thank you. I guess I will."

"Mr. Pickering," said Mrs. Roosevelt, "I have begun to entertain a suspicion I imagine you are going to think rather farfetched. I am going to ask you to indulge me in it, not to ask what it is while you assist me in checking it. If my suspicion proves wrong, I would rather not suffer the embarrassment of having expressed it."

"As you wish," said Pickering. His mind was focused at the moment on something entirely different, which he hurried to tell her. "I spoke with Professor Tracy. He says he did not go home when he left his office last night but went to a movie instead. He even told me what movie he went to see: a sort of fantasy called *King Kong*. He did not arrive at home much before midnight. In short, he cannot account for his whereabouts at the time when Achille Pepino was shot."

"And what does Mrs. Tracy say?"

"Rainey went out to see her. He has not returned."

"I have a question for you, Mr. Pickering. Have you ever heard of what is called the Bertillon System, or the Bertillon Method, of criminal identification?"

Pickering nodded. "I have. It was a method used before the discovery that every person's fingerprints are unique. It involved measuring certain characteristics of the head, face, and body. Rather discredited, I believe."

"Perhaps," said the First Lady. "But not necessarily. I think maybe it was not so much discredited as simply supplanted. If you found a person whose middle finger was ten centimeters long, whose nose was six centimeters, whose face was nineteen centimeters from ear to ear, and so forth, and if your index of criminal records noted a person with identical measurements, it is very likely the two persons were one and the same. They might not *necessarily* be the same person, but—"

"Very well," said Pickering, his tone suggesting a lack of patience with whatever the First Lady was driving at.

"Well, where can we find a Bertillon expert?" she asked.

"I should think nowhere," he said. "The method has not been used for many years."

"But it is still used," said Mrs. Roosevelt. "Not for criminal identification, because fingerprints are more reliable. It is, however, widely used in departments of anthropology, on university campuses. I have two people I wish to match. Please don't ask me who. But be so kind, would you please, as to drive out to the Georgetown campus and pick up Dr. Lucas Graham? I will phone him, and he will be waiting for you."

Mrs. Roosevelt left word at the gatehouse that she was to be notified as soon as Sergeant Rainey arrived at the White House. He was told to come immediately to her office.

"Sergeant," she said as soon as he walked into the room.

"I am going to ask you to break into someone's home and search it for me. I dislike having to ask you do such a thing. But—"

Rainey shrugged. "Police business, ma'am," he said. "Doesn't bother me."

"Will you need a warrant?"

"Well . . . It would be better."

"Then I shall have to explain what you are looking for."

The President was amused but Mrs. Roosevelt was hard put to conceal her impatience when they took half an hour at lunch time to gather on the still-wet lawn to greet and be photographed with Busby Berkeley and a dozen comely young women who were featured in his latest film, *Gold Diggers of 1933*.

The young women were innocently affected to be at the White House—and embarrassed to appear there in the costumes they had worn for the shooting of the picture. Four of them wore imitations of World War army uniforms, complete with undersized helmets they could wear atilt on the sides of their heads. Four wore black sequined dresses. Four—the Gold Diggers, the First Lady guessed—wore costumes made of oversized "coins." All twelve of them wore abbreviated skirts that exposed their legs halfway to their hips, which was why, Mrs. Roosevelt guessed, all of them were giggly and evidently ashamed to appear so costumed at the White House and in the presence of the President and First Lady.

She made a point of speaking cordially to each of these young women, hoping the warmth of her welcome would reassure them.

But she was anxious to be away.

"I dislike dramatic scenes," she said—but it was a disclaimer that meant little or nothing to the people who assembled in the Cabinet Room at six o'clock. In fact, Lawrence Pickering took the liberty of snickering at her protest. She took note of him and added, "I really do wish this could be done some other way."

"You could do it some other way so far as I'm concerned," said George McKibben. He sat in handcuffs, flanked by two uniformed policemen. His face was swollen, and Mrs. Roosevelt had noticed that he moved painfully. "I'd as soon be back in a comfortable cell in the District jail."

"Not your choice, McKibben," said Rainey gruffly.

"Obviously," said George McKibben glumly.

"No one is here by choice, I assume," said Harper Nelson.

"I regret the inconvenience and the embarrassment," said Mrs. Roosevelt. "I think, however, the embarrassment all but one of you has suffered will be eliminated very shortly."

Professor William Tracy shrugged. He sat at one end of the table opposite Mrs. Roosevelt at the other. His friend Harper Nelson sat beside him. Their wives sat to their right, with Barbara Higgins and Lawrence Pickering filling the remaining chairs on their side.

George McKibben sat to Harper Nelson's left, with a vacant chair between him and Sara Carter. The last chair on this side was occupied by Detective Sergeant Wilbur Rainey.

Seated beside Mrs. Roosevelt was Dr. Lucas Graham.

"Everyone here," said Mrs. Roosevelt, "is necessarily deeply concerned about the murder of Judge Horace Blackwell. Although I dislike the dramatic confrontation of a meeting like this, I believe all of you but one will forgive it. We *must* resolve the matter."

"You sound as though you have reached a conclusion about the case, Mrs. Roosevelt," said Professor Tracy.

"In fact, I have," she said. "I am prepared to be proved wrong, but I think I know, now, who murdered Judge Blackwell."

"It is a risky proposition to accuse someone," said Harper Nelson.

"Indeed it is, Mr. Nelson," said Mrs. Roosevelt. "But I will ask you, as a lawyer, to consider my evidence quite critically, as I develop it for all of us here, and tell me if you find it so flawed as to demand I should not have revealed it."

Nelson nodded and smiled weakly, not quite sure if she meant what she had said or was being facetious.

"Please allow me to introduce Dr. Lucas Graham, professor of anthropology at Georgetown University. The professor and I have spent the last two hours together, and he has confirmed, to my mind, a suspicion that began to dawn on me yesterday and became stronger this morning. The professor has had occasion, in his professional life, to make extensive use of the Bertillon Method. I will leave it to him to give such explanation as may be necessary."

Professor Graham bore a slight resemblance to Albert Einstein. That is to say, he wore a thick but precisely trimmed mustache and long hair that burst out in all directions from his large head. He peered at the assemblage through thick, gold-rimmed spectacles; and, being wholly unaware that Mrs. Roosevelt would rather he did not, he puffed on a big brown cigar.

"Bertillon's method of creating criminal-identification records, based on measurement, has been laid aside in the field of criminal investigation," he said. "It has been replaced, quite justifiably, by the fingerprint method. But in anthropology it is still quite useful. We use the method developed by Bertillon to measure the features of primitive peoples—and, of course, of skulls and skeletons. It is useful in identifying racial differences, in deciding for example if a skull is that of a North European or an African. The method is not infallible. But its scientific validity cannot be questioned."

Mrs. Roosevelt nodded as he spoke, as if she were impatient to go forward. "I asked Dr. Graham if he could apply the Bertillon Method to photographs."

"I answered," said Dr. Graham, "that perhaps I could, to a limited extent."

"The question," said Mrs. Roosevelt, "is whether the photograph of a person disguised might be matched to a photograph of that same person not disguised, to see through the deception."

"I replied that was possible," said Dr. Graham. "Possible. I never used the Bertillon Method that way before, but I concluded—" He stopped and smiled. "I concluded, with Mrs. Roosevelt's encouragement, that the method could be used with photographs."

"But photographs come in various sizes," Pickering objected. "How could you match, let us say, a $3 \frac{1}{4}$ by $4 \frac{1}{4}$ snapshot to an 8 by 10 enlargement?"

"Actually, you can," said Dr. Graham. "Mrs. Roosevelt suggested we work with *proportions*. And I believe the method—though I never used it before—is valid and has in this case established a valid identification."

"I will be very much interested in this evidence," said Harper Nelson, failing to conceal a measure of scorn.

"Allow Dr. Graham to go forward, then," said Mrs. Roosevelt.

Dr. Graham nodded. "It is a fact," he said, "that people's faces are variously proportioned. I cannot say that no two people are proportioned the same way, as I could say that no two have the same fingerprints; but I can say that matching proportions on four or five points creates a very high statistical probability of identification.

"I should of course have preferred to measure the subject personally. But photographs do allow one to gain a satisfactorily accurate impression. So we measured—Mrs. Roosevelt and I—about a score of photographs. And came to some very suggestive conclusions."

Professor Tracy shoved his chair back. "How long is this to remain a mystery?" he asked. "It is tiresome to—"

"Shut up, Professor," grunted Rainey.

Dr. Graham fixed a contemptuous eye on the academic who had interrupted a scientific presentation. "Measurement," he said. "With the subject sitting in a chair before me, I would use calipers and take very precise measurements of such things as the length and width of the head, the separation of the eyes, the length of the nose, and so on. With photographs—especially those of varying sizes—it is a bit more difficult. But . . . it can be done."

"With what precision?" asked Pickering skeptically.

"Even on a photograph," said Dr. Graham, "you can obtain a rather accurate measurement between the centers of the pupils of the eyes. We used that as the base number. On you and me, measured in person, and taking the distance from the center of the pupil of the right eye to the center of the pupil of the left, the number will usually not range too far from 8 centimeters. All right? Then we use that number as a base. The length of the nose may vary considerably more. We measure the nose from its tip up to the line between the pupils. A nose 4.5 centimeters long is rather short and perky. A nose 6.5 or even 7 centimeters in length is not at all unusual."

"But," said Mrs. Roosevelt, "since we were working with photographs, the important issue is *proportion.*"

"Exactly," said Dr. Graham. "So we used an 8-centimeter distance between the centers of the pupils as a base figure. A nose 4.5 centimeters long would thus have the value .5625. If the tip of the chin is 12.5 centimeters from the line between pupils, the value of that dimension is 1.5625."

"And the same values would apply," said Mrs. Roosevelt, "if you were measuring a photograph on which the distance between the centers of the pupils was only 4 centimeters. With the same values, the nose would be 2.25 centimeters long. The distance from the line to the tip of the chin would be 6.25 centimeters."

"Very well, very well," said Professor Tracy. "So what have you proved with all this?"

"We measured three photographs of one person," said Mrs. Roosevelt. "We knew it was the same person. The—"

"The proportions matched exactly," said Dr. Graham. "I was in fact myself surprised. I hadn't thought of using the Bertillon Method on photographs that were not life-size. Anyway, on the three measured photographs, the measurements were— Well, I've prepared a diagram."

He handed a drawing to Rainey, to examine and pass down the table.

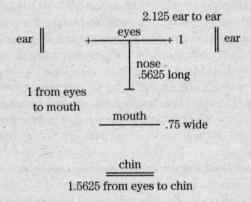

"Quickly explained," he said. "Giving the line between the centers of the pupils the value 1, the head is 2.125, the nose is .5625, the mouth is 1 from the eyes and is .75 wide, and the chin is 1.5625 from the eyes. Those proportions are consistent in every photograph of the person in question."

"Did you check any others, for control?" asked Professor Tracy?

"Absolutely. In two other, typical pictures—that seemed

to be of rather similar subjects—the head was 2.47 and 2.86 values wide, the nose .7249 and .8235, the chin was 1.6 and 1.647 values from the eyes. You see, there is significant variation."

"Assuming the validity of your method," said Harper Nelson, "what does it prove?"

"We used three newspaper pictures that are two years or so old," said Mrs. Roosevelt. "And some recent ones taken here in the White House, for identification purposes. The older photographs were of—" She paused and nodded toward the far end of the table. "They are of your sister, Mr. McKibben. Angela McKibben. Pictures from the New York *Mirror*, showing an attractive blond girl near her father during his ordeal."

"Angela . . ." he muttered.

Mrs. Roosevelt nodded to her left. "Known to us as Barbara Higgins. Angela McKibben with her hair dyed brown and allowed to grow long."

Barbara . . . Angela . . . shoved back her chair and leaped to her feet. *"No!* Dammit, *no!* You won't stick me like you stuck my dad!"

She spun around and ran for the door.

Out of his chair in an instant, Rainey sprang after her. She struck at him and drove a fist into his jaw, but he grabbed her. The uniformed officers who had been guarding George McKibben leaped toward her and subdued her. She spat and shrieked, and Rainey cuffed her hands behind her back.

Mrs. Roosevelt stood, appalled. Angela McKibben spat at her.

Rainey slapped her face. "You do that again, I'll gag you," he threatened.

George McKibben sat sullenly watching. His face was hard and bitter.

Pickering had pursed his lips tightly. He stared at Angela

with the scorn a civilized man reserves for people who shriek
and spit.

Blanche Tracy tossed her head at her husband and
sneered. Then she slid her chair sideways to put more distance
between her and Angela.

The two Nelsons stared at the table.

"There is other evidence," said Mrs. Roosevelt quietly.
She was stunned by the young woman's outburst, and she
could not help but glance down distastefully at the spittle on
her skirt. She wiped it with her handkerchief. "I am most
grateful to Dr. Graham, but his excellent work has served
chiefly to confirm what I had come to suspect."

"Evidence . . ." sneered Angela McKibben.

"Why is your hand bandaged, Angela?" Mrs. Roosevelt
asked gently. "What wound is under there? Do you want to
deny that a physician will find traces of gunpowder under
your skin? You fired a worn-out old revolver, and it burned
your hand with gunpowder residue. That happens, doesn't it,
Sergeant Rainey?"

"Very definitely," said Rainey.

"And when you are examined—which you will be at the
District jail—the nature of your injury will demonstrate that
you did, indeed, fire a revolver within the past day or so."

Angela McKibben twisted her shoulders against the
strain of having her hands locked behind her back. "Will it really?" she scoffed.

"And then, beyond that," said Mrs. Roosevelt, "I am afraid
the matrons at the jail will take a sample of the hair from your
most intimate part. And when that hair is matched against the
sample taken from the body of Judge Blackwell—"

"You'll prove I did it with Horace Blackwell," she said.
"So . . . ?"

" 'Did it,' as you delicately put it, just before he died," said
Pickering.

Angela shrugged.

"Another piece of evidence," said Rainey. He reached in his pocket, took out an envelope, and from that envelope he shook Jimmy Walker's watch fob onto the table. "Guess where I found it, Angela?"

She shook her head. "I don't play guessing games," she said. "Not now, for damned sure."

"You betrayed yourself," said Mrs. Roosevelt. "I asked you if you'd seen the watch fob in the judge's things. You said you'd look in the packed boxes. I suggested you go down to the White House physician's office and have your injury treated. My suspicion—already intense—was heightened when you left the White House immediately after."

"I left . . . ?"

"You left as fast as you could," said Mrs. Roosevelt. "I asked young Mr. Ballenger, Mr. Pickering's junior, to watch you. Not only did you leave, Miss McKibben— Do you continue to deny you are Miss McKibben? Not only did you leave, you went out through the tunnel to the Treasury Building."

"So? Where did I go?"

"I asked Sergeant Rainey to check that. I didn't tell him soon enough to make it possible for him to reach your boarding house before you returned and left again. But—"

"But I had a hunch about where the watch fob would be," said Rainey. "When you've worked in law enforcement as long as I have, a lot of your hunches turn out right. We didn't bother to search your room. Your landlady said you'd been there already. We looked in the trash bin behind the house. And guess what? The fob—"

"Big damned deal."

"When it gets tough," said Rainey, "people make mistakes. You might have handled the watch fob with a tissue. But you didn't. So, Angela dear, you left your fingerprints on it. You might have got rid of it some smart way. But you didn't. You were in a big hurry, so you went out the back door and tossed it in the trash bin. When the woman working in the kitchen told us you'd gone out the back door, that absolutely shouted trash bin. So we searched it."

Angela tugged on her handcuffs. "Dammit! Take these things off me and I'll tell you some things."

"Deal," said Rainey. He unlocked one of her cuffs and re-locked it around the arm of her chair. "Now . . . ?"

"It was my father's," she said. "The bastard stole it. When Mrs. Roosevelt asked me to pack his things, I took my father's watch fob."

"Dear . . ." said Mrs. Roosevelt sympathetically. "The watch fob was not your father's. He, too, stole it. Look at the initials on the back. They are Mayor Jimmy Walker's."

Angela shot a hard glance at her brother.

He nodded. "Not worth a crap," he said. "Not dad's."

Angela closed her eyes tight, squeezing out tears. She bent forward and sobbed.

"You and your brother—"

Angela jerked up her head and screamed at Rainey. *"Not my brother!* Not . . . my brother. He . . . tried to keep me from doing it. That's why he's in Washington. He caught up with me."

"Miss McKibben," said Lawrence Pickering, slowly and with studied dignity. "You stand likely to be convicted of the murders of Judge Horace Blackwell and Achille Pepino. Have you any inclination to speak the truth?"

Angela looked around the room, looking maybe for a sympathetic face. She glanced at the cuff that held her to the chair. "George . . . ?" she asked in a small voice.

George McKibben shook his head. "Baby, you've—"

"Well, *he* didn't have anything to do with it! *I did it!* And I tell you something . . . Don't look for an apology. You're not going to hear one. All I'm sorry for is he died so quick. I killed Horace Blackwell, and it's the best goddamned thing I ever did in my life!"

XIII

"A GREAT MANY QUESTIONS remain unanswered," said Mrs. Roosevelt.

"I've got one in particular," said Rainey. He leaned forward on the table to look past Sara Carter and speak to George McKibben. "Why did you arrange for Chickie Pepino to meet you at that speakeasy?"

"*I'll* answer," snapped Angela. "George had nothing to do with what I did. In fact, the reason he came to Washington was to find me and try to stop me from doing what he knew I was going to do."

"Kill Judge Blackwell," said Pickering.

She drew a breath and glanced at Pickering. Then she shrugged.

"Do you mean to try to tell us Pepino was in town to kill the judge?" asked Rainey.

"Right," said Angela. "He had his reasons, too. Ten thousand of them—if he did it and lived to collect."

"What, then, was he doing in the White House last night?" asked Mrs. Roosevelt.

"He came to kill the judge," said Angela.

"But Judge Blackwell had been dead almost a week!" Pickering protested.

Angela smiled bitterly. "The dumb bastard didn't know that."

"It was in every newspaper," said Mrs. Roosevelt. "The news was broadcast on every radio station."

"Chickie Pepino couldn't read an English-language newspaper," said George McKibben. "He didn't listen to the radio, because the announcers talked too fast for him and used too many words he didn't know. The guy came to New York from Sicily. Illegally. He almost never talked to anybody but Italians. He was brought to New York to be a hit man. He was gonna retire sooner or later and go home."

Mrs. Roosevelt spoke to Angela. "Pepino came to the White House last night for the purpose of murdering Judge Blackwell?"

Angela nodded.

"And you were to meet him and show him the way to the judge's suite?"

Angela nodded again.

"But you knew the judge was dead. It was a trap you set for Pepino."

Angela shrugged.

"I believe," said Mrs. Roosevelt, "that we are never going to resolve the unresolved questions this way. Are you willing to tell the story, as straightforward narrative? It may help you, in the end. It may help your brother."

Angela focused on George. "My brother is no angel," she said. "But he didn't kill Judge Blackwell or Chickie Pepino. He had nothing to do with the death of the judge. Like I said before, he tried to stop me from killing the judge."

Mrs. Roosevelt glanced around the table, her eyes stopping for an instant on everyone there. "Angela . . ." she said softly. "From the beginning, please."

Angela frowned at George.

"I think you better, Sis," he said.

"Okay . . . *Okay!* Blackwell called me Bobby. Know what

I called him? Horsie. Horace . . . Horsie. He killed my father.
Oh, sure, I know what you'll all say. But the truth is he picked
out my father and went after him, because there was publicity to make in it. And because my father's political allies were
fading. Jimmy Walker. Al Smith . . ." She nodded. "You couldn't
have had stronger guys in your corner, once. Then—"

"Then along came Governor Franklin Roosevelt," said
Harper Nelson.

"Yeah . . . He brought down both of them. Eventually he
forced Jimmy Walker to resign. So, okay . . . Honesty is the
new thing. But what my father had done in the twenties was
nothing but what every businessman did. Horsie had just one
reason to go after dad. Politics. Publicity. And get on the right
side of Governor Roosevelt. Hell . . . Horsie could have gone
to Sing Sing just like dad. Easy. *Easy.* But he didn't. He betrayed his friends. For his own advantage. For his . . . own . . .
advantage."

"When your father died in prison—" Pickering began.

"When my father was *murdered* in prison," Angela interrupted. "Murdered. An 'incident' in the yard, they said. Bull!
He was killed to keep him quiet. How naive can anyone be, to
believe my father died because of a quick quarrel in the prison
yard? There are guys in New York living comfortably right now
because—"

"Judge Blackwell?" asked Mrs. Roosevelt.

"On his way to governor," said Angela. "On his way to the
presidency, even."

"Back to the narrative," said the First Lady.

"When my father was murdered," said Angela, "I 'disappeared.' Sure. Long enough to let my hair grow out and dye it.
Long enough to study shorthand and typing in a grubby little
school in Greenwich Village. Then I applied for a job with Horsie. He was *Judge* Blackwell now. First rung on the ladder.
Well . . . Actually, he'd resigned from the court and gone to
work on the Roosevelt for President Committee."

"He hired you? All you had to do was ask him for a job?"

"I let him see I was . . . complaisant," she said cynically.

"On what date were you hired by Judge Blackwell?" asked Rainey, who had begun to take notes.

"It was in July last year. I applied for a job as his secretary when he moved from the court to the campaign committee. I thought he'd be happy to hire a girl who was willing to— How shall we say? Willing to accommodate him." She shrugged. "It turned out a lot of girls accommodated him."

"You secured employment with Judge Blackwell for the purpose of getting close enough to him to kill him?" asked Mrs. Roosevelt.

"Or see what else I could do," said Angela. "There were other people that wanted him. Maybe I could set him up. He was a careful bastard, you know. Shifty-eyed. Always looking for the hit man. Chickie tried him once and failed. Horsie was too alert."

"You came to Washington with him."

"Once the campaign got going, he was on the road all the time. I could have got him some night. I had chances, when he came back to New York and wanted some recreation, as he called it. But I'd have got caught, for sure. I was looking for the chance to get him when it wouldn't be just plain obvious who did it. It's one thing to change from Angela McKibben to Barbara Higgins, another thing to change back again, wanted for murder, and get away with it."

"How did you get him to bring you to Washington?"

Angela glanced around the table, grinning scornfully. "Easy enough. When it came to women, he was a hunter, an adventurer. But the hunt was not always successful. He was lucky to have good ol' faithful, reliable Bobby. Or so he said."

"I believe we understand the relationship," said Mrs. Roosevelt. "Tell us about last Wednesday night."

Angela shrugged. "Opportunity. I knew he had been visited in the White House by Mrs. Tracy and Mrs. Nelson. I also knew he was paying Sara Carter occasionally. For variety, I guess. Or because the man was insatiable. I checked out of the White House, made a point of saying good night to the guard at the gate. Then I went around to the Treasury Building and came back in. I had a key to the judge's room. When he came up from dinner, I was waiting in his bed. He was very pleased to see me."

"And you encouraged him to drink," said Mrs. Roosevelt.

"The more the better," said Angela. "When he passed out—"

"Oh *God!*" muttered Bridget Nelson and turned away, hiding her face in her hands.

"I didn't expect anyone would find him before morning," Angela continued, unmoved by Bridget's revulsion. "By then my alibi—that I'd left early and spoken to the guard on my way out—would be as good as anyone else's. I knew a lot of people wanted his ass. Would all of them have ironclad alibis? Anyway, who was going to figure it out that I was Angela McKibben? Why would Barbara Higgins want him dead?"

"Okay," said Rainey. "So you got him drinking. But not at first, 'cause he—"

"Not at first," she agreed. "Because, as you were about to say, he performed."

"Did he whip you?" Rainey asked.

Angela nodded. "Sometimes he couldn't . . . Sometimes he couldn't get enough interested. That would get him interested."

"So what Beauford heard—" said Sara Carter.

"Was Angela taking a beating," said Rainey.

Angela turned and smiled sarcastically at Bridget Nelson and Blanche Tracy. "He was an artist, wasn't he, girls? He hurt you just enough to satisfy him but not so much you couldn't take it."

"I wouldn't know," said Bridget Nelson icily. "I never let him do that."

"All right," said Mrs. Roosevelt. "You acknowledge that you killed him. Stabbed him when he was—"

"Slobbering drunk," sneered Angela.

"Then you went about the room wiping off fingerprints."

"Off the handcuffs in that suitcase, right?" said Rainey. "How'd you get it open? It was locked when we found it, and we didn't find a key."

"I didn't have to open it," said Angela. "It was already open. I was *wearing* the handcuffs: one pair on my wrists, one on my ankles—another part of his fun and games, right, Mrs. Tracy? I used the keys to take the things off, wiped the prints off, and dropped the whip and cuffs in the suitcase. Then I got dressed and wiped the prints off the glass and bottle. I knew my prints were around other places in the bedroom and bathroom, but that didn't make any difference, because I had good reason for being in that suite."

"The whole scene is disgusting," said Harper Nelson. "*The man* must have been disgusting." He fixed a hard, accusing glare on his wife and muttered, "Contemptible . . ."

"The key," said Angela, "was *in* the suitcase. That was my little joke, Rainey. Give you something to think about."

"When I come in, you was still there, right?" asked Sara.

Angela nodded. "You almost saw me. But you knocked first. If you'd come when I was still handcuffed and— But you didn't. I had finished wiping the glass and bottle and was just looking around, to see if I'd missed anything, and you knocked on the door."

"An' you ran out t'other door," said Sara. "You lef' it open. An' you close it after I went out screamin' an'—"

"You were a big help to me, Sara," said Angela. "My next problem was to sneak past Runkle and get off the second floor. But you got all his attention for a while. When he dragged you into that bedroom, that left nobody in the hall, and I made a dash for the stair hall and down the stairs."

Agent Lawrence Pickering frowned and shook his head.

"I still do not understand why Achille Pepino was in Washington and why you thought it necessary to kill him."

"That's because I haven't told you yet," said Angela.

Mrs. Roosevelt suggested that Dr. Graham need not stay any longer, but he said he was fascinated and wanted to stay. The Tracys and Nelsons left, Professor Tracy in a huff. Mrs. Roosevelt also suggested that Sara Carter could leave if she wanted to, and she got up and walked out of the Cabinet Room—not without a final saucy glance at Angela.

"So . . ." said Mrs. Roosevelt. "Mr. Achille 'Chickie' Pepino."

"I told you before," said Angela, "that Horsie could have gone to Sing Sing just as well as anybody. My father paid bribes? Well, maybe he did. And Horsie accepted bribes. Not from my dad, I don't think, but from plenty of people. Did you think the Cassells hated Judge Blackwell because he got Wilmer Cassell sent to the chair? Well, that's not why. They hated Horsie because he took money from them on a promise to get Governor Roosevelt to commute the sentence to life imprisonment—and Wilmer was fried anyway."

"Are you certain of these facts?" asked Mrs. Roosevelt.

Angela shrugged. "Depends on who you want to believe. That's what the Cassell boys told me."

"I didn't know you were that close to the Cassell brothers," said George.

"A natural alliance," she said. "I went to them as soon as dad was killed. They took care of me while I was letting my hair grow. Rupert Cassell, particularly. I couldn't look to you, George."

"Yeah, I was in stir," said her brother glumly.

"So they sent Pepino to Washington to kill Blackwell," said Rainey.

"With my help," she said. "I was supposed to set Horsie up for Chickie. But I got my own chance and did him in myself. I figured it was safer, for one thing. Anyway, I had my good reasons for wanting Horsie dead."

"God . . ." muttered George McKibben. "You did Chickie out of $10,000!"

Angela nodded. "The Cassells knew the judge was dead and canceled the contract on him. But they couldn't locate Chickie to tell him that. And it didn't take me more than a minute trying to talk to him to figure out that I didn't dare tell him. The $10,000 was going to be his retirement. He was going home to Sicily."

"He told you that?" asked Rainey.

She nodded. "Having lived in downtown Manhattan all my life, I understand enough Italian to get the gist of what he said. He was a crazy man, you know. If he found out Horsie was already dead, that I'd stepped on his contract—"

"He'd have killed you," said George. "Slowly and painfully."

"I still don't figure what *you* were doing in Washington," Rainey said to George.

"I didn't know where my sister was," said George. "Not exactly. I hadn't been keepin' very good track of her. Then I found out she was in Washington, and it didn't take me long to figure out why. I mean, Angela doesn't have to work as a secretary for anybody. The old man left her set up. She was his favorite. Angela has dough. And knowing that, and finding out she'd come to Washington with Blackwell, I knew there could only be one reason. So I came down here to see her, to try to talk her out of it. Why bother? was what I wanted to say. The Cassells will get him sooner or later. So let 'em. I found out where she lived, and I went there to see her. I took her out to dinner two, three times. So Chickie saw me, pickin' her up where she lived or bringin' her back. So he follows me. He wants to have a talk with me. I could hardly understand a word he said, so I knew it'd take some time to talk to him. I told him to meet me at that speakeasy. But you guys grabbed me first and tossed me in jail. And from that point, buddies, I'm out of the story."

"Where'd you get the pistol?" Rainey asked Angela.

"Rupert Cassell gave it to me, before I came to Washington. All wrapped in tape that wouldn't take fingerprints."

"What about the knife with chicken blood on it?" asked Mrs. Roosevelt.

Angela shrugged. "That was dumb. Maybe it wouldn't have been if I hadn't used the chicken blood. You said the only missing element in sticking the case on Sara Carter was the knife. So—"

"Two murders," said Mrs. Roosevelt, shaking her head sadly. "I am afraid it will go badly for you. It won't help that you tried to secure the conviction of an innocent young woman."

"When you're facing the chair," said Angela, "you get scared and do whatever you think might save you. Anyway . . . it didn't work."

The First Lady turned to Rainey. "She belongs to you now. You know all you need to know, I believe. A rigorous interrogation should not be necessary."

EPILOGUE

THREE WEEKS LATER CONGRESS completed passage of the National Industrial Recovery Act, and shortly the Blue Eagle of the N.R.A. appeared everywhere. Until the Act was declared unconstitutional by the Supreme Court three years later, the N.R.A. was perhaps the supreme example of President Roosevelt's idea of how to deal with the Depression—do something, try something, and if it doesn't work give it up and try something else, but the main point is to do *something*.

In July Wiley Post succeeded in setting a speed record for an around-the-world solo flight. Two years later he would try it again, this time taking along his friend Will Rogers. Both of them would die when their plane crashed in Alaska.

Babe Ruth hit thirty-four home runs in 1933. Lour Gehrig hit thirty-two. But Washington won the American League pennant and lost the World Series to the New York Giants in five games.

Professor William Tracy shortly returned to Harvard. Blanche did not go with him. She found a job with the Department of Commerce and continued to rent the little house where she had lived with the professor during his tenure as a braintruster. She obtained a divorce early in 1934 and shortly afterward married Detective Sergeant Wilbur Rainey. They were known for some years as a pair of deliriously happy inebriates, often seen in various Washington watering holes, full of gin and joy.

Harper and Bridget Nelson remained in Washington until June 1934, when they returned to New York and he resumed his law practice. They had three children in rapid succession. In 1940 he was elected to Congress, and they returned to Washington and lived there during the twenty years he served in the House of Representatives.

Agent Lawrence Pickering retired in 1935. He moved to a small house on Chesapeake Bay and spent the remainder of his years fishing.

Sara Carter married George Beauford. He continued as a White House usher until he retired during the presidency of Lyndon Johnson. Sara became the mother of eight children.

The Cassell crime family was literally wiped out during the gang wars of the mid-thirties. At the time when Rupert Cassell was gunned down on a Brooklyn street, he was free on $200,000 bail, having been indicted for sixty-three felonies.

George McKibben was held in the District jail until after his sister's trial. After that the alcohol-possession charges against him were dropped and he was freed. He returned to New York. As he had said, the repeal of Prohibition would put him out of business. So he took a little money he had stashed and went to Southern California to work in the oil fields along the Pacific coast. He made enough money to buy some land. He made a little more money and bought more land. When he died in 1981 his estate was appraised at $85,000,000. He left a $10,000,000 trust for the support of his sister and bequeathed the balance to his second wife and their two sons.

Angela was convicted of the murders of Judge Horace Blackwell and Achille Pepino. The judge sentenced her to life imprisonment, and in July 1933 she arrived at the Federal Reformatory for Women at Aldersonville, West Virginia. She was paroled in 1958, after serving twenty-five years. A woman of forty-six, she went to California, where, through her brother's influence, she was allowed to audition for minor roles as an actress. Soon she was a recognized character actress, appearing on many television shows, usually situation comedies where invariably she played the hard-bitten, tough-talking woman with the heart of gold. She was nominated for an Emmy for her role as Bertha on *Drake and Company*.

In 1961, Mrs. Roosevelt received a letter and an autographed picture. The letter was signed "Angela," but the picture was signed with the name Angela used as an actress—"Barbara Higgins."

Read on for an exciting installment of
MURDER IN THE MAP ROOM,
the next mystery from Elliott Roosevelt . . .

ON JANUARY 31, 1943, German Field Marshal Friedrich Paulus surrendered at Stalingrad.

Ten days later the last surviving Japanese troops abandoned Guadalcanal.

Two weeks later Field Marshal Erwin Rommel defeated an American force at the Kasserine Pass in Tunisia. It was the last German victory in North Africa. A week after Kasserine, American forces drove Rommel back and exhausted his dwindling army. He reported to Hitler that North Africa was lost and asked for permission to evacuate what was left of the Afrika Korps.

Though few realized it, the tide of the war had decisively shifted. Hard and costly fighting remained, but after February 1943, the Axis powers were in retreat. How the war would end was no longer in question.

On the same day when Paulus surrendered at Stalingrad, President Franklin D. Roosevelt returned to Washington after a mysterious absence of more than two weeks. Only after he was back in the White House was it announced that he had been to Casablanca, where he had conferred at length with Prime Minister Winston Churchill, General Charles de Gaulle, and with Allied military leaders, including Generals Dwight Eisenhower and George Patton.

His visit to Casablanca also had a personal significance for him, and for Mrs. Roosevelt, since in Casablanca he had been able to spend a little time with two of his sons. The destroyer on which Franklin junior was serving happened to be at Casablanca. Elliott's air unit was stationed in North Africa. The President came home with a cheerful report of how the boys looked, what they said, and what they were doing. Mrs. Roosevelt was pleased. Her sons, she sometimes complained, were not the best of letter writers.

She was not as well pleased with the President's health. He was obviously exhausted. Churchill had insisted they drive 150 miles across the desert to Marrakech, which he regarded as a romantic town, famous for its fortune-tellers, snake charmers, and brothels—plus one of the world's most beautiful views: the sight of the sun setting over the Atlas Mountains. The President had endured this drive and had allowed himself to be carried to the roof of a villa, to view the sunset Churchill had brought him all this way to see. The next day he had flown to the British colony of Gambia, where he had insisted on taking a cruise up the Gambia River. Later he would tell Churchill he had contracted "Gambia fever." He flew on to Liberia for a luncheon with its president. From there he flew to Brazil and conferred with *its* president.

The President did not enjoy flying. He enjoyed travel by ship and by train, but he complained that staring at the clouds was boring. "Anyway, it affects my head," he told Mrs. Roosevelt—by which he meant it caused sinus pain. He had managed to rest on the train ride to Washington, but when she saw him she saw a man tired and fevered and in need of rest.

Which he could not have—not the President of the United States in the second year of a major war.

She had been surprised—pleased and surprised—by the way he had so far carried the immense burdens of his office in wartime. He was sixty-one years old. The very simplest things in life—rising from a chair, sitting down again, taking a bath, going to bed, getting up—not to mention entering or leaving a car or boarding an airplane—were physical ordeals for him, no matter how much help he had. Still, he met the challenges of leadership and even seemed to thrive on them.

Seemed to thrive on them . . . She saw, as others less sensitive to him did not, that his burden was taking a toll.

The President had lost many of the people who had helped him. Louis Howe was of course long dead. Jim Farley had decided he didn't want to be a friend any longer. The children were scattered all over the world. Missy LeHand was gravely ill and no longer able to give him the companionship that had meant so much to him through thousands of evenings that would have otherwise been unbearably lonely. Harry Hopkins and his wife lived in the White House, but he *was* living with his new wife and was besides overworked and in failing health.

The First Lady had long since accepted her own shortcoming: that she simply was not capable of easy banter over cocktails and dinner, the kind of relaxing conversation the President needed and loved. She could never forget that some problem needed his attention, and she could never resist the urgent impulse to bring it to his attention. The unhappy fact was that she and the President could not relax together.

And they could not this evening, the evening of the thirty-first of January, when he lay in his bed, propped up on pillows, taking his dinner from the usual tray. She sat beside him but would not eat, since she was dining with friends downstairs a little later. He frowned skeptically over the unappetizing meal he found on his plate—another dinner of what he called "rubber chicken."

Mrs. Roosevelt continued a conversation they had already begun. "I think you may find," she said to the President, "that the visit by Madame Chiang will prove refreshing as well as useful."

"I'd as soon confront a black widow spider," he said. "If Winston's heaviest cross is the Cross of Lorraine, one of mine, if not *the* heaviest, is that shaven-headed egomaniac and his harridan wife."

"Franklin!"

"I wonder what, exactly is the relationship between her and Henry Luce. Why does he sell out to her and her husband so unconscionably?"

"Franklin . . ."

"I've seen *Time* and *Life*," he said. "Oh, our country is immeasurably blessed. Saint Mei-ling of Chungking has deigned to set foot on our soil."

"I visited her at the hospital in New York," said Mrs. Roosevelt. "She's a very dear woman, really. Kind and generous. She's at Hyde Park now. I offered her the use of the house until she is sufficiently recovered to come to Washington."

"Well . . . mother's dead. At least *she* doesn't have to tolerate the woman."

"Franklin . . . Madame Chiang Kai-shek will be addressing a joint session of Congress during her visit."

"Of course. All she'll ask for is that we abandon the war in Europe and concentrate all the armed forces of the United States and Britain on the war in the Pacific. Well, she can forget that. That's settled. Given a choice between being knifed by Chiang or bludgeoned by Stalin, Winston and I decided to be knifed. And so we will be. And he's sent the Dragon Lady to do it."

"Well, you have about two weeks to improve your disposition and develop a warmer attitude toward a woman I have come to know as a gentle, sweet character."

"I shall think of nothing else till the day she arrives," said the President.

That day was February 17.

Madame Chiang Kai-shek had been born Soong Mei-ling forty-six years ago. She was the daughter of a shrewd Chinese businessman who had amassed a fortune by selling Bibles. She was one of three sisters. Soong Ai-ling was married to H. H. Kung, seventy-fifth in direct lineal descent from K'ung-Fu-tzu, who was known in the West as Confucius. H. H. Kung was

China's minister of finance, though it was widely reported in the West that he understood nothing of money that was not made of copper, silver, or gold. Soong Ming-ling was the widow of Dr. Sun Yat-sen, nationalist leader and the most popular president the Chinese republic ever had.

Madame Chiang had been educated at Wellesley (class of 1917) and spoke fluent, unaccented English—coping with every nuance of American English from the most obscure diplomatic subtleties to the coarsest vulgarities. She was a Christian—a Methodist—and had convinced her husband to convert.

Madame Chiang was a political power in her own right. Her family connections had contributed immeasurably to her husband's rise. When the Generalissimo, as he styled himself, was kidnapped by rebels in 1936 and held prisoner for two weeks, Soong family prestige and Madame Chiang's determination and diplomatic skills were important factors in securing his release. She was the darling of the China Lobby in the U.S. Congress, and she enjoyed what amounted to adoration from Henry Luce, the publisher of *Time* and *Life*. No Chinese was better known and better liked by Americans than Madame Chiang Kai-shek.

The President had to keep her popularity in mind as he received her at the White House.

She had been injured in an automobile accident in China and had come to the United States for medical treatment and spent her first weeks in New York, where she and her staff occupied a whole floor of a prestigious hospital. Then she spent some time at Hyde Park. February 17 was a Wednesday. She would be a guest at the White House the rest of that week and all of the next, after which she would tour the States for several weeks.

Her chief of staff arrived on the fifteenth. His name was Weng Guo-fang, and he was a fragile little old man with a deeply wrinkled face, wispy white mustache and goatee, a hunched posture, and a dry cough. He wore beautifully tailored suits of soft wool. His speech was elaborately polite and deferential when he spoke to Mrs. Roosevelt but—though still polite—quite curt and firm when he spoke to anyone he supposed was a servant. It was quite plain that he divided people into classes and treated them accordingly. The First Lady found that difficult to tolerate—though she made a due allowance for his age and for the cultural difference.

He inspected the suite Madame Chiang was to occupy and asked for changes. He explained that Madame Chiang carried her own bedclothes—silk sheets and pillow cases. If she lay down on her bed even for a few minutes, her servants would strip the bed and remake it with fresh silk. All her sheets had to be ironed several times a day, to be sure she did not lie down on a wrinkle. She would not eat the ordinary White House diet. The housekeeper, Mrs. Nesbitt, was given detailed instructions about what Madame Chiang ate and how it must be prepared.

Weng Guo-fang was apologetically tactful; yet he made it plain that Madame expected these concessions.

"Just who the devil does she think she is?" the President asked irritably.

"Let me remind you of something, Franklin," said Mrs. Roosevelt. "When our son Jimmy was in China, he was suffering a great deal of pain from his ulcer, a problem that had been compounded by the food he had to eat as he traveled. Madame Chiang found out about this and saw to it that he was given a proper diet for an ulcer patient. She prepared many of his meals with her own hands. If she can do that for us, I guess we can tolerate her dietary requirements while she is our guest."

"Even so, I wish she were not coming," said the President. "Her dietary demands will be the least of her demands."

Mrs. Roosevelt was long accustomed to how her husband could change his colors, as dramatically as a chameleon and infinitely faster. Meeting Madame Chiang at Union Station, he treated her as if she were an old, old friend he had long yearned to see again. In fact, as soon as they were in the car together, he asked her with a sly smile what she thought of Wendell Willkie.

Wendell Willkie had been the President's opponent in the 1940 election. Subsequently he had toured the world, meeting the leaders of various nations and gathering the impressions that would become the subject of his book *One World*. Among those he had visited and apparently impressed with his personal magnetism was Generalissimo Chiang Kai-shek and Madame Chiang.

"Ah, Mr. Willkie is charming!" Madame Chiang replied to the President's question.

"Of course. But what do you *really* think of him?" the President persisted.

"Well," said the First Lady of China, after a brief hesitation, "he is, after all, still an adolescent."

The President laughed. "Oh, ho! So, then, what do you think of *me?*"

"Mr. President," she said instantly, "*You* are very sophisticated."

In that exchange, a new relationship was born. The President's hostility toward Madame Chiang, if it did not die, was significantly diminished. Hers toward him—arising from the fact that the Generalissimo had not been invited to the Casablanca Conference—slipped away into invisibility.

In any case, as the First Lady had anticipated, Soong Mei-ling, Madame Chiang Kai-shek, was the sort of woman the President instinctively liked.

She was, to begin with, diminutive. That was part of her charm—and her charm was formidable. Her skin was pale and soft. Her makeup was understated but exquisitely contrived and flattering to suggest she was younger than her forty-six years. Her nails were rapier long. Mrs. Roosevelt wondered how a woman who carried the burdens this woman had to carry could manage to find time during each day to undergo the beauty care she obviously required. She was like a fine automobile or airplane that required constant maintenance. No doubt she was massaged each day from head to toe with creams and oils. Her hair must have required half an hour's attention every day. Her cosmetics . . .

Obviously she regarded all these things as essential.

She wore an ankle-length black silk dress, ornamented with chips of jade sewn here and there. The collar was fastened just beneath her chin and ears. Yet, the dress was not modest. It clung to her figure. Also, the skirt was slit on each side. When she sat the slits exposed her bare legs to the knee and sometimes even a little above.

It would have been foolish to use the term *modest* about this woman. That word meant nothing to her. She was steel-hard, aggressive, and ruthless. She was also crafty, subtle, and wary. She identified her advantages and used them. She had sometimes done so at the risk of her life.

She used the fact that she was an exceptionally handsome woman, just as she used the fact that she was a Christian (and a Methodist at that), to dazzle men far more perceptive than the senators and representatives she was going to meet on this trip, far more perceptive than the dull-witted Henry Luce.

She was the wife of a "generalissimo." No queen was ever more regal. As the First Lady was shortly to observe, when she entered a room, she dominated it. What was more, there was no question but that she meant to dominate.

"I am very much looking forward to Eleanor's visit to China," said Madame Chiang in the car.

The President glanced past her and for an instant caught the eye of the First Lady, who was able to convey that she had no idea what China's First Lady was talking about.

"Well, that's something we're looking into," said the Pres-

ident. He did not say that he had no intention whatever of al-
lowing Mrs. Roosevelt to travel to China. "There are some
arrangements to be made."

"Of course," said Madame Chiang, who entirely understood the implication of what he had said.

At the White House, confusion reigned. Which suite the
famous guest would occupy was well understood: the elegant
Queen's Suite that had been occupied by Queen Elizabeth on
the occasion of the visit of King George VI and the Queen in
1939. The difficulty was with Madame Chiang's staff.

She had brought with her a nephew and a niece, invariably referred to as Mr. Kung and Miss Kung, as private secretaries. (They were the children of the seventy-fifth lineal de-
scendant of Confucius and were never modest about
informing people that they were the seventy-sixth lineal de-
scendants.) The difficulty was that Miss Kung dressed as a
man, always; and being slight, with her hair cut short, was
taken by many Americans as a young man. Mrs. Roosevelt had
assigned Miss Kung to a room and instructed the White House
staff to take her there and unpack her things. Shortly, an usher
came to the First Lady, flustered, saying a mistake had been
made, that the person assigned to *that* room was a young
man. While Mrs. Roosevelt was dealing with that embarrassed
usher, another arrived, saying that the maid unpacking the
young man's luggage had found that nearly everything in his
bags—underclothes, nightclothes, cosmetics—were a oman's!

The guests for dinner that first night of Madame Chiang's
visit were only the President and Mrs. Roosevelt, Madame Chiang, Weng Guo-fang—dressed for the evening in black silk cap,
embroidered yellow silk jacket, and black silk trousers—Mr.
Kung and Miss Kung, Harry Hopkins and his wife, Louise, and
Congresswoman Helen Gahagan Douglas. They met first in the
President's study, the oval room adjacent to the family suites.

The President, as always, took delight in the convivial-
ity of the cocktail hour. This evening he took delight also in

the company of the glamorous and sophisticated First Lady of China. Wearing another black silk dress, this one with even higher slits in the skirt, she stayed near the President throughout the hour and encouraged him to talk about the war and the strategy he believed would win it.

She said nothing of the resentment Mrs. Roosevelt knew she felt about the Casablanca Conference. She had spat that out in the hospital in New York, when she had told Mrs. Roosevelt there was no point in China staying in the war and fighting the Japanese if China were not to be regarded as an equal partner in a great, four-power coalition: the United States, Great Britain, Soviet Russia, *and China.* We are equal partners, she had said bitterly, or we are not partners at all. So, how dare the President and Churchill meet without the Generalissimo? That Stalin refused to meet Chiang was understood, since the Soviet Union was not at war with Japan; but the United States, Great Britain, and China were allies in a grand coalition, so how could Roosevelt and Churchill meet alone to discuss strategy? No decision they could take could possibly be valid without the concurrence of Generalissimo Chiang Kai-shek.

Tonight, though, she showed nothing of the tough Madame Chiang. She charmed the President. Mrs. Roosevelt almost regretted she had given the First Lady of China some instruction into winning the confidence and support of the President of the United States.

One awkward moment. Madame Chiang introduced her nephew and niece to the President. He did not quite hear what she said, and he smiled and nodded to Miss Kung and said—

"Well, it's very nice to meet you, my boy."

Harry Hopkins quickly scribbled a note and slipped it to the President—in time for the President to say to Miss Kung, "You understand that I address all interesting young people as 'my boy.'"

It was weak, but it worked. Miss Kung smiled and said she had heard that he did.

The truth, as Mrs. Roosevelt guessed, was that Miss Kung was not in the least offended. Dressing as a man, as reportedly she invariably did, helped her to overcome the male prejudices that still very much governed society and government in China. Weng Guo-fang's heavy-lidded eyes expressed his disapproval of Miss Kung; but no one else, once the matter was understood, either approved or disapproved.

Over dinner, Madame Chiang did gently raise with the President the question of the strategy agreed upon among the other three leaders—what was called the "Germany first" strategy.

"This country," she said to the President, in a voice so low she obviously meant to be heard by him alone and not by anyone else at that dinner, "entered the war, not because of anything Hitler did, but because of what Japan did at Pearl Harbor, followed by Japanese atrocities in the Philippines, Hong Kong, Singapore, and so on. Americans hate Japan. To let Japan continue to run wild in Asia while you concentrate your resources on defeating Hitler—"

"We have committed major forces to the Pacific Theater."

"Will you deny, Mr. President, that your overall strategy for winning this war is to defeat Germany first?"

"I cannot confirm or deny it."

"Well, Mr. President, there are those who believe—I am not among them—that the United States is far more concerned about aggression against the British, the French, et cetera—the white races, in other words—than about aggression against Orientals."

"Hitler is the greater threat," said the President. "If he should defeat Russia and—"

"What if Japan defeats all our forces in Asia and becomes the ruler, not just of China, but of Burma and India?

Which is the greater threat then? Australia and New Zealand fall, of course. And then what?"

"It's been considered," said the President.

Madame Chiang let the President see a cynical smile the First Lady had seen before and he had not. "All of this *must* be carefully considered, Mr. President," she said. "What concerns me is that when you meet with Churchill—or meet with Stalin, as you will—you will be meeting with the leaders of countries threatened only by Hitler. They will convince you that *their* salvation is imperative. All I ask, Mr. President, is that you consider what results will befall if Japan attains its goals in Asia."

The President glanced at Mrs. Roosevelt—an "I told you so" glance.

"But let us not darken a lovely dinner with talk of global strategy," said Madame Chiang. "I will welcome the opportunity of talking with you about it again. For now—"

She raised her glass of wine. "Mr. President. Your health and success—and those of the American people."

Five minutes later, Mrs. Roosevelt had to lean close to the President and Madame Chiang to witness another element of her character.

"Do you enjoy little jokes, Mr. President?"

"I do, very much."

"Well . . . It seems there was this American Indian. A doctor advised him that he should have been circumcised as an infant and suggested the operation should be performed now. The Indian was skeptical, but he asked what the fee would be. "One hundred dollars," said the doctor. "Ugh, too much," said the Indian. So he went to another doctor and asked what his fee would be. The doctor said eighty dollars. "Ugh, too much," said the Indian. A third doctor asked only sixty dollars, but— "Ugh, too much." So . . . "Do him myself," said the Indian. He put his male organ on a stump, wielded his axe, and, looking down in horror, exclaimed—*"Ugh! Too much!"*

The President laughed, but Mrs. Roosevelt doubted he had enjoyed the joke. He had never appreciated that kind of humor. As for herself— Well . . . By reputation, she would have been offended. In truth, she shrugged and chuckled and promptly forgot the little story.

Weng Guo-fang's lips tightened, and he did not laugh. The First Lady took note that Madame Chiang's chief of staff was a man with sufficient stature to show his disapproval of her. She wondered who he really was.

The joke was not interesting. That Madame Chiang told it was decidedly interesting. She had a catholic armamentarium.

The First Lady watched the President closely, trying to judge to what degree he had changed his mind about this woman he had called "Dragon Lady." She had hoped he would find some sympathy for this magnificent woman and her besieged people. Now, though her sentiments toward China had not changed in the least, she was not sure she wanted to see Franklin influenced by—

By what? Whom? A woman who had broken free from male constraints and made herself a popular leader? A jezebel?

Her visit to the White House was going to be more interesting than anyone had imagined.

"I beg your pardon," said Mrs. Roosevelt. "I shall return in a moment."

Statecraft requires, almost above all else, unyielding control of the bladder. The statesman who must abandon the conference table from time to time to make a visit to the bathroom earns the contempt of his fellow statesmen. It is with them a matter of pride. Hold your water and negotiate. Hold it until the other fellow can't.

Of such things is international policy concocted.

The American First Lady ordinarily played the game well. Tonight, for some reason, she was compelled to go.

The intimate dinner for Madame Chiang that first night of her visit was in the small private dining room, north of the State Dining Room. Leaving that room, a quick visit to her own suite on the second floor—where she could check her makeup and hair and even look at her telephone messages—was as convenient as any bathroom on the ceremonial first floor. She walked out through the east door of the private dining room and into the small private elevator the custodians of the White House called Elevator Number 1.

The usher who operated the elevator appeared oddly nervous but said nothing.

Leaving the elevator, she walked into the Center Hall. To her right was the West Sitting Hall, where the President usually sat in early evenings and enjoyed his cocktail hour. To the left and some ten yards to the east were the double doors that separated the private quarters of the White House from the second-floor public rooms.

The rooms were laid out like this—

A uniformed White House policeman stood guard at the double doors. That was unusual, and she walked over to ask why.

"Excuse me, Ma'am," he said. "Let me ask Mr. Kirkwal to speak to you."

He stepped away from the door for a moment and went into the Map Room just beyond. A Secret Service agent the First Lady recognized as Robert Kirkwal came out.

"What's going on, Mr. Kirkwal?"

"I'm sorry, Ma'am. There's been a murder here. Ugly sight, I'm afraid. In the Map Room."

MURDER IN THE MAP ROOM—
Coming soon from Elliott Roosevelt
and St. Martin's Dead Letter Paperbacks!

As storm clouds gather over Europe and FDR receives such guests as Albert Einstein, Joe Kennedy and crime buster Eliot Ness, Eleanor is thrust into danger much closer to home. One of the President's staff has been found dead, poisoned by cyanide mixed in his evening bourbon. Even worse, the accused killer is another White House aide, diminutive beauty Thérèse Rolland.

Although the police are determined to pin the crime on Thérèse, Eleanor is immediately convinced she is innocent. Calmly, but firmly, the First Lady uncovers a web of lies and secrets swirling around the Louisiana political machine . . . until another shocking murder is discovered. Suddenly, the investigation is taking Eleanor Roosevelt places no proper First Lady would ever go— to the darkest underside of society, and toward a shattering truth that lies within the White House itself!

ELLIOTT ROOSEVELT
MURDER IN THE WEST WING

An Eleanor Roosevelt Mystery
"Compelling!" —*Kirkus*